TRACED

Megan Squires

Kindra,
I hope you love
every minute of
Traced!

To my husband and children for graciously dealing with overgrown laundry piles, last minute dinner plans, and late night writing, all so my dream could come to fruition.

To my dear friends and family for mentoring, inspiring, encouraging, and uplifting me throughout the process by offering their prayers, their insight and their amazing editing skills.

To my Heavenly Father for orchestrating more events than I can count and for placing people in my life to make this all happen. To Him be all glory and praise.

Luke 2:34

PROLOGUE

Sixteen year olds aren't often afraid of much. Don't people always say we think we're invincible? We don't fear the consequences of our actions, the authority of our parents, or the longevity of our decisions. We just live, guided by our immediate actions, and we aren't afraid of the process and where it takes us.

Or at least that's what we want everyone else to think.

Because when faced with the glaring truth of it, we all have something that sets our hearts racing, causes our fingers to tremble, and rushes chills up our spines. It's always there. Maybe some of us do a better job stuffing it down and keeping it hidden than others, but we're all afraid of something. Heights, the dark, falling. Some around here say we should even be afraid of our own government, and most my age probably are. Whatever it may be, fear manifests itself in many different forms, but the emotions evoked are always the same.

While no one is completely immune to fear, some of these reservations are just more reasonable than others. On a return flight from California three summers ago, the elderly woman sitting in the middle seat was visibly held captive by the fear of flying. She didn't have to say anything. Her posture, her long, precise, deep breaths, and the way she held her eyes shut as the rumble and vibration of the tires disappeared and the wheels were lifted back into the undercarriage, conveyed it all. She was utterly terrified, and I imagined a thousand different thoughts were racing through her mind as the plane gradually tilted upward and left the safe harbor of the runway.

There was an unspoken understanding that this fear was completely acceptable—maybe even logical—and definitely nothing to feel ashamed of, as evidenced by the stranger in the window seat who slowly offered her hand, palm up, for her to grab hold of. To cling to. To reassure her that everything would be fine. She understood her distress and was there to calm her anxieties and to offer comfort.

It's reasonable to be fearful of things like flying. But to be terrified of something that isn't physical—to fear time itself? That seems illogical. We are afraid of things that have power over us, and time doesn't. Or at least it shouldn't.

But for me, that just doesn't seem to be the case.

So tonight when the red lights from the digital clock pierce the black canopy of my room, my heart stops, even if just for a moment. When it starts again, it's ragged and out of sync like an old, stalled vehicle requiring countless thrusts on the gas pedal before it finally lurches to life. I feel my once frozen blood begin to surge through my body, burning my veins from the inside out as it weaves and climbs to the icy tips of my fingers and toes. Sweat slides off my brow, catching on the fibers of my pillow, dampening it, serving as a wet, clammy reminder of my unwarranted emotions. Nothing about how I feel—the panic that rages over me, a tidal wave threatening to swallow me up in its uncontrollable current—none of this reaction makes sense.

And when I roll over onto my back, starting to drift slowly away again, and my hand slips from its tight grasp on the covers and falls to the side, landing palm up on the cold sheets next to me, I'm even more helpless. All I want is to be like the woman on the plane three years ago. I need someone to take hold of my insecurity, my fear, and my worry by reaching out for my hand. To tell me everything is going to be okay.

But for this to happen, I suppose someone has to relate to my fear; they need an explanation for this anxiety. Such an explanation requires sentences and words strung together.

And I'm not even entirely sure those words exist.

ONE

"I think everything left after the estate sale is in storage. There should be no problem if they want to start moving in today. Give 'em my number if they happen to run across anything, but I think it's all outta there." Uncle Mark switches his phone off, hanging up with the caller on the other end, and slumps down into his seat at the kitchen counter with a huff. "They're in for a real treat. That place has been empty for two years. I can only imagine the amount of work they'll have to put into it to get it up and running again."

The way he refers to my childhood home—the house that shaped me, sheltered me, and protected me for fourteen years—as "that place" makes my stomach physically turn, twisting inside my gut. I try to choke back the blueberry muffin that involuntarily makes its way back up my dry throat by swallowing a large gulp of orange juice. But the acidity just adds to the bitter taste already present in my mouth.

I know he doesn't mean anything by it. Everyone tried to move forward after my parents' death. Selling their items was the first phase in that process, even though it was over a year before we were allowed to get to that point. After a death, our government sends officials to go through the deceased's possessions before any estate sales are permitted. Apparently, their duty is to reclaim any items that might have been government property. I wasn't there when the agents descended upon the ranch, but from what I could tell, they hadn't really taken much—just my dad's old laptop with his flight logs and recordings, his pilot license and certificates, and his uniform. Everything else still seemed to be intact when we were finally given the green light.

Going through their belongings was like stepping back in time. Their relics—that's what we call so many of the objects from my parents' era—were items that you just don't see any more. The compact discs they used to listen to music on, the watches they wore to tell time, and the phones that were bolted to the walls in their house. My parents always reminded me that though times were changing, it was still important to hold on to the past. But as I looked through their things, I couldn't see how some of them could ever be of any use to me, even though I longed to keep them. My generation, we're the in-between. We're the ones living in the transition times. The times between tradition and technology. To hang on to so many things that society deemed useless just didn't make sense, so we sold them. It seemed like the first necessary step in moving forward.

The second was putting the ranch on the market. That was a year ago. And for two full years, the hundred-year-old ranch remained vacant, silence penetrating its walls. It was as if the moment my parents passed and I was swept away to live in Madison, the ranch ceased to exist. No more memories made in the yard; no more footsteps running up and down creaky stairs. Everything at the ranch was frozen in time.

Part of me is glad for this news of the sale. It's wrong that a place once full of so much life could sit empty for so long. Sometimes, when I jolt awake in the middle of the night, I lie in bed, dreaming about a family with a young girl making the ranch their own. The thought of those rooms hearing laughter again makes the sting of leaving my home a little easier to endure, even though I had no real choice in the departure.

"Shouldn't be too bad," Uncle Mark continues. "The realtor said they've got four boys. I'm sure they'll have plenty of extra hands to help with renovations."

Well, there goes the hope of a family with a young girl. Four boys. Not exactly my idea of pigtails and tutus twirling in the yard. It was always such a magical, ethereal place for me as a child. To think of it being overtaken with dirt bikes and skateboards and who knows what else...well, that's just too much testosterone.

"And they're turning the hangar into a barn. Guess they want to make the place a working ranch again and need a shelter for their horses."

My breath lodges in my throat. It takes everything in me to clutch my glass of orange juice, to prevent it from shattering onto the counter, slipping from my shaky hold. The glass. My life. It's all unsteady. What I wouldn't give for some stability.

So they're turning the hangar into a barn. I try to mask the shock that must be so evident on my pale face—the hollow stare that, although it appears completely vacant on the outside, works to cover the astonishment underneath.

No one ever talks about the hangar.

I'm not sure why it never comes up. Uncle Mark and Aunt Cathy often speak of the ranch and the bank account that they set up in my name, to which they would route the money once the ranch finally sold. They talk freely about the house, but the hangar never edges into dinner conversation. Maybe out of respect—maybe because they can't bring themselves to say the words either—but it never comes up.

Not until today when its new identity is revealed. A barn. A place for horses. A home for a bunch of animals. I can't think of a more inappropriate use for the spot where my parents spent some of their final minutes, not knowing it would be the last time they would ever take their two-engine prop plane out for an afternoon flight.

"I'm sure whatever they do to the old place will be lovely." Aunt Cathy saunters into the kitchen, her melodic voice reaching us before she does, like musical notes dancing into the crisp morning air. The coffee pot begins to fill up with her favorite blend as her index finger lightly grazes the "on" switch.

"It's always been a beautiful house—it's a shame that it sat vacant for so long." Aunt Cathy slides a piece of whole wheat bread into the toaster. "It will be good to have some life in there again."

Finally, someone articulates the thoughts spinning through my muddled mind. It *will* be good to have a family living there, even if it is filled with a bunch of boys, I guess. That part I can get past, but the horses— that will take a bit more effort.

"Any of their kids going to East Valley? I haven't heard of any new students." Trent plops down next to Uncle Mark at the counter, grabbing Aunt Cathy's piece of freshly crisped bread when it jumps out of the toaster, apparently not caring that it was made specifically for her.

Sunday mornings are like this at the Buchman household. Slow and relaxed, no official wake up time, no pre-planned breakfast—just everyone coming and going as they please. I would have loved this sort of thing back at the ranch; being able to sleep in as late as I wanted, set my own schedule, and make my own food. But my mom always had a strict agenda to adhere to, so I followed it, with only a grumble or two here and there. It was important to her to have family time, and that time had to be carefully planned. I've never really been one for planning.

"I think I heard the older two boys are going to East Valley. But I'm sure they're having a tough time getting in. The school lists were finalized last month, so I don't know how easy a transfer is right now." I inadvertently close my eyes while my other cousin, Bailey, continues. "One is a freshman and the other a junior. Someone said that the younger boys were homeschooled—I think they're little."

That makes sense. The ranch is a good twenty minutes from Madison where the local high school, East Valley, is located. Any elementary school is another twenty-five minutes further. When I lived at the ranch there was a small, private elementary school up the road that I attended, but it had been shut down in recent years. All of the youth are older now and the demographics have changed so much that there isn't a need for the elementary school anymore, though I'm a little surprised our government has allowed for homeschooling. But I guess every case must have an exception to the rule. In my old county's instance, childhood had literally grown up and left town. Must have been a good enough exception.

"What are their names?" I inquire, my words muffled by the dry bits of muffin I still haven't managed to swallow. I'm not hungry at all. All of this talk of hangars and horses has stolen away any appetite I might have originally had.

Bailey answers, but her words swarm around me, like bees knocked from their hive, ready to engulf and disorient me with their piercing stings and deafening buzzing. I can only hear the inarticulate hum of their talk. I'm certain there must be meaning that goes along with the sounds emanating from their mouths, but all I see are lips moving and hands motioning. No significance, just buzzing.

Snap out of it, Tessa! I need to rejoin their discussion and pull myself out of my head. Sometimes it's much too easy to get lost in there.

"Liam is a junior and Joshua is a freshman. They're trying to transfer from Superior."

Superior. What a ridiculous name for a high school. Didn't anyone stop to think how pretentious it might sound to name a school Superior? "Superior High Sweeps the League Again" is printed across our newspapers every year at the close of football season. With a name like that, it makes all of the other schools sound like a joke. East Valley High is so much more straightforward. The high school is literally on the east end of the valley and thus appropriately named.

"I think Liam is in our journalism class, Tess. I was talking to Mr. Crawford after school on Friday and he was reworking the seating chart." Bailey takes the orange juice pitcher and grabs a muffin from the basket. "Ooh, thanks Mom! These are my favorite!" Funny how a meal that's almost inedible to me is something Bailey loves. Then again, Bailey and I are so different lately that it shouldn't come as a huge surprise.

We're just a year apart in age, so for as long as I can remember she was always there. We've fought and we've made up, knowing that the blood we share as family will always cover over any argument that we might ever have.

For years we were inseparable. When she got her ears pierced, I begged my mom to let me get mine pierced that same day. And when I learned how to ride my bike without training wheels, Bailey called later that day to tell me that she no longer had use for hers. Our little lives paralleled one another in nearly every aspect.

But then junior high hit. That time of transformation, when you don't feel like you are your own, but still aren't quite sure who has control over you. Maybe it's your peers, maybe it's your teachers, more likely it's the government—but whoever it is, it's not you. Those two years belong to someone else and it isn't until you emerge from that time that you understand just how much influence others have on your life.

Prior to middle school, Bailey and I never attended the same school, so while we seemed to lead similar lives, we also each had an aspect of our own that remained separate. That was until junior high and Chris Fenton. Looking back, I honestly don't remember what it was about him that we were both drawn to—he was just a scrawny, twelve-year-old boy—but what I do remember was the realization that no matter how similar Bailey and I once thought we were, the fact that Chris preferred me over her taught us both that there must be real differences.

Bailey's always been beautiful, a total head turner. Her big green eyes and her perky little nose, covered with just the right amount of freckles, make her appear innocent yet not completely childlike; the perfect complement to her cropped red hair. And she is tall—she's always been tall and lean just like her twin brother, Trent—an athlete's body from the time she was a little girl. Her beauty is made even more apparent by the confidence she exudes. She knows her mind and she isn't afraid to let people see it, like a peacock that spreads its train in a dizzying, iridescent array of teal, green and blue, showing off its splendor for everyone to gawk at. Bailey proudly wears her own confidence in similar fashion, parading around her thoughts, opinions, and self-assurance in a gorgeous, if slightly obnoxious, display. Even in junior high, when the rest of us lacked this confidence, she had it. Maybe that's why the battle over Chris was such a blow.

If Bailey is the peacock, I guess I am the hen. I'm less extravagant, less showy, but more intentional. While the peacock uses his lustrous plumage to strut around, showcasing himself and his own impressiveness, the peahen, her feathers dull and short, fans her tail only to ward off danger and protect her young. That's much more my style. Intentional and deliberate. Not flashy and extravagant.

At the same time, though, I'm not entirely unlike Bailey. I do have opinions on things—and strong ones at that. But I also have some sense about me and know when to keep my mouth shut. Like when the accident happened and Aunt Cathy and Uncle Mark came to the ranch to help me pack up my things in two of their own medium-sized, brown leather suitcases, I did just that. I folded my favorite knit sweater, a few pairs of jeans and the yellow sundress I'd just purchased with my mom the week before, and gathered my album of photographs, my dad's old box with his memoirs from the war, and my laptop. I packed the contents of what was left of my life at the ranch in just two suitcases. *Their suitcases.* I couldn't even take what remained of everything I once knew with me in my *own* luggage.

Even though I longed to stay, I didn't make my wishes known, and I didn't blame Aunt Cathy and Uncle Mark for any of it. I'm completely convinced that they were doing the best they could, or at least what they thought was best for my life. That was always the plan. If anything were to ever happen to Mom and Dad, there would never be a question as to where I would go. I'd have a family. I'd never be completely on my own. I have always been so grateful for that foresight; I've heard so many stories of kids who lost their parents and the government made the final decision as to who their "family" would be. And from what my dad was always saying about our government, I am certain I wouldn't have wanted that. Even though he's not physically here now, I guess my dad is still looking out for me.

Uncle Mark reminds me of Dad, too. He was my mom's big brother and her protector from the time she was born. So it came as no surprise when Uncle Mark later went on to become a paramedic and then eventually a firefighter. He's just cut out for that sort of thing, for coming to the rescue of those in need. He'd done it for my mom on countless occasions, and I know that's what he was doing for me when we drove off in their SUV that summer afternoon, leaving the ranch in the rear-view mirror to head toward Madison, the suburb where Aunt Cathy and Uncle Mark lived just twenty minutes away. He wasn't trying to wrench me away from everything I once knew to be real, everything I had built my life, my hopes, and my dreams around. He had a plan for me. A new plan. A plan to protect and take care of me. How can I be anything but grateful for that?

I never let anyone see my disappointment and never mentioned how much I wished that I could have stayed at the ranch a little longer. How I longed immediately to go through Mom's closet, to hold her favorite worn and tattered sweatshirt up to my nose and breathe in what was left of her. I wanted to fill my lungs with her being—the scent of her honeysuckle shampooed hair that I used to bury my face in while she cradled me when I was sick. I would snuggle in close with my cheek resting on her collarbone so my forehead would settle in right by the crook of her neck. It was a place of safety and warmth and a mother's love.

I never mentioned to them that I needed that. But I'm sure Uncle Mark needed it, too. I'm sure he desperately wanted to go through her things right away to find the tangible memories that remained of their childhood in the form of a photograph or a letter. I knew that he didn't want to let go any more than I did, so I followed his lead. If this was the path that was best for him, then it was good enough for me, too.

And what Uncle Mark and Aunt Cathy could provide for me was immeasurably more than I could ever have expected from a family in the midst of grieving as well. They had purchased their current home just a year before the accident, so when I came to live with them everything was still new, still smelling of fresh paint. I sensed that they were only in the beginning stages of making the transition from a house to a home.

I was glad to be part of that process. I could only imagine how different it would have been if the tables were turned and my cousins, Trent and Bailey, came to live with my parents and me at the ranch. They would have felt so out of place being in a home full of so many years of history and memory-making. The marks etched in the doorframe indicating my growth each year, the wall of school photographs proudly framed and displayed in the entryway, and the huge tire swing hanging from the Heritage oak in the front yard would all serve as daily reminders that they were entering into an already established life and routine, one that they weren't born into, but suddenly and unexpectedly thrown into.

I'm sure there's no way Bailey would have been quiet about her unease and forced transition if the roles were reversed. And that's where we differ; I've mastered the art of knowing when to speak and when to keep silent. Bailey certainly hasn't. My mom once told me that a wise person does what is best for the whole and not just what is good for her. Her confession was in secret, out of my dad's earshot, and I knew it was some mantra she'd probably picked up from our government handbooks. But it seemed like sound advice, so I've always heeded it. No strutting, no parading. Only purpose in my actions.

Aside from our demeanor, Bailey and I differ in our appearances, too. We don't really look related. My wavy, long, chestnut hair is such a contrast to her short, red tresses. And she stands a good five inches above my five-foot-four stature. I had been so jealous over her freckled nose as a child, even spending one night praying for a nose like Bailey's. I remember looking in the mirror that morning after my prayers, brokenhearted and in tears, and then running to the phone to tell Bailey that my face remained un-freckled. "Good! I'm so glad," she'd snickered from the other end of the line. "I prayed for your rosy, red cheeks, and I didn't get those either!"

It didn't take long for us to learn to accept the differences between us that we discovered during the "Chris Fenton Days." And even though we made our own friends in high school and began to develop our separate interests, we still share a relationship that I am so grateful for, now more than ever. She's one of very few constants in my inconsistent world. And right now these memories of our childhood together provide a hint of comfort, even in the midst of this morning's uncomfortable hangar discussions.

Breaking out of my reverie, I pick up another piece of the muffin but I can't eat it, even though I know it's not the muffin that's making me ill. It isn't even the conversation. It's the idea that a complete stranger is beginning a new life in the home where I was supposed to build my future. That some guy named Liam will be turning the hangar into a stable. That he will lay awake at night in one of the rooms in *my* house and will plan out *his* future. That he is allowed a new start to his life at the ranch while I have to live out mine in Madison.

The enormity of it all is more than my head, or my stomach, can bear.

TWO

2:34.

Seriously? Not again.

It's so frustrating that those three numbers harbor so much meaning. For anyone else it's just one of 1,440 other minutes in a day. It quickly ticks by in sixty seconds, and chances are, a normal person is completely unaware of its coming and going. But too many times those numbers stop me in my tracks. Or wake me out of a sound sleep. No other minute of the day causes me anxiety, but 2:34 sets into motion a full range of emotions so vast that every time it passes it's as though life comes skidding to a halt, yet again.

2:34 p.m.

I never read the coroner's report, nor cared to know the details. I knew they had crashed—that something in one of the plane's engines malfunctioned shortly after takeoff. When I saw the officers pulling onto the long, dirt drive just as I had placed the last plate left from lunch into the wire dish rack, I knew it was bad news.

That's all I needed to know. I didn't want more details because I didn't want my last memories to be about the facts of how they died. They lived life too fully to be summed up in a two-sentence statement regarding their death. So all I inquired about was the time of the crash. That I did want to know—the precise minute when my life changed forever.

Since then, things have continued to change. I'm no longer the skinny, knock-kneed, quiet girl they left at home that day, charged with cleaning up the house before our company came over for supper. I'm sixteen now, three weeks shy of seventeen, and I'm a woman. Or at least a more grown-up version of the girl I once was. Her distant existence is like a shadow to me now—still attached, still part of me in some way, still bound to me even, but forever behind me. That shadow is only slightly visible when I look back, which I seldom have the ability to do anymore.

I'm thankful I have Mom's eyes. I guess I've always had them, but the older I get, the more their shape seems to transform into hers. My mom had long, dark lashes that framed her blue eyes and curled all on their own without the aid of any instrument. Over the past two years mine have become so much like Mom's that at times, when I look in the mirror, it is her staring straight back. I'm so grateful to share this likeness. It's comforting to have those physical characteristics as reminders of her presence and to help me keep my hold on parts of my past—like that shadow of the girl I once was.

But this morning my eyes don't reflect those bright, crystal ones from my memories. They are swollen, puffy and tired, and the deep, purple circles encasing them tell the story of my struggles for sleep. I groan inwardly. *Tessa, you've got to start getting some rest.*

2:34 a.m.

It was yet another night where those numbers burned on the digital clock on the wall. Sleep doesn't come easily for me anymore. Just two years ago I would spend half the day under covers, my mom nagging me about how I was "wasting the day away" by hiding out in my room until noon. But that's just what fourteen-year-olds did. We were programmed for it like robots—preset to stay up all hours of the night talking on the phone to the same friends we had just seen moments earlier at school. Then we'd attempt to catch up on our lost sleep during those morning (and early afternoon) hours. It was a ritual of sorts. It just went with the teenage territory.

All that has changed. My life has been altered and sleep is now a luxury, one that I never seem able to afford. The routine that was so comfortable and predictable has vanished, leaving behind few remnants with its departure. In reality, any routine remaining from back then is all but completely gone. Even after two years of searching for a new sense of consistency, I am still out of sorts. Trying to make the daily tasks fall into place is exhausting, like attempting to put a square peg in a round hole. It's so much easier to abandon it altogether.

So I just take one day at a time. But even one day is too big of a chunk to bite off and swallow and feels completely capable of lodging itself in my throat and choking me to death. An hour—I can handle that. I can probably take things one hour at a time. Or a minute. That feels much more attainable. To take things as they come and to live each minute as its own, separate moment. *Just roll with the punches.* That's what I've been trying so hard to do these past two years, however unattainable or unrealistic that goal may be.

But all this nightly waking has been challenging to adapt to. At first I figured it had to do with my new surroundings. It took a little while to get used to this spare bedroom Aunt Cathy set up for me. It's fully furnished, which is a relief considering I only had two suitcases worth of belongings to fill it. The mahogany, queen-sized, four-poster bed takes up the majority of the room with a large, distressed armoire to the left of it. On the wall across from the bed sits an old, upright piano that had been my great-grandfather's. It seems strange to keep a piano tucked away in a spare bedroom and not proudly on display in the main living area, but I enjoy having it here. I love the worn, ivory keys and the solid, wooden bench with its many scratches and divots, each imperfection telling a story. Its history reminds me so much of the history of the ranch, so it is a welcome fixture in my new room.

Night after night of interrupted sleep indicates that it is more than unfamiliarity and the newness of my surroundings that keeps me up all hours. For the past four nights, when my eyes immediately lock on the clock, those three numbers jolt me wide awake, like I've placed my fingers in a socket and the current is surging through my body. The first few times, I wrote it off as mere coincidence, or thought that maybe I'd fallen into some strange sleep cycle that caused me to wake at the same time every night. But now, by night number four, something in me suspects it's more. I can't explain it away as random chance any longer—it has become too patterned and precise to be haphazard. Things of this nature rarely are.

Grateful that it's now morning and no longer the dead hours of night, I drop my bare feet off the edge of the bed onto the cold hardwood floor beneath me. The grooves between the planks are familiar under my toes, though they were most likely machine-made in a factory a few years ago as opposed to the hundred-year-old floorboards back at the ranch, carved by hand, the craft of someone's sweat and labor. But even in their newness, something about this floor still reassures and calms me, especially after such a fitful night. The soles of my bare feet glide over the boards as I shuffle out of bed. Everyone else is already up, their lighthearted chatter echoing off the rafters in the kitchen down the hall. *Oh, you are so not a morning person, Tessa.*

I trudge to the adjoining bathroom to wash my face, hoping to slough off some of the morning grogginess with an ice-cold douse of water. As I twist the knob on the faucet, I drag my toe across the grooved floorboards, finding comfort in their seemingly insignificant familiarity, wanting to cling to the memories they draw out of me.

And I guess it's natural to want to cling to the past in some form, especially when it feels like everything else in life has completely changed. I know I'm not the only one who's gone through this. My parents' entire generation experienced this shift on some level after the war. I remember my dad telling me how vastly different life was growing up for him.

One day in particular is still vivid in my memory. The sun had been blistering in the sky during one of his accounts, and I was drawing water from a hose on the spigot at the side of the house. After twenty seconds, and well before the container was completely full, the water flow instantly shut off, leaving the bucket half-empty and still greatly underfilled. I'd twisted the handle on the faucet in an effort to start it again, but when I did so, nothing poured from the spout.

"It wasn't like this years ago, Tess." He'd pulled the metal pail from my hand and poured it over the windshield of Mom's car. "We *used* to be able to manage on our own. We *used* to be able to make decisions for ourselves, like how much water we needed. Things like this were never regulated." He leaned his head closer to mine, emphasizing his words with his posture and his tone, and as he recalled, his eyes gleamed with remembrance. "The war in the East that happened right before you were born changed all of that. We *used* to be a democracy, Tess. But those days are long gone."

I'd loved the way that word sounded. *Democracy.* The way it rolled off of his tongue—the way it hinted at a freedom my generation has never really known. I'd longed for my dad to tell me his tales of the past, like the year that he'd turned eighteen just in time to vote in the presidential election. Presidents. Elected officials. Those notions seemed like ancient history.

Once the war started, all young men my dad's age were recruited for the efforts. He never shared war stories with me, though I have his box containing those untold memories tucked away on a shelf in my closet. I've just never had the courage to open it. Something about it feels dishonest; I know he avoided those discussions for a reason. I know that war changed everything, and that it changed him. And I liked his freedom stories so much more.

"You teenagers don't know any different, but this isn't the way our lives should be run, Tess." My heart had leapt within my chest that day, as if his words had literally compelled it to quicken. *He shouldn't be talking like that,* I remember thinking. *You can't speak out against the government, Dad. You can't challenge those in authority.*

Whether it was my own sense talking that day, or the refrain ingrained in me throughout my years of schooling, I could never be sure. Likely it was a little of both. After all, it didn't seem too farfetched to believe that my generation had been indoctrinated to accept the way things were as fact; we'd been taught it in our classrooms and were instructed to believe it as our truth. It was all we'd ever known.

"These fifty states, Tess? Each one used to have *real* people—senators and congressmen—representing us, looking after our best interests." Dad's tone had grown heated. "We weren't just some voiceless group of citizens being forced round and round like a wheel, the spokes pushing and turning us monotonously, robotically."

His illustrations always painted such vivid pictures of our reality. In this case, the analogy was perfect. Our government *was* like a wheel with the powerful at the center and the civilians on the periphery. Even the division of government Sectors bolstered the comparison: Technology, Medicine, Agriculture, Defense and Protection, Education, Transportation, Media and Entertainment, and Commerce and Industry. Eight different Sectors, with just one authority figure from each representing them at the Hub. Even the name for the powerful elite—the Hub—paralleled the analogy. Like the hub of a wheel, all power resided in the small center that moved and controlled the spokes protruding from it, which in turn governed the rest of the population.

"Everything changed during the war. The idea that a shift in power was necessary once we started losing battles—it changed everything, Tess. Even the creation of the Sectors was a direct result. Where do you think the Defense and Protection Sector originated? They just funneled us from our war responsibilities into our own separate divisions. Well, most of us anyway." Dad had wrapped up his diatribe that day as he swept the towel over the frame of the sedan, as though he was sweeping away any hope he'd had for our society's future right along with it. I'd wanted to ask him how he ended up in the Transportation Sector since I knew he was a soldier in the war, but I just couldn't interrupt him. Dad commanded an audience when he spoke, and I was a captive listener. "We lost our voice the year the Hub took over, Tess. Life as we knew it had completely restarted."

Maybe Dad was right. Maybe things did restart for our country. Maybe governments actually did have the ability to start over, morph and transition. But I seriously doubt individual people do. We just continue on, maybe changed by the effects of the transformation, but as my dad's reminiscing evidenced, the past is always a part of who we are.

Because people just don't start over; they don't reboot like a computer when it freezes up and the only solution is to kill its power and start things fresh. People don't forget and resume functioning again as though nothing has happened. They continue on—

maybe in a different direction, but they still move forward.

Yet as much as I've tried to convince myself of this truth, somehow that just hasn't been my case. I felt that pause, the frozen screen in my life where my reboot·happened. It wasn't in a form of a simple click on a keyboard, or even a complete power shift of government authority. It was an SUV and an old, dirt-covered, two-mile road. And when that dust cleared and the horizon appeared, all that was left of me was gone, vacated.

Much like the vacant face that stares back at me from the mirror this morning.

"Holy smokes, Tessa! What were you up to all night?" Trent peeks his head into the room, still holding the side of the doorframe for support, as he edges in and snaps me out of my trance. The water gushing into the sink shuts off simultaneously, as if my memory and his voice trigger it.

"Is it that bad, really? How awful do I look?" I don't break my gaze in the mirror to glance back at him, knowing he doesn't need to answer to confirm that I really do look *that* bad. I pinch my cheeks between my index finger and thumb until the skin underneath begins to tingle. It's an attempt to give them some color—a rosy glow—any indication of life on my tired face.

"A little sleep wouldn't hurt you, you know."

Thanks, Trent. That's fantastic advice.

"Oh, okay," I mock as I slug him upside his shoulder, following him into the hallway like a little duckling trailing behind her mother. "Are we picking Joel up on the way today?"

Joel McBrayer. Trent's lifelong best friend. Just like Bailey and I, Joel and Trent have always been an inseparable duo. But unlike the two of us, they never seemed to go through any rough patches. I guess guys are just easier that way. If they had a fight, you'd never know it, because chances are they would just physically duel it out and probably forget the real reason why the altercation started in the first place once all was said and done.

Joel and Trent also share many of the same interests. Both are seniors this year and play on the varsity football team; Joel is the quarterback and Trent is a kicker. But while Trent resembles his twin sister, Bailey, in stature—tall and lean, bordering on scrawny—Joel has grown into his six-foot-two body quite nicely. Had there ever been any quarrel between them, I would bet it was over this physical difference. But Joel wouldn't initiate a fight. In fact, it would probably be all of the high school girls that obsess over him who would, fighting for his attention. He has quite a fan club. Not to mention the fact that Sectors are already scouting him, too.

Despite his many adoring fans, he remains humble, which probably explains why he is held in such ridiculously high regard. Even the Hub itself acknowledges his athletic abilities, and I bet the recent scouting has something to do with the Media and Entertainment Sector. Talent like Joel's doesn't go unnoticed, and I'm sure the Hub wants to claim their right to it.

But it's as though Joel has some sort of blinders on and can focus his attention elsewhere. Even in the midst of utter adulation, he keeps his eyes straight forward, not allowing himself to slip and teeter off the pedestal that the town, and our government, has placed him on. How he does it, I don't know, but everyone—citizen and official alike—loves him for it.

Joel spends a lot of time at the Buchman house. His parents are both doctors, part of the Medical Sector: his mom at the hospital in Dalton, a neighboring town, and his dad at the new pediatric practice that opened in Madison last spring. As such, their hours are long and unpredictable. So Aunt Cathy asks Joel over to the house for dinner at least once a week, often inviting him to stay the night when he and Trent have to travel for away games the next morning. He is around a lot, and easily manages to make himself right at home.

That's something I still struggle to do. Maybe I can take a few pointers on assimilation from him. There must be a trick to falling into place that he knows and I don't. But then again, even though he spends so much time here, he still has a home and his own life to return to. For Joel, our house is more like a vacation from his daily grind. For me, it's a permanent relocation.

I snap out of my Joel-induced daydreaming and wait for Trent to answer my question about our

29

carpooling plans. Some days it seems like my brain has made a permanent relocation, too.

"Nah, I'll meet him at school today," Trent says, yanking his backpack off the hook and opening up the door to the garage, stepping out of the way, and motioning for me to go ahead of him. "He had another Sector recruiter come out early this morning to talk with him. He's probably already there."

I pull on the passenger door of Trent's Chevy truck, and it falls open. I climb into the seat and buckle myself in, settling into the worn leather. The truck is a hand-me-down from Uncle Mark, though Trent claims it entirely as his own, rarely giving credit where credit is due. A twinge of resentment toward Trent spikes through me for taking advantage of Uncle Mark's generosity. But Trent's just that way, and after seventeen years, I doubt he'll change. People seldom do.

Trent and I ride to school together daily, picking up Joel en route about half the time. Today Bailey's already been at school since before sunrise. She is the editor-in-chief of our yearbook staff, so she has a zero period class. Of the four of us, Joel and Bailey are the early risers. Trent typically wakes up ten minutes before we leave for school, and I would never dream of signing up for anything that requires a zero period. These days I take every ounce of extra sleep I can get.

Things will change for Trent next semester though. He's a senior, and all graduating students are required to attend the Sector Exposition held at the end of December. There they'll be interviewed, prepped, and recruited for a specific Sector, though it's been rumored they are technically allowed to decline admittance and choose their own Sector if they wish. I've never heard of that happening before, and I think it's more myth than fact. We all typically do as we're told. After all, if a certain Sector shows interest, it's probably because you show promise in that field. While it's intended for graduating seniors, all juniors are required to visit the Expo so the Chairs can scout upcoming aptitude and potential. It's never been done before, either, but if a Sector recruits you as a junior, you are required to discontinue your studies and graduate a year early from school. I'm sure that won't be the case for me. The Chairs look for students who show promise and stability, two things I'm severely lacking.

I pull down the passenger visor in Trent's truck and flip open the mirror, hoping this time I'll be greeted with a completely different version of the fatigued face that stared back at me earlier, but no such luck.

"Seriously, Tess. Stop it—you look fine. I'm giving you a hard time." Trent doesn't glance my direction but scans the parking lot of East Valley High for an open spot. His fingers tap nervously on the top of the steering wheel, the annoying sound of a woodpecker thrusting its beak into a solid, oak trunk, and he begins to chew on the inside of his cheek. It's a nervous habit he's had since he was little, and an immediate indicator that he is visibly anxious.

Trent isn't good at masking his emotions. Honestly, I'm not sure he even tries. It surprises me, especially when everyone our age seems to hide behind a self-created façade. I've always assumed the upkeep is too much for Trent. It's easier to wear your real self on the outside rather than have two versions of the same person to maintain—one true persona hidden away underneath, and the other false identity coating the visible surface. Trent can't uphold that front. Sometimes I wonder if anyone actually can.

"Mrs. Morton told me one more tardy and I'll have to stay after to write an apology to the Ed Sector Chair. I'm supposed to meet Coach for weight training—he's not going to be so gracious if I miss again." Trent pulls his truck into an empty space, hops out of the cab, and grabs his backpack from inside the truck bed, all in one smooth motion. "Joel will take you home. Wait for him by the oak tree out front, okay?"

I nod my understanding and make my way to first period biology class. Luckily, Mr. Harrisburg's classroom is at the entrance to campus, so I don't need to make the sprint across the school grounds that Trent is about to. And even if I did need to, I probably wouldn't. One tardy wouldn't be so bad. And for some reason, today I'm not as afraid of the Hub as Trent is. Maybe I should be.

I slide into a metal chair at the second table from the back just as Mr. Harrisburg emerges from the adjoining teacher's lounge to commence class. I can feel the cold from the seat through my jeans and I shiver. The disparity between my body's temperature and the chair's sends a sudden chill through me, sloughing off an outer layer of the sleepy fog I'm under. It'll take more than the cold to pull me out of my haze completely, but it's a slight help and I welcome it.

Bailey's already in her seat, her instruments and notebook neatly lined up, and she's waiting for me to settle in. "I have to stay after today to meet our deadline. Tell Trent I'll get a ride home with one of my staffers, okay?" The perfect way she organizes her things and talks of her yearbook responsibilities and her "staffers" as though she owns them—it's like she's fanned out her gorgeous plume of feathers once again to strut around in front everyone. I'm tempted to pluck one of them out.

"Oh, Trent's got weight training. He told me to catch a ride with Joel," I reply, searching in my bag for my notebook. As much as her flawlessness aggravates me at times, I do wish I had Bailey's organization skills. Her precise penmanship, her anal retentiveness—okay, maybe I'd do without that—but it would be nice to be a bit more put together.

Bailey sees me fumbling, yanks my backpack out of my hands, and begins to comb through its contents. "Sometimes, Tessa," she huffs, a slight note of annoyance in her tone. "Wouldn't it make life easier to be a tad bit more organized?"

She's probably right. It *may* make things easier, but at this point in my life, I don't really see the need. There may come a day when a type-A personality like hers would come in handy, but since I haven't yet reached that point, I'm happy with my ways.

"Here." She shoves my notebook, pencil, and dissection tools into my hands after mere seconds of searching. "Weight training again? Poor Trent—he's gotta be frustrated that Coach makes him come in so much more than the others."

It's true; of the entire football team, Trent probably spends the most time in the weight room, yielding the least results. He's such a lightweight. Not so for Joel. I suppose he is in there often, judging by the looks of him, but I would guess that the majority of his stature and physique is genetic. Though everyone on the team is required to clock a certain amount of time lifting, Joel seems to avoid spending the countless hours doing the hundreds of reps that Trent is obligated to.

"If everyone will go to the back of the room and retrieve their pigs from their trays, we'll get started on today's lesson," Mr. Harrisburg commands, pulling the reins on his chatty class.

Fetal pig dissection at 7:55 in the morning—what a way to start off the day. Like clockwork, Jake Connell, our resident class clown, quips, "Anybody hungry for some bacon?" His all too predictable joke results in the usual chorus of humoring laughs and customary eye rolls.

It *is* a pretty revolting way to begin the day, but Bailey and I have actually grown to enjoy this section of our biology unit. It's hands on and intricate, so it helps me stay awake, which is desperately required on a morning like today's. The cold from my chair has already worn off, and the seat radiates the same temperature I do. I'm starting to get too comfortable and drowsy. Maybe a little pig dissection will strip away another layer of my fog.

"I was up again last night, Bail," I say, turning our pig over on its back and using the scalpel to pry open its already exposed ribcage.

"Same time?" she asks. She takes her glove-covered finger and helps me pull apart the pig's chest and it makes an awful cracking sound as it's ripped further open. "Tessa, I'm so sorry that you have to go through this. Two years isn't very long, you know. I wouldn't think you'd be sleeping easy after all the changes."

But it *is* a long time. Two years is an eternity.

"Once you and your partner find the duodenum, I want you to raise your hands so I can come around and check it off your worksheet." Mr. Harrisburg paces the classroom and peers over his students' shoulders, his hot breath reeking of a mix of coffee and sausage, and it wafts my direction from a few rows up. I look at Bailey, hoping one of us knows where to locate this part of our pig's digestive system, so we can avoid Mr. Harrisburg's examining eyes and nauseating breath. Her blank look confirms she doesn't, and I feel stuck, certain we'll be getting another just-barely-passing grade on this assignment. Even that will only happen if Bailey is able to sweet talk Mr. Harrisburg into it. I'm sure she'll be able to just fine.

Joel hasn't arrived to class yet; most likely he's still meeting with his potential recruiter. He usually sits at the table immediately in front of us, and his familiarity with medical terms contributes to our ability to keep up our grades in Mr. Harrisburg's class. He told us before that growing up, his dad would use a medical dictionary to quiz him on spelling, and also to help him study for his exams. Joel's dad had been in the running for the Medical Sector Chair years back, and a rigorous set of tests and evaluations was a large part of that process.

Though Joel hated it at the time and quickly grew bored reciting, and even memorizing, obscure medical terms, the fact that he has this random knowledge locked away in his memory serves both himself, and his classmates, quite well. I'm sure Mr. Harrisburg knows that Joel is the reason for our higher than to be expected class average, but he never makes it apparent, nor does he stop Joel from helping the other students when we need it. I bet somehow Mr. Harrisburg is reaping the benefits that trickle down from the Hub for producing a group of students with such outstanding GPA's.

I once thought this favoritism—or at least the ability to overlook any flaws in Joel—was due to his being one of the stars of the football team. Everyone at East Valley, and in all of Madison for that matter, praises our high school football team. There is a stereotype of those Midwestern towns where daily life seems to revolve around football—where everyone eats, sleeps, and breathes passes, yards, and touchdowns. Madison is no exception to the rule. Sometimes I even wonder if we may have created it.

It probably also helps that for the past two seasons, with Joel as quarterback, the varsity team produced a record number of wins and even a state championship, shutting out Superior High for the first time in six years. Our school gets additional funds from the Education Sector, as well as Media and Entertainment, for every win our team earns. So everyone applauds Joel's incredible talent on the field, as well as his respectable conduct off it. Not that he has done anything heroic by throwing a football, but it really does seem as though everyone views him as a hero.

Well, he is a hero for me—at least when it comes to biology class. Bailey and I are lost as we pull back our pig's rib cage again, lifting up the heart to look under it for the illusive duodenum.

"Part of the *digestive tract,* class," Mr. Harrisburg reiterates, unmistakably glancing our direction over the rim of his wiry glasses as we fumble our way around the pig's circulatory system.

"Sorry I'm late, Mr. Harrisburg. I hope I didn't miss much." The classroom door yawns open and Joel passes through it. The click from it latching back into its frame draws my attention. A buttoned down, light gray shirt with the sleeves rolled up to his elbows exposes his muscular forearms. He's wearing dark, denim jeans and has a slate tie fashioned smartly around his neck. Obviously his attire was for the meeting with the recruiter earlier this morning, but it sure helps bolster the idea that he isn't your average high school senior. Especially in contrast with the rest of our class, casually dressed in hooded sweatshirts and worn jeans, the typical dress code of any East Valley High student. It's easy to see why he is a favorite on more levels than one.

"Not a problem at all, McBrayer. Have a seat. Maybe you can help your floundering classmates find their pig's duodenum." Just the way Mr. Harrisburg phrases his reply indicates his preference for Joel over the rest of the class. I guess it's hard not to like someone who aces every quiz and exam you create. Not that Joel is a superstar in every class—he isn't by any means a straight A student—but when it comes to anything involving medical facts and terminology, he definitely stands out among the rest.

Joel flashes Mr. Harrisburg his infamously bright smile, adding to his already-present charm. I draw in a sharp breath. If I hadn't been staring before, I unquestionably am now. It's hard not to gawk at him—his strong, commanding presence simply demands it. I'm powerless to look away. He's like a magnet that's charged and locked in on its counterpart, with his chocolate eyes and that magnetic field they create. I wonder how many other classmates are in its range.

"Fisher gone again?" Joel asks, as he slides out his chair and sits down at the empty table in front of us. His lab partner, Caden Fisher, has been out with the flu all week, and apparently isn't any better today. "You gals mind if I partner up with you for today's worksheet?"

His eyes, dark and brown, lock with mine, and he raises his eyebrows to a point as he asks the question. I still haven't broken my original gaze with him. My mind begins to daydream and I yank myself out of it quickly. I've been doing way too much of that lately. I suppose I am making up for the lost dreaming I should experience at night, but either way, I force myself to stop. Every time I let my head go that direction the barrier between reality and fantasy is blurred, and I can't afford to have things slipping back and forth between the two. It's difficult enough to stay fully in the present moment. I don't need illusions confusing my realities even more.

"Oh Joel, whatever would we do without you?" Bailey teases, batting her eyelashes and speaking with a high, southern accent, mockingly playing the damsel in distress. But it's true; without his help in the class, we probably would be failing. I'm grateful for all the assistance we can get.

His eyes roll and his chair spins around, as if one act has to do with the other, and he joins our table, his statuesque body positioned directly in front of me. "But seriously, what are you trying to do here? We're supposed to be biologists, not butchers," Joel teases, taking the scalpel out of my hand without asking permission. Chills rise up from the soles of my feet and I'm half tempted to look down at the floor to see if there's some exposed wire my shoes have brushed up against. Joel's touch shocks me.

He holds onto my fist with his left hand and releases the instrument from my grip with his right.

Even after he has full possession of the scalpel, his left hand lingers on mine for a second or two, his palm damp with sweat. Intentional or not, it sends my heart racing, a thumping that originates in my chest but culminates in my ears, so loudly I glance up at Joel to make certain he hasn't picked up on it, too. His eyes are focused on the pig in front of him and I shake off the notion that a pulse can beat strongly enough to physically be heard. *My goodness, Tessa. How tired are you?*

"Look. It's right here next to the pancreas," he says, skillfully moving around the organs that surround the anatomy in question. He grabs our sheet and Bailey's pencil from the table and begins to draw in the duodenum, as well as several other organs that are part of today's assignment, furiously scribbling away. "Hey, Tess—I'm taking you home today. Trent said Coach needs him to stay after."

"Yeah, he told me. I'll meet you out front after sixth period," I respond, pretending to dig around at our pig with the tweezers, hoping Mr. Harrisburg doesn't notice that Bailey and I have completely abandoned any responsibility we once had over our assignment. Joel is perfectly capable of finishing today's lesson, and I'm much too tired to even attempt to focus on any schoolwork. Plus, it's kind of fun to watch him poke and prod at the pig, getting excited every time he's able to draw an obscure term out of his memory bank. He certainly has a gift—I'm not sure how useful it is unless he hopes to join the Med Sector like his parents, but it is still a gift.

What wouldn't I give to possess a gift like that? Not necessarily one that involves random medical knowledge, but to have something that is all yours, that sets you apart. This wistful desire is enough to make me wish for a brief moment that I was a little more like Joel McBrayer.

But from what I've seen, gifts typically result in expectations, so I think I'm content with being gift-less for the time being. And Joel has another gift, one that's more well-known. And when you become known for something, it starts to define you; it even starts to determine your path in life.

Everyone assumes that Joel's plans for his future involve football, which isn't too surprising considering his obvious talent. I've never spoken with him directly about his plans after high school—he's a senior and will be recruited this winter—but I figure from all the recent visits and meetings with Coach that football is something he won't be able to get away from. Everyone always talks to him about what team he will play for, what colors he will wear, and what mascot he will represent. Little old grandmas stop him in the grocery store and encourage him to join their Sector, though he likely won't have any real choice in the matter. The Hub makes those calls, especially for talent like Joel's. I'm sure the Sectors will all be fighting over him at his Expo come December. Everyone seems to care about Joel's future plans after East Valley High. Everyone wants a piece of his guaranteed success.

I wonder if those are his hopes and dreams, too—if football as a profession for the Media and Entertainment Division is what he wants out of life. Or maybe he just does what's expected of him, like I guess we all should.

At least he's able to have a plan. *That* I respect. I know all too well that planning is something I can't do—something I've actually sworn off—since my parents' death. I am so grateful that I'm only a junior and don't have to make any "path in life" decisions any time soon. The Hub won't officially be interviewing me for any of their Sectors for another year. The term "floundering" that Mr. Harrisburg uses to describe our class may actually hold more truth than he realizes.

One moment at a time, Tessa. That's all that's expected of you right now. And in this moment, Mr. Harrisburg is expecting me to pass his biology class.

Luckily, I have Joel to rescue me.

THREE

"You'll help me edit the *Day in the Life* spread this weekend?" Bailey asks as I walk her to the yearbook room, the final bell of the day ringing into the late autumn air. Our steps are in unison, but hers exhibit a bit more bounce, a little more life, as she floats across the ground. Her heels never completely make contact with the pavement below.

Bailey's thrilled that I signed up for journalism as my elective class this semester, and she loves to take advantage of my editing skills for the benefit of our school yearbook. After spending six periods—plus zero period—at school, I can't see how she could want to spend another minute on campus. But she loves being editor, and the endless hours never seem to bother her. In fact, I think she thrives on deadlines, drafts, and editing. It's like some sort of drug that produces a rush of creativity, drive and determination. Her responsibilities as editor do that for her. I wish I had something that would do that for me.

"Yeah. Wanna plan for Sunday?" I reply, landing on the tips of my toes rather than the balls of my feet, attempting to recreate Bailey's sprite-like walk, but it's not natural on me. I resort back to my usual shuffle, my worn soles scraping the tiny bits of gravel and dirt under their rubber tread.

"Perfect! First copy is due on Monday. Thanks Tess, you're the best!"

Bye-bye, peacock. The words almost sneak from my lips.

I turn and walk away, heading toward the parking lot to meet up with Joel, but my feet glide in another direction, almost as if I'm not controlling them. I find myself in the girls bathroom, staring squarely into the mirror, and I look slightly more awake than my first encounter with my reflection earlier this morning. My cheeks have regained their typical rosy glow—a permanent blush. Maybe I should be thankful for that right about now, since getting in the car with Joel draws even more crimson up to my cheeks.

Joel's driven me home countless times before. Why does today feel so different? What are these nerves that tingle through me at the thought of us alone in his car? Maybe it has to do with the scalpel exchange earlier in the day during Mr. Harrisburg's pig lab. It's not like our hands have never touched before. I'm sure over so many years Joel and I have brushed hands—probably even shaken hands, but today is different. Those other occurrences never felt electric or made my heart thunder. I wonder if it caused the same reaction in him.

Stop it, Tessa. You're reading a million different things into a four-second act.

And most of these jittery nerves have to do with the fact that I have never actually held hands with a boy before. I'm nearly seventeen, and I don't know what it's like for someone to intentionally take me by the hand, to intertwine his fingers with mine and hold them tight. Like we're woven together in some small way, hand in hand, a visual and physical indication that we belong with one another.

But it isn't for lack of opportunity, this empty handedness. It's the fact that commitment scares me to death. Not that holding someone's hand means that you're about to say your wedding vows, but to me it's the first step in forming a bond with someone, letting them in and giving them part of yourself emotionally. I'm not ready to do that. Or at least none of the guys I've dated were ones I wanted to open myself up to in that way. My last boyfriend (if you could call him that), Tanner Weston, had reached out to hold my hand on our second date, and I actually gave him a high five. *A high five? Seriously? Who does that?* Sometimes I frustrate even myself. But I know that the high five reaction was more than me trying to dodge his handholding. It was a way of intentionally blocking him—or anyone else, for that matter—from getting too close to me emotionally.

Bailey always says that relationships are games, and emotions are just pieces in them. And once the game is done being played, it's boxed up and placed on a shelf only to be forgotten or one day thrown out. I've been discarded before, though maybe not intentionally nor romantically. But I think being left alone emotionally has got to hurt just as much; at least it feels like it does.

I push myself off of the sink counter in the girls room and fold my arms tightly across my chest, hugging my palms into my sides. No. I think I'll keep my hands to myself. At least that I do have some control over.

***

Joel is already out front by the tree when I emerge from my pre-ride prepping. *You made him wait. Nice one, Tess.*

"Hey Tessa—you ready?" He has his gym bag slung over his broad shoulder and his head is cocked to the side. *Wow, he's totally hot.*

"I gotta get out of here before Coach sees me standing around and puts me to work." He leans toward me, a coy grin spreading across his face as though the corners of his mouth have strings attached and a puppeteer is pulling on them. His teeth are perfect, distractingly so. But everything about him seems to distract me today. I seriously need to get a good night's sleep tonight to start seeing things more clearly.

We walk to his truck. I try to decide whether or not I should attempt Bailey's step again, rising on the upbeats instead of the down, but I've never been good at trying to be something I'm not. Why would trying to walk like someone else come any easier? I make my way through the parking lot to Joel's truck, neither sauntering, nor marching, nor prancing, just walking, and I'm surprised when I match Joel step for step. His truck is nearly identical to Trent's, just white instead, and as he unlocks the passenger door for me, its metal frame creaks upon opening. My breath hitches in my throat.

Stop trying to read anything into it, Tess. He does this every time he drives you.

Joel coolly meanders his way to the other side of the car and slides into his seat, shoving the key in the ignition. Nearly everyone has cleared out of the parking lot already, no one wasting any time getting off campus, which reinforces the fact that it's just the two of us—that we're alone.

Almost immediately, I'm uncomfortable with the silence between us. There are some people that you can sit with and be comfortable without the need for words to fill the quiet spaces, but I'm not to that point with Joel. He is so interesting, so full of character; he's Joel McBrayer. I feel the nagging tug of inadequacy, like I need to present myself the same way. I know I can't. Each time a topic worthy of conversation comes to mind, I immediately second-guess myself and shove it out of my head. After several minutes of shoving, the silence can't really be ignored.

I look at the clock on his dash. 2:30 p.m.

At least it's only been two minutes; that seems like an acceptable amount of time without forced words or false chitchat.

Maybe he is thinking about our interaction in lab today. I definitely still am. I rub my hands subconsciously together, pulling them out from their folded position in my lap, as the silence expands between us. It was so thrilling to have him touch them earlier, even if just to steal my scalpel from me. I glance over to his side of the car where his two, strong hands are wrapped tightly around the steering wheel, knuckles bared. For a moment I feel jealous of an inanimate object, if that's even possible. The close contact, the control he has over it, something in me craves that from him. I blink hard, try to rejoin reality, and commit to getting a better night's sleep once more.

Start talking, Tess, before your thoughts twist further out of control. Phrases float through my mind like clothes in a washer on the spin cycle, rotating round and round, quickening with each cycle. I decide I need to force open the lid in an attempt to regain control over my own thoughts before they become a tangled mess that I'm powerless to straighten out. Unfortunately, I just can't seem to stop.

Joel's not into you, Tessa. Joel could have any girl he wants. Joel doesn't want you.

I keep up this inner dialogue until the lack of audible conversation becomes glaringly apparent. But Joel seems perfectly content with the silence as he flips his turn signal on and pulls into the left turn lane. To sit so closely in the quiet with him and not know what he is thinking is racking my nerves to no end. To hear his breathing, smell his musty, yet pleasant, scent of sweat and cologne, but not know what occupies his thoughts, overwhelmingly distracts me. I would give anything to get a glimpse into his mind right now.

The light turns green and he steadily pushes his foot down on the gas pedal. My book bag folds over itself on the truck's floorboards, and I mentally make note of the assignments that I need to finish for tomorrow's classes. If I occupy myself with a mundane task, then maybe I'll be able to relax a bit. Five paragraph assignment on the final act of Hamlet for English, color-coded pig anatomy diagram for biology, family member interview outline for journalism…

That's when I feel the tightness of my shoulder harness begin to pull. It all happens so suddenly that the cutting of the seatbelt's fabric into my hipbones, and the firm pressure of Joel's arm across my collarbone and shoulders, all feel like one forceful movement. Had I not been so keenly aware of his presence before, and the fact that the strap pushed me back into my seat slightly more quickly than he did, I would have thought it was Joel's protective arm, rather than my seatbelt, that kept me from catapulting into the dashboard.

We both jolt to a stop and our eyes lock for a fleeting moment, trying to process what just happened.

"I'm sooo sorry, Tessa! I don't know where my brain was. I seriously did not even see that bird!" Joel apologizes, a sincere pleading in his tone, as he motions out the window to an enormous hawk that's landed three feet in front of the truck to scavenge on some sort of debris littering the road.

I don't know where your brain has been either, but I hope it was the same place mine just came back from.

But before I have time to slip deeper into my wishful thinking, my left hand, which had found its way back onto my lap, is engulfed in his—his strong, warm fingers tightly lacing through mine. Firm, intentional, and deliberate. My palm sweats in response, and I realize this calming gesture is just as much for his benefit as mine. His carved chest rises and falls, gradually decreasing in intensity until he's breathing at a normal pace again. Something about our hands as one calms him.

But as Joel steadily regains his composure, I am perilously close to losing mine, though I'm not sure I could even stake a claim on it to begin with. My blood begins to pump even faster than when the car jolted to such a sudden stop, my heart rising up into my throat as the beats echo out from it. I don't have any words, but I'm sure if I did they would croak out of me.

"I've wanted to do that for a long time—not almost hit a bird in the middle of the road—but you know...*this.*" He lifts up our linked hands. It's the first time I have ever seen him blush or fumble through his words. Fumbling isn't something Joel does. But me, on the other hand—well, the idea that he has actually thought about holding my hand before is almost too much to process. And that additional phrase, "for a long time," immediately turns my face scarlet. I pray that it doesn't appear as flushed as I feel, and am relieved when I realize there isn't even a shade in existence that's red enough to accurately reflect the true temperature of my cheeks.

I suppose I should say something affirming, something to let Joel know that I feel the same way. At least I *think* I feel the same way. I don't really know what these feelings are. They are foreign and not my own. This is the sort of thing I've read about in romance novels, never experiencing it, and not entirely convinced the author hasn't fed me a lie for the sake of entertainment. Still, I hang on to the hope that it does exist because I want it to. *I need it to.* Because if it doesn't, then what on earth has purpose anymore? Isn't this what people live for? To experience a rush of emotions like this? I can definitely see how they would now.

I had imagined what it would be like to have Joel's tight grasp on my hand just like any other girl at East Valley has. In truth, most of them probably daydream about a lot more than just handholding. But even my tame fantasies always seemed like such unrealistic delusions, so I never actually played them out to see what I would do if they ever became a reality. So I sit here now, thinking how unfair it is that I'm not saying anything back to him—just trying to soak in all that has happened. He deserves some type of affirmation.

Before I can give it to him, I break out of my contemplation and nearly leap out of my hot skin for the second time in less than five minutes. The driver in the car behind us impatiently blares his horn. Joel also snaps out of his own silence and yanks his hand out from mine. It lands loudly on the leather-covered steering wheel. He peers out of the corners of his eyes in my direction and his mouth curves up into a smirk. "We sure have had our share of surprises this afternoon." He puts the truck back in gear.

I nod in agreement—but one thing isn't a surprise as I do so, my head bobbling on top of my shoulders, still feeling muddled and still trying to process the past few moment's events. I know what three numbers I will see when I glance at the clock on the dash, and it comes as no great shock when I discover I'm right.

2:34 p.m.

I should have guessed.

But for the first time, those minutes that have filled me with so much panic and anxiety stir in me an entirely different reaction, setting my heart racing again, but for a completely separate reason.

FOUR

"What? Joel held your hand? Wait 'til I tell Trent—I wonder if he knew about this!"

Bailey isn't the one to confide in about the recent turn of events. She's fixated on the idea that Joel and I held hands. On the one hand, so am I. I honestly can't get my mind off the notion that it happened either, but what I really want to talk to someone about is numbers, not emotions.

I want her to understand that correlation and the fact that I constantly wake up at 2:34 every night. That my life always seems to come to a screeching halt when those three numbers appear on the clock. That for so long, the memories that flood back each time I relive that minute, even on a new day, make me feel hopeless and helpless. That for two years, all I've wanted was someone to comfort me in that minute. And that today I experienced a whole new emotion at 2:34 and I want someone to process it with me. Bailey's clearly not going to be that person.

It isn't as though anything about today's events could erase all the memories I associate with that time. When you experience something so traumatic, even if you appear fully healed to everyone else, you're left with a scar. And scars, though not as painful as open wounds, carry their own sting. They don't stretch; they don't disappear. They just do their job of covering the original injury. I've been wounded, and 2:34 is my scar.

So I'm not naïve enough to actually think that suddenly everything could be right in my world again. If anything, I'm incredibly conflicted, guilty, and confused by it all—a sensation both numbing and exhilarating at once. I really just want to talk to someone about it, because even though life seems so haphazard at times, it is starting to feel much more systematic than I'd ever thought possible.

"He said he'd wanted to do that for a long time? I wonder how long! Did he say anything else when he dropped you off? Do you know if he's coming over for dinner tonight? Doesn't it weird you out a little bit—I mean, doesn't he kind of feel like a big brother—"

"No—no, he doesn't feel like a big brother," I stammer, the words flying out of my mouth and interjecting themselves into Bailey's diatribe of outspoken questions. Joel is definitely no brother figure for me.

"I guess that's probably true. I mean, for *me* he does. But he's been around here a lot longer than you have, so that makes sense. Do you like him? What're you going to say to him tomorrow? What're you going to wear?"

The questions fire like bullets and I realize they aren't about to stop any time soon, so I humor Bailey for what feels like an eternity. It's probably just fifteen minutes or so in reality. I finally make up some excuse to go shower before dinner, which she follows up with a comment that I might not ever want to wash my hand again. *Oh Bailey, you certainly have a flare for the dramatic.*

At times like this, I'm grateful for the downstairs spare bedroom Uncle Mark and Aunt Cathy gave me. Having my own bathroom offers me some privacy, and on days like today, I want a hideout where I can think without interruption.

So I stand there under the cascade of hot running water and hope the steam will cleanse my mind as well. Unfortunately, clarity doesn't come. The vapor, as it curls and twists and fills the shower with a plume of smoke-like condensation, rises toward the ceiling, spills out of the stall, and creeps to the mirror to coat it with a thick, beaded mist. I peer from behind the shower door and can't make out my own reflection in the mirror anymore. The whole bathroom has become a fog—not much unlike my life, just more contained, with the ability of completely dispersing the moment I open the door and release it into the expanse of the house. I wish for a moment that my life had that same type of release.

One thing is clear—even in the midst of the bath-room haze—Bailey can't see deep enough into my situation to help shed any light on what concerns me most. In truth, Joel is the one I really want to talk to, but how can I possibly do that without scaring him away?

Hey, Joel, so you know how you held my hand today? I have this theory that things in my life happen at certain times. My parents died at 2:34 p.m. and you held my hand today at 2:34 p.m., so what do you make of that? Talk about a surefire way to make sure that he never holds my hand again *and* thinks I am the absolute freak that I'm beginning to prove I might actually be.

No, I have to wait to say something to him. It isn't fair to unload two years worth of baggage on him just because he assumed I might actually be a normal sixteen-year-old girl. Clearly, I'm not.

The water flow shuts off before I'm ready to join the real world again. *Stupid Sector regulations.* I step out of the shower and remember Bailey's question earlier about whether or not Joel was staying for dinner. It probably shouldn't change my plans for attire, but for some reason, tonight it does. I open the old wardrobe; its door creaks in response. I hesitate, and for a moment I'm unsure of what I should wear. My style has always been simple but feminine. My mom once said, "Wear your clothes tight enough so they know you are a woman, but loose enough that they still consider you a lady," and that stuck with me. I decide on a fitted scooped-neck, pale pink sweater and jeans. I sit down at the vanity to brush my hair, still wet from the shower, when there's a knock at my door.

"Hey, Tess? Can I come in?" Immediately, I know the male voice on the other side of the bedroom door isn't Uncle Mark's or Trent's, which only leaves one other option. My breath accelerates along with my pulse. *Pull yourself together, Tessa.*

"Yeah, Joel. Come on in." I swiftly smooth my hair back into a ponytail and make my way toward the door, reaching for the handle at the same time Joel pushes it open. The unexpected assistance rolls me back on my heels and I stumble as he enters the room.

"Um, hey, dinner's almost ready. I told the others I would tell you. But I wanted to talk with you for a sec first, if that's okay." He's two feet inside the doorway, clearly not knowing whether to sit or stand, his eyes darting back and forth. He's visibly nervous. The idea that I make him even the slightest bit anxious gives me the confidence I need to assure myself that I won't blurt out any of the things I'd wanted to tell him earlier. I must have a little power. It makes me feel a bit more at ease knowing that the guy who is always so calm and collected seems a bit off when talking to me, as terrible as that sounds. What does that say about me that I can find joy in his discomfort?

"So, about this afternoon—I'm sorry if that seemed out of left field for you." His voice is apologetic and sincere. "I just kind of freaked out. I'd been daydreaming about you, so much so that I almost ran over a bird in the middle of the road." He edges closer to me and I suck in a breath. I don't let it out.

"And then I think because my mind had completely been somewhere else, it didn't really seem so out of place to hold your hand," he explains. "But the more I thought about it, there was no way you could have known what I was thinking. So it may have totally caught you off guard. If I offended you, I'm really so sorry…and…Cathy said to tell you dinner's ready."

His nervous, rambling explanation makes me feel horribly guilty. I should have said something reassuring earlier in the truck. Why did I have to go and leave him to try to figure things out all on his own, and then even take the slightest bit of pleasure in his unease just moments ago? *Really, Tessa?* I had no idea I could be so inconsiderate. I'm not used to this relational stuff at all.

"No, really, Joel, it's okay. I mean *yes*, it was totally unexpected, but you have no idea…it was exactly what I needed in that moment."

"I know, right? I mean, I practically got us in an accident over a stupid bird." Even though the almost-accident wasn't the real reason for my need for comfort, I resolve to let Joel believe that for now. I know that after this conversation, it won't be long before I'll be able to tell him why holding his hand meant so much to me, but for now I'm just grateful to know that we share some mutual understanding, even if it isn't as deep as I hope it will one day become.

I don't share mutual understandings with many people. But somehow Joel seems like just the person to try it with.

FIVE

I could feel his breath caress my face as he pressed his solid chest against mine. He wrapped his arm around me and pulled me in at the waist, bringing my face within inches of his. His heartbeat through his shirt quickened and mine immediately raced to catch up with it. Nerves. Maybe it was nerves I was feeling, but it didn't stop me from wanting him to draw me in even closer—if that were possible—until my lips were practically touching his. Before I could even think of how to react, his full, warm mouth was pressed heavily against mine, and if I had any breath in me at that point, it was now completely gone.

Dizzy and drenched in sweat, I try to open my eyes, hoping they might stay glued shut, because I know what it will mean when I finally manage to open them. Not only have my waking hours become overrun with daydreams, but my wishful thinking is now working its way into my nighttime routine as well. I roll over and force my right eye open, but I might have to enlist the help of a crowbar in order to fully pull the lids apart.

4:47 a.m.

I'm both shocked that I have managed to make it almost until morning without waking, and angry that my dream has been interrupted. I pull the sweat-soaked, down pillow over my head and try to drown out the night. I really want to pick up where I left off.

Unfortunately, my dreaming continues with Mrs. Norris lecturing on the motif of action and inaction in Shakespeare's "Hamlet," which ends up being not too far from her actual lesson plan for the day in reality. Biology comes and goes as usual with limited interaction between Joel and I since Caden Fisher, Joel's original lab partner, is back in school. The other classes are their typical blur of quizzes, assignments, and essays, but they are good distractions to keep my mind from spinning out of control. And before I know it, the final bell rings and school is out for the day.

Both Joel and Trent have football, and Bailey is locked away in the yearbook room for another deadline, so I situate myself on a painted blue bench under the old oak tree at the periphery of the football field. Its finish is weathered and worn, and the top layers of wood peel back, curling up like ribbons on top of a present. A ragged splinter lodges under the cuticle on my thumb and I suck the fresh drop of blood from it. It stings like crazy. My schoolwork is a mess of papers inside my bag, so I pull them out with the hand that's not bleeding in an attempt to organize and pass the time until football practice finishes at 5:00 p.m. I create six different piles, one for each class, and space them out on the bench accordingly. Bailey would be so proud.

"If this is the amount of work they expect us to do here, then I may just go to the Education Sector and put in for a transfer back to Superior." I jump out of my skin, the unfamiliar voice pulling me from my immersion in my organizational efforts. "Is that what you do to comfort yourself?" Spinning around, I spit out my thumb, still holding onto my English assignments, and cross my arms tightly over my chest.

My eyes engage with those I can only assume belong to Liam, the new kid. *Wow, are they green.*

"Sorry to startle you. I thought you heard me walking up, but it looks like you're pretty focused here, huh?" He smirks, his pale eyes illuminating as he shoves his blonde hair back from his forehead with his right hand. He works his fingers through the twists of golden coils that interlock strands as they pass through one another. His hair is a mess of loose, wavy curls that reach down to the nape of his neck. Mess really isn't the best word to describe it. Captivating is probably more appropriate. His skin is tanned; a light golden kiss from the sun. I rake my eyes over him, half in awe, half in aversion, because I know who he obviously is. Even without a formal introduction, it's clear that he's not from East Valley High. I've never seen any guy on campus that looks anything like him. I definitely would have noticed.

So you're Liam. You're the boy who stole my home. I didn't know you'd be so cute.

I shake my head, hoping to shake the hormones right out of it.

"I'm Liam," he introduces, extending a rugged, yet welcoming, hand to me. "And you are?"

"Oh, sorry. I'm Tessa—Tessa O'Donnell." I thrust my loose papers back into my bag. My attempt at order will have to wait for another time. "Have you started here yet? I haven't seen you around campus."

I plop back down on the bench, release my book bag so it falls to the ground, and bring my legs up, folding them to sit cross-legged. Liam drops down next to me—literally *right* next to me—even though the bench has a good five more feet of free sitting room available. There's ample space. Why does he feel the need to encroach on mine? *Maybe they don't teach about those things where he comes from*, I muse wryly. I scoot over a few inches, but he follows in the same direction. *Who the heck is this kid?*

"Nah, haven't started yet. I had a few group projects to finish up at Superior. I didn't want to bring my classmates' grades down by skipping out on them," he explains. "Plus, the Ed Sector doesn't make it very easy to transfer. I start here tomorrow. Wanna take a look at my schedule to see if we have any classes together?"

Shoot. He's seriously thwarting my attempt at hating him with that genuine, warm smile and overly-friendly disposition. And he stuck around at his old school because he didn't want his classmates' grades to suffer? Who does that? I don't get this guy.

I snatch the sheet of paper out of his hand and give it a cursory glance. "Yeah, we've got journalism and biology together. My cousin, Bailey, is also in those. And Joel is in biology with us, too."

"Joel McBrayer?" Liam's eyebrow quirks up. "He's the football guy, right? Everyone at Superior knows him, and I'm pretty sure all the girls want to date him. You guys are friends?"

The football guy. It annoys me that someone would sum up Joel as 'the football guy,' though I'm sure he gets that far more often than he cares for and yet he never seems to complain.

"Yeah, he's the quarterback. And yes, we're friends. He's best friends with my other cousin, Trent. He's around our house a lot."

"Your house? You live with your cousins?" Liam unabashedly pries, sliding his hair back behind his ear as he turns to look at me. Our close proximity leaves only about a foot between his face and mine. It should be too close for comfort, but strangely, it's not. And even if it was, I don't know that I'd be able to scoot my way out of his personal-boundary intrusion. He's unintentionally cornered me, and if I move at all, I run the risk of falling off the bench completely. Not wanting to make an utter fool of myself, I opt to stay put, slightly draw my head back as I answer, and all but turn my nose up at him.

"Yeah—I live with my cousins. My parents died two years ago. They took me in."

Hello self-disclosure!

Why am I so willingly sharing my life's history with this guy? Admittedly, his close-talking tendencies don't give me much room to bury myself and hide. I've got to activate my guard quickly if I'm going to continue any type of conversation with him.

"Oh wow, Tessa, I'm so sorry. That's sucks. How are you now? Are you okay?"

All bets on hating him are completely off, the sincerity in his tone stripping them away. I don't think it's just an act; his inflection truly seems to indicate concern about my well-being. As much as it's possible for one stranger to feel concern for another, I suppose. Liam's intentions seem pure. Maybe it's okay to divulge a little. And even if I don't really want to, I'm not sure I'll be able to resist.

"Oh, um. I'm okay I guess. One day at a time, right?" Even though I know one day is much too ambitious.

"If you're able to take things one day at a time, then I'd say you're doing pretty well. So what should I expect from these teachers?" He yanks his schedule back out of my hand and scrolls his finger along the list of classes, pointing to the teachers that coincide with them. I'm grateful for the changed subject matter; if I'm not careful, I'll end up telling this guy my ATM pin number and where Uncle Mark hides the handgun. Something about Liam just feels too familiar and safe, and apparently I don't do well with safe. I don't have boundaries with safe.

We sit together and talk for the next half hour or so. Liam tells me he moved into a ranch with his family last weekend, just twenty minutes outside of town. He describes the wrap-around porch and the bedrooms that hold so much history, and how his littlest brothers are sharing a room on the second floor. He says that Joshua, a freshman, claimed the larger suite on that level, and that Liam chose the upstairs room with the slanted ceiling. "It has the best view in the whole house," he says. "From that window, you can see for miles."

He doesn't need to describe it to me. I know the view. That had been my room.

"Seriously, Tessa. This place is amazing. It's historic—not anything like the cookie cutter homes here in Madison. No offense if you live in one. You're just missing out is all I'm saying."

I know I am missing out, and I want to tell him just the extent of how much I know, but I hold it in, buttoning my lips, keeping the words tucked behind them. No more self-disclosure—not with Liam—not with a boy I just met whose last name I don't even know.

"Dad's thinking of carving a big sign that says 'Hollander Ranch' for the entrance to the property. I told him that might be overkill."

So he does have a last name.

Liam Hollander. It suits him well, strong and confident like he appears to be. He has all the makings of a modern-day cowboy, and though I'm not sure if that's the look he is going for intentionally, he fits the bill. Rugged, yet heartfelt. Charming, yet intriguing.

He tells me a bit about his time at Superior High. Somehow it comes up that he was homecoming king, and I snicker at the idea of him wearing a crown. And the fact that his hair probably looked so much better than his queen counterpart. I playfully tease him and say that his locks must have been "quite luxurious under that royal crown," and he briskly jabs me in the side, right under my ribcage. I'm not ready for his elbow and it nearly knocks me completely off the bench. Liam instinctively reaches around my waist and pulls me back up before I hit the ground.

My eyes dart toward his. Panic and butterflies keep them moving along and don't allow them to stay connected with his for long. I've disclosed so much already, I'm not sure what my eyes would give away if he could read them right now. I worry they might reveal even more than I'm ready for.

"Seriously, are you trying to injure me?" I stutter, situating myself back on the bench. His hand is still planted on the curve of my hip. His palm is unusually warm.

I think about Joel immediately. About how nervous I had been the day before in the car with him. How I struggled to find conversation worthy to be spoken. How my heart surged the instant his hand touched mine. And how strange it all feels in comparison to my lighthearted interactions with Liam, this boy I've only known for an hour.

"You make it too easy," Liam jokes back, his hand still lingering on my side, his fingertips hot against my shirt. Whether conscious or not, I don't want him to move it and silently will him not to.

The truth is that *he* makes it too easy—too easy for me to relax, let my guard down, and let him in. And I'm not ready for that, especially not with someone I am still trying so desperately hard to dislike. There has to be something intolerable about him. I resolve to find out exactly what that might be.

His easygoing nature and ability to draw me out of myself doesn't change the fact that he is still the guy who is living the life that I was supposed to live. It doesn't change the fact that he's turning the hangar into a barn and that he falls asleep at night staring at the same ceiling on which I once counted sheep as a child. Though Liam appears to be a nice enough guy, he isn't anyone I want to let too close. I plan to keep him at arms length. But the heat radiating on my hip under his touch makes that a bit difficult.

He's slowly seeping in through the cracks in my self-made barricade.

"Hey, do you know what time it is?" I change the subject in my mind and in our conversation. Joel and Trent are probably almost finished with football practice. I guess it has to be close to 5:00 p.m., but the marching band typically takes to the field right before that time to practice once the football guys clear out. I haven't heard any of their instruments warming up yet.

"Yeah, it's 4:47." Liam pushes up his sleeve and glances at his wrist. I unintentionally gasp, my heart tugs and quickens within me, and apprehension laces through me. Alarm registers in my mind and likely on my face, too. A watch, probably from several decades back, is wrapped tightly around his wrist, its leather band worn and aged. I haven't seen anything like it since going through my father's belongings to sell, and he was one of the only people I'd known to wear one—his small attempt at insurgence, as he called it.

The Hub doesn't allow watches. They outlawed them years ago once the Technology Sector gained control over the national standard time. "To create consistency in our time management efforts," they'd touted, reasoning that it was only necessary for all citizens to sync with the Tech Sector's standard of time by using the digital clocks they provided for homes and places of business. Apparently, watches allow for misinterpretation because the user can manipulate them and the Hub can't guarantee their accuracy. Seems a little farfetched if you ask me, but I'm not usually one for challenging authority. I smirk inwardly at the memory of my dad's quiet rebellion. Oh, how he'd hated the Hub.

"How does that work?" The words spill out of my mouth without permission as I gawk at his seemingly ancient artifact. "My dad had one, but I've never seen anyone else with a watch before. We aren't supposed to have those. Where did you get it?" Involuntarily, my fingers reach out to brush the glass face, tracing the minute and hour hands with the edge of my nail. I recoil, realizing I've now broken the personal perimeter rules that Liam bounded through earlier.

"I'm not too worried about the Hub, Tessa. It's not like they're going to come after a kid with a watch. I mean, really, what kind of threat could this pose?" Liam twists his arm, and the watch's gold rim catches the light. "It's kinda crazy to even see one anymore, right? It belonged to my grandpa. We lived with him before buying the ranch. As a little boy, I would always ask to borrow it. When I turned sixteen he gave it to me."

His form unexpectedly changes; his shoulders square and close off, and for the first time in our conversation, there is an invisible wall between us. Something about his grandpa, maybe their relationship, summons a protective response in Liam. The freeness with which he shared and spoke earlier is now veiled with a thin layer, and I want to tear it down—to rip right through it. I want to be on that same side as Liam, not on the outside looking in. But that's not my right. How could it be after only knowing him an hour?

This silence feels strange and thick—audible almost—certainly louder than the words that filled our earlier conversation. As if on cue, the first notes of "Eye of the Tiger" echo through the air, interrupting our brief pause. Joel and Trent will soon be emerging from the locker room, ready to take me home. I have to figure out a way to wrap up my time with Liam. But part of me is content to sit on the bench until sundown if he continues talking about the ranch or his grandfather's watch. I like that there's a touch of rebellion in his act of wearing it. It reminds me of Dad. It reminds me of home.

"I should probably go check on Josh. It's his first football practice and I'm hoping they didn't kill him. Thanks for keeping me company, Tessa. I'm going to look for you in biology tomorrow, okay?"

"Oh yeah, sure. You won't have to look too hard, though. I'll be the girl in the back with the clueless expression on my face." Clueless or captivated. Probably a little of both. "Any chance you have a secret talent for identifying fetal pig anatomy?"

"Nope, not even a little bit. I'll be just as lost as you."

My heart sinks in my chest and I nearly feel it hit bottom.

I actually won't be lost in biology because I have Joel to guide me. It's unfair, and even wrong, to ask Liam questions that directly compare him to Joel. Unfair to both of them, in fact, because they are two entirely different people.

Yet somehow they both stir in me a similar feeling, a feeling of wanting more. I'm just not sure which one I want more of right now.

SIX

Liam is already gone when Joel and Trent emerge from the locker room to make their way to the parking lot. Something about waiting on the blue bench for Joel makes my stomach churn, a hint of guilt coursing through me. So I opt to perch myself on the open tailgate of Trent's truck instead, trying my best to act nonchalant. But all I think about is my much too easy conversation with Liam—a boy that neither Joel nor Trent knows exists at this point, but one to whom I feel oddly connected.

I hop down from the rusty truck bed to welcome the boys and all but stumble straight into Joel's solid chest, tripping over my own clumsy feet. He grabs both of my shoulders to steady me and chuckles, "Hey, did you miss me?" Trent tosses his gear into the metal bed with a thud.

I smile my answer, knowing the truth is, had there been no Liam to keep me company, I *absolutely* would have missed him. I would have spent the past two hours organizing my book bag in an effort to distract myself from my wandering mind. I would have played last night's dream over and over again in my head, desperately hoping that at some point it would become a reality and not just some faraway fantasy. I would have devoted every minute to Joel.

But I can still feel Liam's warm, assuring hand on my hip. And the spot where it rested throbs in longing for its return.

"How was practice? Was Coach hard on you guys today?" Dodging the question altogether seems to be the most logical approach—the best way to spare Joel's feelings, and the best way to avoid facing mine.

"It wasn't so bad. But the end of the season is coming. Coach is gonna crack down harder on us, I'm sure," Joel replies, slowly releasing me. He opens the passenger side door for me to climb into the back of the cab.

"Speak for yourself, McBrayer. Today's practice was a killer—I'm seriously not going to be able to walk tomorrow," Trent groans. "And I'm kinda getting tired of Mrs. Morton yelling at me for being late to class every day, not to mention her threats about reporting me to the Ed Chair. There is no way I'm going to be able to run across campus tomorrow morning with my quads like this!"

Trent slides into the driver's seat. "We can't be late tomorrow, Tessa." He speaks directly to me, maintaining eye contact in the rear view mirror, glowering at me like he is my father. "Please try to get a good night's sleep so we can get here early." I half expect him to scold me and tell me that I need to start cleaning up the dishes or put away the laundry as well by his tone. But I know he is channeling his inner Mrs. Morton and that my sleep schedule can't truly affect him as much as he lets on. And the longer, un-interrupted duration of sleep I had last night as opposed to my routine 2:34 a.m. wakeup call honestly makes me feel like a new person. Or at least a less fatigued version of myself than usual. Maybe it was that or the interaction with Joel from the day before—whatever it is, I feel more at peace and well rested than I have at any given point in the past two years. So I, too, hope for another good night of sleep, as much for myself as for Trent with his half-threats.

***

My cheek is numb against a hard surface; the resulting pins and needles sensation draws me out of my unconscious state prick by tickly prick. I lift my head off the kitchen table, but the weight of sleep makes the effort more difficult than expected. I wipe the drool from my biology textbook, my makeshift pillow for the last two hours.

7:36 p.m.

There go my chances for the full night's sleep both Trent and I wished for. My early evening nap might make that a little challenging.

Two heavy footsteps resonate down the hall. I hastily pull the elastic band from my wrist and twist it around my tangled mess of hair. I cover my mouth to yawn and feel the thick lines creased down my cheek, indentations that give away my textbook-pillow-slumber.

"Hey Tessa, I'm headed home. Is everything okay?" Joel doesn't mention my disheveled state when he enters the kitchen. I'm grateful he's always a gentleman, though it's glaringly apparent that I'm not at my finest. "You seemed a little off this afternoon. Didn't know if it had to do with yesterday. I was hoping we'd be able to chat tonight, but you looked so sweet drooling on your biology book that I just couldn't wake you."

I vow to start doing my homework in my room. I embarrass myself enough when I'm alert and awake. The last thing I need is to betray myself while I'm sleeping.

"Nah, everything's good. I'm sorry I slept the whole time you were here," I mutter, pushing myself up from table.

"Tess, I'm pretty much a permanent fixture here. Don't worry about entertaining me. I was just glad that you were able to get some sleep. Trent was telling me how you haven't slept much since your parents—" Joel stops abruptly, hesitating before he says the word "died." It isn't as if it's a big secret. Everyone knows.

But Joel's trying to guard my feelings and I can identify a sensitivity in his voice that feels oddly familiar. Liam's tone held that same warmth earlier today.

"Well, I'm glad that Trent could keep you entertained since I couldn't," I interject so Joel doesn't have to finish his sentence. "You coming over tomorrow? Maybe we could hang out after practice."

Joel flashes his infamous smile. There it is again—that fluttering feeling from yesterday when his hand brushed mine in biology. It resonates in both my stomach and my heart in unison.

"That sounds great. Maybe I could take you out somewhere after practice? Like maybe we could get something to eat? That is, unless you have plans to sleep through dinner again."

"No, no scheduled naptime for me. I would love that."

"Okay, I'll plan to pick you up here at 6:00 then. Is it weird to admit that I'm actually kinda nervous?" Joel asks. I bite my bottom lip to pin back a giggle.

"No, not weird at all. But don't be nervous. It'll be fun." I place my hand squarely on his forearm, an attempt to calm his nerves. My own go skyrocketing.

"Perfect. I'll pick you up tomorrow at 6:00. It's a date."

***

The repetitive drone of the alarm clock draws me sluggishly out of unconsciousness, but I have to concentrate hard to focus my eyes. The sleep gradually sloughs off and the numbers edge into view.

I've slept through an entire night—the first full night in two years.

I can hardly believe it, and I don't know whether to do a victory dance or gawk at the clock in awe. I don't have time for either. School starts in twenty minutes.

I rush to get ready, hoping Trent will recognize my efforts and cut me some slack, but no such luck. He is too much like an annoying big brother to let me off so easy.

I have my book bag packed and ready to go when I decide I have time to pour a glass of orange juice before Trent makes his way downstairs. I lift the jug out of the stainless steel refrigerator and am just about to tilt it slightly to pour into my glass, when Trent's thunderous voice enters the room before he does, like a train whistle warning as it approaches.

"*Tessa!* Let's go! It's *7:36*!" Trent bellows. "We don't have time for orange juice—we have to leave *now*!"

He's right. I don't have time for this glass of juice. All my spare time will be spent cleaning up the sticky mess I've just created. Trent's voice practically made me jump out of my skin and caused the jug to literally jump out of my grasp, too.

"You don't have time to clean that up. *We have to go, now!*"

Trent's visible fear—maybe not necessarily fear, but respect—of our government is even more apparent than usual in his nervous nature this morning. Mrs. Morton's threats have really gotten to him. I guess we all should fear the Hub to some extent. It's hard not to fear something that ultimately controls your future, even though that future is seemingly far off and at a distance.

Maybe since Trent's a senior, his future doesn't feel as remote as mine does. Maybe that's why he's so concerned about jeopardizing his good standing with the Hub. He talks about his upcoming Expo often, so I know he hopes to be recruited. The last thing any student wants is to be one of the unchosen. It's happened before, and those students are forced to select their own Sectors, but they never fully assimilate. We call them the Discards, those who aren't picked up or actively recruited by a specific Sector. They're discarded and snubbed, and they're the only ones forced to look out for their own future. It doesn't actually sound so bad to me. I think I could do without the guidance of the Hub in my life. But society would look down on such a thought as rebellion, so I know I can never express it.

"Trent, don't be so high-strung. I'm not going to leave orange juice all over your parents' counter. If you're in such a hurry, I'll just see if I can get a ride with Joel," I retort, unwinding the roll of paper towels around my hand. I fold them and drop them on top of the counter to sop up the spilled juice.

Trent jumps at the chance to leave and heads to school alone. I retrieve my phone to call Joel, my fingers inadvertently quaking as I dial. *Hi, Joel. Can I get a ride with you?* My voice shakes the five times I recite it, but when he picks up on the third ring, I'm able to make my request without much trembling in my tone.

Part of me is excited about showing up to school with Joel, just the two of us. I like the idea of all the eyes that will be on us. People don't eye me too often. But out of the high school population, there's one set of pale green eyes that I don't want on Joel and me. Unfortunately, we all have biology together. I'm not sure how I'll be able to avoid that interaction. My mouth goes dry at the thought, and I almost regret calling Joel in the first place as his truck eases into the driveway outside.

It isn't as though I would have called Liam to pick me up, though. I don't even have his number, for one thing. And he might already have a girlfriend, for all I know. How ridiculous of me to assume that someone who had just been nominated his school's home-coming king isn't already involved with a girl, or even a few different girls. After all, he *is* pretty smooth. And even if he isn't already taken, how forward of me to think that he would even be interested in driving me to school.

The car ride with Joel is quick and uneventful, especially when compared to the near-disastrous episode from two days before. When we arrive at school, he swiftly gets out of his seat and meanders over to the passenger side, holds the door open for me, and then effortlessly slides his hand into mine. *Whoa.* My heart leaps inside my chest, and a small, quick

breath releases from my lips. Joel makes me nervous—
a good nervous—but nervous nonetheless. I want to
feel comfortable with him. Maybe at some point, a
warm, fuzzy feeling will edge out all of these
butterflies. But right now, the butterflies are clearly
winning.

We walk hand in hand to Mr. Harrisburg's
biology class and I can literally feel the eyes on us—all
those glances I thought I desired earlier, but which
now feel prying and intrusive as opposed to envious
and interested. But the whispers are even worse. I'm
hot with discomfort and incredibly out of my league.
I'm pretty sure everyone else thinks so, too. Joel is sort
of a town hero, and who am I compared to that?
Granted, I am his best friend's cousin, so I guess I rank
a little higher than the girls who've never even spoken
a word to him, but have their names plus his scrawled
across their notebooks. Even still, Joel is an icon, and
pretty much any girl he has at his side is instantly
viewed the same. I don't know if I'm ready for that.

And I definitely am not ready to see Liam sitting
in Bailey's seat upon entering our biology classroom.
Instinctively, I pull my hand from Joel's, pretending to
fumble with something in my book bag, and I make
my way to my seat near the back of the room.

"Hey Tess," Liam smirks, running his hands
through his golden hair. *Stop doing that.* My knees go
even weaker than they were the entire hand-in-hand
walk to class with Joel. They're nothing but Jell-O
now. "Mr. Harrisburg said Bailey's taking pictures of
the academic decathlon for yearbook. He'll have an

extra desk for me tomorrow, but I get to sit in her seat today. What d'ya say, lab partner?"

Liam shoves his hand at me across our desk. I can still feel the heat from Joel's protective grip minutes earlier pulsing in mine, and I hesitate, but I finally succumb and reach out toward Liam's. It's an entirely different gesture than Joel's, but it causes that same warm ache inside me. I wish it didn't, because it's so confusing. I decide to view it merely as the formal beginning to our new friendship and nothing more.

"So, what do we do with this thing?" Liam picks up the cold, metal scalpel and stabs at the ribs of our fetal pig. He reminds me all too much of myself and my own floundering in lab. Though he hasn't turned around to watch any of our exchange, I can sense Joel's curious eavesdropping. He hasn't been formally introduced to Liam, but it must be evident that I already have—that this clearly isn't our first encounter. A remorseful pang pokes me in the gut, as though Joel has taken that same scalpel and pierced me with it instead of the pig

"Hey Joel, this is Liam. We met yesterday during practice when I was waiting for you and Trent." I introduce them in an attempt to make things right. Some kind of clarification is necessary to explain Liam's overly-friendly nature, though it appears he's this way with everyone he meets by the looks of it. Maybe I'm not an exception to that rule. I blush at the idea of even briefly hoping there might be something more.

"Hey Liam—good to meet you." Joel, ever the gentleman, extends his hand to Liam. His consistent sincerity overwhelms me. "Your family moved into Tess's ranch, huh?"

Liam, immersed in the guts of our pig, stops in his tracks, and his head whips up to meet mine. "Seriously? That was your place, Tessa? How come you didn't say anything yesterday?"

Because it didn't come up. Because it didn't seem important. Because I didn't have the chance. All of those explanations are lies, and I know that both Joel and Liam would see right through them. *Because if I told you, I'd be letting a piece of you in and I'm not ready for that.* Nope. I'm definitely not about to say that to a near-perfect stranger.

"I don't know. I think I didn't say anything because you were so excited about the place. I didn't want to put a damper on that or taint your view of the ranch."

"Well, now I feel like a total jerk," Liam says. "I was going on and on about how great the place is. Apparently, there was no need for that. Clearly, you already know." Joel rotates back to his desk and his assignment, and Liam and I are left to our conversation. But I know Joel still has a listening ear tuned into our discussion. "Seriously, Tess. I really do feel like such a jerk. I honestly had no clue."

"Of course not. You couldn't have known," I reassure. "Plus, it was kinda nice to hear someone talk about the ranch again. I've always known what an

81

amazing place it is—it felt so good to hear that the person who lives in it now feels the same way."

Liam nods, understanding my reasoning, and leans back in his seat, stretching out his arm and placing his hand on the back of my chair. I shudder. It feels like the in-class equivalent of putting his arm around me, and I'm overcome with embarrassment, both for myself, for Joel, and for Liam who doesn't seem to have any idea that there is anything going on between us. Luckily, he suddenly feels the urge to tuck his hair behind his ear once more, so his temporary hand placement doesn't last long enough to draw any unwanted attention.

"I want you to come see it," he blurts. "In fact, I'd *love* for you to see it. We haven't done much to it yet, but we've got some great plans. It would be nice to have your input."

I gather that Joel doesn't like where our conversation is going when he interjects, "So, Tess, did you have any thoughts on where you'd like to go tonight for dinner? I really want to try the new sushi place, but I've heard it's pretty hard to get into."

Being tangled in a spider web must be pretty much the same feeling I'm currently experiencing. I'm stuck, unsure of which direction to go or whom to answer, but I know the longer I sit here without doing anything, the greater the likelihood that I will be paralyzed forever due to my inaction. Like prey in a web.

"That sounds great, Joel. I'd love that." I lift my scalpel off the table and nudge the organs around inside our pig, bumping into Liam's utensil to get his attention as I murmur, "And I'd love to come see the ranch. Seriously, you have no idea how much I've wanted to go back."

Liam leans in, as though my words literally draw him closer to me. He's just out of Joel's earshot, reenacting his close-talking from yesterday. His breath tickles the edge of my ear.

"Good. It's a date then."

SEVEN

"Tessa, I have to be honest with you. I really don't think I can do this anymore—the whole thought of it is starting to make me feel physically sick," Joel says. "I've been pretending for a while now, but it's becoming nearly impossible for me to keep this up much longer."

And it's true. He looks ill, as though all of the color has left his face, replaced with a greenish hue. The thought of Joel being physically sickened by it all makes me uneasy and my stomach free falls.

He picks up another pink slice of raw salmon between his chopsticks, draws it closer to his mouth, and gags, a gurgling belch wet with disgust. The sushi falls back onto his plate. He covers his mouth with his napkin to catch the seemingly imminent vomit but nothing comes.

"Nope. I *really* can't do this. Do you care if we go to Burger Bill's instead?" Joel's brown eyes are wide with embarrassment. "I feel like I've ruined our evening—I don't know why I suggested sushi—I've never had it but it seemed like the impressive place to go. But obviously none of this is impressing you. And I really don't want to throw up in front of you."

I conceal my own mouth with the cloth that's blanketed across my lap, masking the giggles that involuntarily escape. That Joel McBrayer wants to impress me makes me laugh out loud.

"Yes, please, let's get out of here. I'm so not cut out for this kind of food, if you can even call it that." My stomach thanks me. "I definitely prefer my dinner cooked. Burger Bill's sounds amazing."

Joel pulls several crumpled up bills from his wallet and tosses them onto the table, grabbing my hand to lead me out of the restaurant. The chill of the cold night air is refreshing against my skin. I hadn't realized how stuffy and stifling it felt inside that box of a restaurant. Maybe it was the act of trying to enjoy something I truly didn't, but it's now freeing to be out of the building and in the open air. It's easier to breathe, like a binding corset has been untied and my rib cage is free to expand and contract again.

"Usually I can just suck it up, but I really don't think raw fish is my thing. I'm glad that doesn't disappoint you."

Joel, not much about you can disappoint me.

"Are you kidding me? I'm relieved to be out of there. I was worried that it would become your new favorite place and I'd have to spend many more dinners trying to suppress my gag reflex."

Joel smirks. I think it's because I mentioned more dates. This grin of his is becoming much more frequent and easier to predict. *Joel McBrayer is flirting with you, Tessa.* I wonder how many times he's given me this look before and I have failed to make the obvious connection.

We pull into the drive-thru of Burger Bill's, and a crackly, somewhat robotic female voice echoes through the speaker. Without hesitation, Joel orders for both of us. I like the idea of him taking charge—something about it feels protective and intentional. He guides the car around the curve and a brace-faced girl at the window stretches the hot, steaming bag of food out to Joel, her hand lingering just a little too long during the exchange. I actually think I hear an audible sigh slip through her lips. He hands the food off to me, not acknowledging his most recent admirer's affections.

I sit in the passenger seat, my eyes involuntarily transfixed on him. The way the moon shines into the car focuses all of the available light on him. For a moment I just sit there, gazing at his strong illuminated profile. This perfectly moonlit, gorgeous boy. It really is easy to see why every girl in town dreams of being with him—even metal mouth back there couldn't take her eyes off of him. He is incredibly handsome, no doubt about it.

"So…I'm not ready to go home yet. I want to take you somewhere—is that okay?"

I startle, surprised by his voice.

"Yeah, of course. We gotta eat this food anyway. I'm up for whatever." And I truly am. I *am* up for anything with Joel. I feel safe with Joel. Nervous and filled to the brim with butterflies, but safe. Even though we have to work harder at conversation and things don't always come naturally, I know I'm protected when I'm with him.

And I've never really felt that way with a boy before.

I've desperately wanted someone to protect me, for years now. For someone to *choose* to protect me. I know without a doubt that my Uncle Mark would do anything for me—that he would probably even give his own life for mine—but I know that stems from an obligation. An obligation he made to my mom and dad so many years ago when they wrote up their wills and decided whom my guardian would be if the unthinkable ever happened. Though Uncle Mark and Aunt Cathy warmly accepted me into their family, they didn't choose me the same way my parents had. They stopped expanding their family once they had one boy and one girl. A third child hadn't been in their plans any more than it had been in mine to lose my own parents.

So the thought of someone *choosing* me, of someone *wanting* me, is foreign. Very much welcome, but foreign still. There is a sense of security and safety in that. And that's the exact security that Joel offers me.

We drive for a while in silence. It's not quite as awkward as the previous car rides. I think Joel might actually be okay with quiet. He looks quite content from his post in the driver's seat. I wonder if he is daydreaming again like he admitted to before. I hope he is. It makes my dream from earlier a little less foolish when I pretend he is thinking and hoping for the same thing, too. And it makes me feel closer to him—to think that our thoughts are sharing the same time and space.

The amber-colored storefront lights morph into starlight as we drive up the twisting roadways just outside the valley. Joel's truck begins to climb and the engine struggles up the incline of the mountainside, growling in its efforts. Trees blur into one fuzzy, dizzying evergreen scape outside my window. It's like a painted forest on a canvas and the artist has decided to wipe it all away, blending the leaves, the shades of green, and the textures into one mass of woodlands. It's a confusion of color, but equally, stunningly beautiful.

"Okay. We're here." After fifteen minutes without noise, Joel's voice cuts through the now welcome, comfortable silence. He steers off the side of the road; the wheels slowly find their grooves in the dirt.

I look around.

It is absolutely breathtaking. Surrounded on all sides are the tallest pine trees I've ever seen. Their large, formidable trunks and dense branches force my eyes directly up to the white canopy of glowing stars overhead. In all of my life, and even when I lived at the ranch, I've never been somewhere so dark, yet equally as illuminated, all coexisting in the same space. I'd been expecting Joel to take me to some mountaintop with a view of the valley—a typical spot for many teenage date nights. But this is an entirely different scene, and it overwhelms me to the point of speechlessness.

"It might not seem like much, but this is my favorite place on earth. I come here a few times a month. I don't know about you, but I've never seen so many stars at once. Here, hop up." Joel reaches for my hand and helps me into the bed of his truck. I set down the bag filled with our dinner, still keeping my eyes on the stars above. I have a crazy urge to count them all, but I know even if I begin at this moment there will never be enough days to total their number.

Joel retrieves a tattered, blue and gold gym bag from the cab of his truck and tosses it into the bed. He jumps up into the back and sits down next to me, finding his place in the ruts of the cold, corrugated metal.

"I like to come here because it makes me feel small. Small might not even be the right word—it makes me feel normal." His eyes flicker with the same intensity of the stars blanketed overhead. "Sometimes it seems like there are so many expectations for me, like I'm supposed to be some hero or something. I don't know—I almost feel kind of silly even admitting that." Joel pulls out a hamburger and begins to eat it, speaking around his bites of food, as though our conversation can't even wait until he's done eating. "But sometimes it feels like everyone has this idea about me—my future, my Sector—who I'm supposed to be. I don't want to be larger than life. I don't want strangers to care about what Sector I join or what football team I play for. Sometimes I just want to blend in like all of those stars up there."

His eyes meet mine and I can't look away, not that I want to. But even if I did, I know it would be impossible. I'm staring so much deeper into those brown eyes than ever before. They reveal so much more of him as he speaks to me, and he's so much more than I have ever given him credit. I could have just as easily been lumped into the category of Joel supporters, of those people who idolized him in some silly way. But it is hard not to. And saying things like this makes it even more difficult not to place him on the pedestal he deserves.

"I don't know. Don't get me wrong. I'm grateful for it all—for all of the opportunities and the trust that everyone puts in me. To know that I won't be a Discard and that the Sectors are actively seeking me out. But sometimes it would be nice to not have so many expectations, you know?" He crumples up the wrapper to his hamburger and shoots it back into the bag as though the bag is a hoop. A perfect shot of course.

I am voiceless, stunned into silence by Joel's unsolicited confession.

"I bet." I find my words. "That's a huge responsibility to bear, I'm sure. To carry our whole town's hopes and dreams—even our government's—I don't know how you do it." I shake my head. "But I do know that you're cut out for it. It honestly just

90

seems to come so naturally for you. I don't think any other high school guy in your position would be nearly as humble or do what you do with such grace. It's like you were made for it, Joel."

His neck cranes back and his face bathes in the starlight, a soft, white glow reflecting on him, highlighting his form amid the surrounding ebony cover of the forest. "I don't know. Sometimes I think so, I guess. Sometimes it does feel like I've been set apart for a reason. Like there is a bigger plan for me than what I can see right now. But sometimes I just want to be a normal high school student, you know?"

He slides down onto his gym bag, folding into the fabric grooves like a pillow. I sit still, self-conscious and unsure of what to do with myself and my awkward limbs. For some reason it's like I have extras at the moment—I've never been so aware of my extremities before, at least not so intentional about where to place them. I teeter back and forth, crossing my arms over my chest, then thrusting my hands into my pockets. I'm fidgeting. Joel wraps his hand around my wrist and draws me down next to him, pulling me into his warm, welcoming body.

"Sorry Tess, this gym bag reeks—you're not going to want to get anywhere near it," Joel advises as my head finds its home on his solid chest. I inhale deeply. I can't smell his gym bag at all, just his warm mix of cologne and sweat, and I am comforted by the intoxicating scent.

"No worries, I'm fine."

He weaves his fingers through my hair and we both stare up into the cloudless sky. If I got flustered by Liam combing his own hair with his fingers, then Joel's act just about sends me over the top. My stomach squeezes and my palms grow damp.

"Seriously, Tessa. I don't think you have any idea how long I've wanted to be here with you. I mean, literally here in this exact place," Joel says. "There are so many times I've come here by myself and wished that you were here with me." His honesty catches me off guard.

"Seriously?" I'm shocked. "I had no idea. Honestly Joel, I thought all I was to you was Trent's cousin."

"You're kidding. You had no idea? Why do you think I'm always at the Buchman's?"

"I don't know—because you and Trent are best friends."

A grin spreads across Joel's face and his eyes roll slightly. He pauses before he speaks. "Come on, Tess. I mean, Trent's great and all, but I don't like him *that* much," he teases. "And why do you think I'm always trying to talk to you in pig lab? Or convince Trent to drive me to and from school? You seriously had no idea? Am I really that subtle? I thought it was pretty obvious."

"No, not obvious at all. Or maybe I'm just dense—that could be the case, too," I say. "But honestly, Joel, why me? I mean, it's no secret that you could have any girl at East Valley. Or any other school in Madison for that matter. What I don't get is why you would be interested in someone like me?"

"Why wouldn't I be? Tess—I think you're even more clueless than you might realize." He suppresses a laugh. "Seriously, all of the guys talk about you in the locker room. How beautiful you are, how innocent you seem. How you're one of those girls that's gorgeous and doesn't even know it. Plus, there's always been something about you that just feels familiar. Like you have the ability to make people feel instantly comfortable. Why wouldn't everyone want to be around someone like that? It's kinda hot."

The only thing that feels hot about me is the temperature of my flushed cheeks, radiating my embarrassment right out of me.

"But even all of that isn't really why I first noticed you. I know your story—I know what you've been through. And for some reason, I've always felt a connection with you," Joel divulges. "Like how everyone seems to have certain expectations for you, too. I feel like I can relate to that. How you're living a life that has to be so different from the one you imagined. I feel that way a lot—like I've been shoved into this role and have to keep playing the part for the benefit of everyone else. I don't know. I thought maybe you felt that way, too." Joel offers an out for his explanation through his wavering tone.

But he's right. I have. Even if I haven't known it or verbalized it out loud, Joel articulates everything I know to be true about myself. And it startles me. I am okay with Joel serving the protective role. Knight in shining armor I'm good with. But Joel the counselor? I hadn't counted on that.

"I don't know what to say," is all I can force out.

Joel's frame sinks, his shoulders dropping.

"I'm sorry, Tess. I feel like I've just unfairly projected all of these assumptions on you. That's exactly what I just said I hated. I guess I'm no better."

"No—no, you are—you're a whole lot better." I sound ridiculous, but I can't conjure up anything else to say and I need to reassure him. The last thing I want is to have him take back all of the things he's just confided in me. "And I think you're right about all of that. I'm not sure I ever put those pieces together on my own, but I agree with you."

"Tess, you really are incredible," he sighs. "I hope you know that about yourself. Everyone else does."

It's crazy that Joel could think I'm incredible. It is even more farfetched that anyone else in school gave me a second thought. I'm not incredible. I'm ordinary. People don't pay attention to ordinary. Ordinary doesn't get noticed. But here I am, alone with Joel, and I feel incredibly noticed.

This has got to be some kind of act. I can't possibly be the first girl Joel has brought to this place. I bet he gives everyone the same speech and has the same coy grin and stares up at the same stars in wonder. Maybe this is his thing; maybe it is his ploy to win the hearts of half the school's population by telling them how wonderful they are, how insecure he actually is, and how they are more alike than it seems.

But as quickly as my theory surfaces, it's extinguished as I roll over and prop myself up on his chest, finding his eyes. Joel's authenticity can't be masked. He rises up a bit so our faces are inches apart, and his breath caresses my chilled skin, warming my cheek where it touches. Visions from my dream flood in and my heart picks up tempo. Joel places his hand on the back of my neck and pulls me toward him as he plants his soft, full lips on my forehead. He closes his eyes and breathes deep. My body, tense in anticipation, relaxes under his embrace. He keeps his lips there for a moment, then pulls slowly away, locking his eyes with mine as he draws back, gazing at me intently. Both muscular arms wrap around me, and he pulls me in and glides back down against the truck bed. I want to kiss him, to feel his lips against mine and not only on my forehead.

"Tess—you seriously are so beautiful." Joel sweeps away a stray lock of hair that falls across my forehead, draping into my eyes. The backs of his strong, yet gentle, fingers graze my cheek as his hand slides across my face and sits at the crook between my neck and my jawline. They linger there, then rotate over and cup my chin in his broad palm. I close my eyes, responding inadvertently to his touch. "I mean it, you're breathtaking."

For someone to use those words in the midst of actual breathtaking beauty is wrong.

"I'm really glad sushi was such a flop. This is so much better than trying not to throw up in front of you," Joel says, squeezing me as he continues to play with my hair.

"I have to agree with you on that one," I tease, fiddling with the button on his shirt rather than planting my hand on his chest. I'm new to this physical affection thing and I hope he doesn't notice. It gives me more butterflies than I feel like I can contain. Part of me wants these butterflies to go away and part of me welcomes them—I have never felt as alive as I do now, and their fluttering presence is a tangible reminder of that.

"Ugh, what time is it?" Joel groans. "We should probably head back—I don't want Mark to think I've kidnapped you or anything."

It must be close to 9:00 p.m. I assume we've spent at least an hour in the mountains, though I'd be happy to stay here until morning. I think I would get a better night's sleep in Joel's arms in the back of his truck under the cold night sky than in the comfort of my own bed. But I know that isn't reality. Maybe none of this really is. Maybe tomorrow Joel will realize what a huge mistake he's made pouring out his soul to me. Maybe he will take it all back. Maybe I'll be left alone again.

But maybe things won't go back to the way they were. Maybe this changes everything for me. And for Joel. *For us.* Maybe it is a new beginning. And for once, the thought of starting over doesn't evoke a sense of fear in me.

Because this time I won't be alone.

EIGHT

"I don't see how that theory holds any water." His tone was unflinching, his stance firm. Mom reached across the wood tabletop, lightly touching his arm, a gentle reminder for him to keep his cool. Somehow her touch did just that and Dad's eyes and voice softened simultaneously. "Yes, I understand, Mr. Chairman. But we don't have it. How you think we can produce that amount of money in that timeframe is ludicr—I mean, it's near impossible."

From my vantage point in the hall, the voice on the other end—inaudible up to that point—raised slowly, becoming heated and authoritative. *Retroactive. Taxes. Responsibility and duty. Integrity.*

Dad's eyes rolled, meeting my mom's, and his hand opened and closed, mimicking a blabbering mouth. Mom dropped her head and giggled quietly into her scarf.

"Like I said before, I understand. I'll do my best to gather the funds. Thank you, Mr. Chairman."

Dad hung up the phone, anger and frustration, along with a bit of mockery, emanating from within him. I stepped into the kitchen, giving away my eavesdropping, and sat next to him at the table. I rested my head on his shoulder.

"Sorry you had to hear that, Tess," he apologized, stroking my hair. "I know I'm probably the worst example of respecting the Hub, but the hoops they want us to jump through now are impossible."

He was right. He was a textbook case for what my teachers called a "Silent Disobedient." Though I should have been afraid of his dissent, I'd actually admired it.

"What is it now?" Fourteen-year-olds weren't often privy to government information but my dad always openly shared his knowledge, unless I were to ask him about his time as a soldier in the war.

"The Transportation Sector is instituting a fifty percent, retroactive tax on all commissioned flights during the war." He thumbed through the cream-colored sheets in his flight book, landing on the pages from that timeframe. "That's completely unjust in my opinion. The Hub wasn't even fully in power at the time. They have no right to the money earned during those years. They were just coming into being."

"Then why are they asking for it? I thought you were part of Defense and Protection when the Sectors formed during the war. Weren't all soldiers?" I'd asked. "Why should you have to pay Transportation Sector fees if you weren't even in that Sector?" Curious and confused, I'd never understood my dad's staunch opposition to the Hub until that point.

His eyes widened with the realization that I knew more than I'd always pretended to let on. "You're right, Tess. I wasn't part of the Transportation Sector during the war. War is a complicated and messy beast. Sometimes things happen and decisions are made at the top without your consent and you just have to follow them. And sometimes that involves Sector Reallocation."

He'd been Reallocated. Better than Discarded in a sense, but dishonorable and shameful nonetheless. Dad had never told me that before and I wanted to know more, but it wasn't my right. I was just grateful that a different Sector had recruited him. Discards not only carry their disgrace but their families wear it, too. They're the unwanted. At least Reallocates have the opportunity to be recruited and picked up by another Sector that sees promise in them. I suddenly felt an uneasy indebtedness to the Transportation Sector for choosing my dad and saving our family from that immanent dishonor.

"So what they're saying now is that the power shift actually began the day the war started, not during it." He punched numbers into the calculator with his index finger and slid it across the table to Mom. Her eyes widened and her shoulders dropped in resignation. "And honestly, Tess. It doesn't matter what their reasoning is. It's the Hub. They do as they please. We're just puppets in their game."

His assertion had haunted me during our original conversation, and now again as I draw my covers up to my chin—not certain if I've been dreaming or am experiencing some kind of déjà vu. It sure feels like déjà vu, reliving those exact words, that same dialogue, feeling his warmth all over again. I squeeze my eyes shut and send up a thank you to whomever gave me this small gift, this revisiting a brief moment of my past, however melancholy it may be. My eyes pop open again and I turn to the clock.

11:12 p.m.

***

"You have three minutes to find a partner and read over the first five questions on the handout. And you have to interview someone different than last week's assignment. Learn to make friends, people!" The alternating clicks of Mr. Crawford's boot heels against the avocado-colored tile floor produce an antique 'tick-tock, tick-tock' sound of a clock. It implies that time is of the essence just as effectively as his tone does.

"And please, feel free to get creative. You are not bound to the questions on that paper. Be inventive! Tell a story! Let your voice be heard!" The assignment sheet drops out of his hand and flutters onto my desk. I shove it to the side and continue to trace the familiar numbers carved on my tabletop, etched by some student decades ago, I'm sure.

11:12.

The same time I awoke last night and the same time third period ends. I'm sure whoever wrote those numbers was watching the numbers on the wall, too, anxiously counting the minutes until class was over. I follow the lines with the tip of my pencil, small pieces of graphite lodging themselves into the grooves, and avoid looking up to find a partner. Bailey and I interviewed one another last week so I know she is out of the running according to Mr. Crawford's explicit instructions. I don't like being put on the spot and the idea of choosing someone scares the heck out of me. Maybe I can wait it out—there is an odd number of students in the class. Maybe I won't be paired with anyone.

"Hey, we worked together so well in biology yesterday. Whatdya say?" Liam slides into the empty desk next to me, leans in and raises his right eyebrow to frame his inquisitive green eyes. They match his celery colored t-shirt so perfectly. It's as though the shade of his irises are pulled directly out of it, like the seamstress fashioned the shirt specifically to reflect them.

"Yeah, sure. I always hate these things. I think I work much better independently."

"Then you're in luck. I'm the group project king. No man left behind, right?" A smile rises from the corner of Liam's mouth and crinkles his eyes. "Seriously though. This will be fun. I get to know you a little more, you get to know me. Win-win."

He holds the sheet of interview questions in front of him and squints as he scans the assignment.

"Hey, Tess," Bailey whispers from two rows up, mouthing her words so as not to draw Mr. Crawford's unwanted attention. "Do a *Day in the Life*. That way we can use it for yearbook, too." She winks.

Bailey always has yearbook on the brain. Somehow every assignment for her remaining classes always links back to yearbook. Her teachers never seem to have a problem with the crossing over so she continues to do it, and does it quite well. I wonder how her journalistic talents will aid her in the future. I'm sure she'll be recruited for the Media and Entertainment Sector at her Expo next month. And now she's even recruited me to submit my own work for the school yearbook, without even getting credit for it. The things you do for family.

I answer her with an approving nod.

"So, this all looks like junk," Liam says. "What do you say we do something else? No offense, but I don't care much about your favorite color or what you want to be when you grow up." Straightforward. That's one way to describe Liam. What you see is what you get.

"Yeah, I agree. What if we do something like a *Day in the Life*? Like I follow you around for a day, you follow me? Or is that silly?"

"Nah, that's a great idea, Tess. Plus, it'll get you to the ranch even faster, so I'm all for that." Our eyes meet and Liam's lips twist into a scheming grin. "It says this is due a week from today. What do you think about working on it this weekend? How about Saturday?"

I stifle a snicker, but it works just about as well as trying to hold in an impending sneeze. *A day in the life with Liam on Saturday. A day in the life with Joel on Sunday.* I already promised Bailey I would help her edit the yearbook spread about Joel this weekend. Now I'm taking on that same assignment with Liam, too. The irony isn't lost on me.

"Sure, yeah. I don't have anything going on. There's the football game in the afternoon, but I guess I can skip it." *You're skating on thin ice here, Tess.*

I wonder how Joel will feel about me spending the day with Liam as opposed to standing on the sidelines, cheering him on during one of our last home games. It isn't as though we have any firm definition as to what we are. I'm not even sure that we are anything at all. After last night's conversation it seems like we are well on our way to becoming something. But still, up to this point we aren't officially labeled, so what's the harm?

And this with Liam is strictly schoolwork. That can't upset Joel. If he had to spend his Saturday at some girl's house for a school project, I would be totally supportive of that. Wouldn't I? Or am I trying to justify what I know to be wrong? Maybe not necessarily wrong, but deceitful. Or at least not entirely honest. Either way, Joel will understand. And truthfully, I can't think of anywhere I'd rather be than at the ranch. Even if there was no Liam. Though the thought of spending the day with him is entertaining.

"Okay. So my days start pretty early with all the animals. You sure you're up for this?"

"How early are we talking? And how many animals? I'm not much of a morning person."

"My parents are part of the Agriculture Sector. Us Aggies are morning people by nature, and you're going to have to become one if you plan to spend any amount of time with me."

"Why would I be spending more time with you, Liam?" His confidence surprises me, though I don't know why. He has been nothing but self-assured from the moment I met him.

"Because I'm irresistible."

My heart hiccups.

"Teasing, Tessa. Teasing." I hope he hasn't noticed my pause. "No, I just figure you'll probably want to spend more time at the ranch. I mean, if I were in your shoes I would. And my parents love to entertain. I know my mom would enjoy having another female around the house. She's definitely outnumbered."

"I'm sure your house has been filled with girls, Liam. I mean, come on, you were homecoming king and all. I bet they were knocking down your door and you had to fend them off with a stick." Our exchange is teasing in nature, yet I knot my fingers in my lap and hope for a serious answer.

"I don't know. Maybe. But I'm pretty picky—I don't just date to date or go out with a girl just to have a girlfriend. That's not my thing."

"So you don't have a whole list of admirers back at Superior then, huh?" I chew nervously on the gummy, rubber eraser secured to the end of my pencil, not sure why I've decided to be so bold in my questioning. Our interviewing process hasn't even officially started and I've already begun the interrogation.

"No, I probably do," he grins coyly, absolutely sure of himself. "But I've never dated any of them. I actually became pretty notorious for being on my own. I think the girls there gave up on the idea of me since I never picked any of them."

"Like you've never had a girlfriend?" I gape.

"Is there something wrong with that?" He shoots a fast glance. "Like I said, I'm picky. I have standards, okay?"

"And none of those girls met those standards, huh?" I keep the questions coming, however inappropriate it may be to pry into Liam's personal life. My own interest in the answers won't let me stop.

"No, they didn't. I just figure, why waste my time with someone that isn't worth it, you know?" His shoulders shrug up to his ears.

Of course I know. That is probably the main reason why I've hardly dated much either. It doesn't make sense to spend time with someone, to let them in, only to know that it won't last. Relationships at our age rarely do. I don't want heartache like that.

"No, I get it. It's just—there aren't many guys like that around here. You're kind of different."

"Gee, thanks Tessa. You're different, too," Liam mocks. He stretches back in his chair and rests his brown, leather boots on the rusted wire basket under the desk in front of him. If it is possible to appear at all comfortable in these ancient desks, Liam is certainly able to do it.

"No, you know what I mean. It's good. It's refreshing."

It's safe.

"So…you good for coming to the ranch at 8:00 a.m. on Saturday? I'll have already been up and at 'em for two hours by then, but I'll let you sleep in a bit if you like."

"No. It's a *Day in the Life*. If we're going to do this assignment, we need to do it right. If you're up at 6:00, I'll be there at 6:00." What am I committing myself to? I haven't seen 6:00 a.m. in years, let alone started my day at that hour.

"That's awfully early. You're going to need a nap by lunchtime."

"It's fine, I can handle it. I'll see you at sunrise."

Mr. Crawford is just finishing up his classroom rounds as the bell sounds.

11:12 a.m.

"Students, those of you who haven't told me who your interview partners are yet, please write your names on a piece of paper and bring it up to my desk so I can record it in the grade book."

Liam tears a piece of binder paper from his spiral notebook and scribbles on it with his left hand. He folds it in half, rips it into two equal pieces, and shoves the paper toward me as he rises from his desk.

"I gotta run to meet up with the counselor during lunch. Would you mind turning this in to Mr. Crawford for us?" he asks. "Oh, and I won't be in class tomorrow. Something was messed up with my transfer at the Education Sector. I have to go back to Superior to pick up my files and get a few letters from my old teachers. They sure make you jump through a lot of hoops to attend this school."

"I don't think it's the school that's causing the hang up. Nothing is easy when it comes to dealing with the Sectors. You're just lucky it hasn't escalated to the Hub." The words fly out, betraying my reason and my volume's much too loud. I hope no one else has heard me.

"You're probably right," Liam nods. "And you sound an awful lot like my mom, talking out against the Hub like that. You should watch yourself or you'll make yourself a target, you know." He's teasing, of course, but the weightiness of his tone remains evident.

"I doubt they care much about a sixteen-year-old girl's idle talk," I reassure myself. "And I can take notes for you in biology, if you like, so you don't fall behind." I take the sheets of paper from his grip and gather the rest of my things as well, yet my eyes remain fixed on Liam as he heads toward the door. He pauses before exiting the classroom.

"See you bright and early on Saturday, Sunshine," he calls across the room, his voice mixing in the air with the shuffling of feet, scooting of desks, and chatter of our fellow classmates.

I look down at the two pieces of paper in my hands. Both of our names are written across the top on the first.

Liam Hollander and Tessa O'Donnell

I'm not sure why seeing our names on the same page strikes me; it is clearly what Mr. Crawford has asked us to do and Liam is just following his instruction. But there they are, written out in his own slanted, chicken-scratch handwriting. And I like it. I like the way our names appear together, as though there is some meaning to them sharing the same space on the paper. I shake my head, literally trying to shake away the conflicting emotions that surface from that vision.

I flip over the second sheet.

This time it isn't the lettering that causes my stomach to lurch. Seven numbers stare up at me. It is Liam's phone number. That he wrote down his number for me isn't what makes my hands tremble as I cling to the paper, now rustling audibly under my uneasy grasp. The phone number exchange makes sense—I will be going to the ranch on Saturday and he won't be in school on Friday—I'm sure he wants me to be able to contact him if anything changes between now and then. The act is actually quite thoughtful, and an unintentional smile plays on my lips at his gesture.

But it's those actual numbers.

If I hadn't previously thought there was some sort of meaning, some type of reason why my life seems to be played out in numbers, this half-sheet of binder paper would have changed all of that for me. My eyes memorize the digits on the page, though it doesn't take long to engrain them in my memory. One set I have been staring at for nearly two years, the others I spent all class tracing their outline.

234-1112.

There they are, strung together in a row. *Liam's phone number.*

I know it has to mean something more. And there has to be more to Liam as well. I just have no idea how I am going to go about finding out exactly what all that is.

Maybe the ranch is the best place to start.

NINE

I think it would be nice to wake up all at once—to have all of my senses fully present the moment my eyes pop open. That has to be the norm for most people, right? But my senses rarely wake all at the same time. It's as though each one gradually regains consciousness piece-by-piece, layer upon layer, until I'm a fully functioning human—well, as close as I can be to one. And most times, it's sight that ushers in that slow beginning when my eyes open to their glowing clock greeting.

But this morning is different. The metallic echo of raindrops hit the steel gutter outside my window, then transform into a whooshing stream of collected water. That's the first sound to reach my ears. I breathe in deep—my eyes still closed—and the crisp air floods my nostrils, tingling with cold as it fills up my chest. I forcefully push the air out of my mouth, now hot from its brief stay inside my lungs, and clench my eyelids shut. I smooth the ruffled comforter that spreads across my body, winding a loose thread around my index finger. I can almost taste the first autumn rain on my tongue as it soaks the dry earth outside. Its familiarity makes my mouth water, making my dry throat thirsty, and it begs to be quenched.

Sound, smell, touch and taste.

But not sight. My eyelids remain tightly sealed, and I don't plan to open them again any time soon. This morning seems to be beginning in reverse from its typical start and I welcome the unexpected change. I bathe in the calm that's traded places with the panic usually rousing me from my slumber.

All week things have slowly started slipping into a pattern, a type of routine—however random it originally seemed—and I welcome anything that diverges from that. Awakening at night and recalling that same time during each day, though it all appeared unsystematic at first, is strangely working itself into a familiar repetition.

I lie in bed, enveloped in the heat trapped under the patchwork quilt, and have no intention of throwing back my covers to officially start my day. Through the sheer skin of my eyelids I can't even tell if it is the dead of night or early morning—the storm outside casts a darkness across the room that makes it impossible to decipher the hour.

'See you bright and early, Sunshine.'

His voice rings in my ears, so clear that it's as though my mind has recorded his tone. If the weather continues this way, it won't be bright—though it might still be early—and I'm sure he won't be calling me Sunshine if I have to drag myself out of bed to face the cold and wet. There is nothing sun-shiney about that.

Today is a new beginning. The irony of that strikes me as my mind wanders to the ranch. The thought of spending the day there with Liam tomorrow doesn't feel like a new beginning; it feels like an old memory. It feels like a return.

It feels like going home.

The rain outside lulls me in and out of sleep. I slip back and forth between wakefulness and oblivion. I'm content to stay there, to rest in the in-between, all day.

So I think I will. School won't miss me and it shouldn't raise any flags at the Education Sector. I've only skipped one day earlier in the year due to a stomach virus. No one should question my non-attendance. We're allowed two unexcused absences a semester before the Ed Sector sends a representative to our home for commitment questioning. It's all part of the preparation and grooming process—teaching us to be upstanding citizens by reinforcing the notion of dedication to our classes and schoolwork. It makes sense that the Hub would want to keep tabs on us in this way. Once we enter the Sector working world, attendance will be essential to a prosperous, cohesive government. Cogs in a wheel; we all work together.

Liam already mentioned he wouldn't be there, so I won't be abandoning him in journalism. A twinge of guilt pangs me. I'd offered to take notes in biology and now won't be able to make good on my promise. But with both Bailey and Joel in that class, I am sure we can get the assignment from one of them.

Joel. He might notice if I ditch. At least I hope he will. I hope he will wonder about me, think about me, and maybe even miss me. I'm beginning to miss him. After our date on Wednesday and his confession, we haven't had much opportunity to reconnect. He was out late at football practice and Bailey and I spent the evening at the mall just outside of Madison. For once she wasn't locked away in the yearbook dungeon, so I jumped at the chance to have some girl time. I'd planned to tell her about Joel and about our conversation in his truck bed, but I couldn't get the words to come out of my mouth. I couldn't think of a way to adequately describe the emotions he stirred in me. I couldn't put into a coherent grouping of sentences the way it felt when I was with him. I still can't.

And I am okay with that. Because for some reason, keeping that moment between just Joel and I seems important—it seems necessary. I am protective over it, as though saving it for myself guards him in some way. As though it guards *us* in some way.

I probably wouldn't have even been able to adequately convey to Bailey what we talked about, what I learned about him, and how he came alive to me that night. To her, Joel is practically another brother. She can only see what everyone else sees of him from the outside looking in. I doubt she'll ever be able to know him the way I do. And that's fine. I prefer it actually. To think that I am one of the few people that gets to witness this hidden side of him makes it all the more valuable. In truth, it makes *us* all the more valuable.

The longer the rain continues outside, the more resolute I become in my decision to stay home. Faint footsteps resonate down the hall, increasing slightly in volume with each step until they are immediately outside my door. The rhythm steadily trails off as they make their way past my room, heading toward the kitchen. The first familiar sounds of our house beginning to awake. Based on the lightness of the paces on the hardwood, I predict the footsteps belonged to Bailey. That means it is likely around 5:30 a.m., though I don't bother opening my eyes to confirm. If I can fall back to sleep, I'll have another two solid hours before Trent comes bounding downstairs in the hurried flurry of his morning rush. I'll tell him that I'm not feeling well, that I've decided to stay home, and ask if he can relay that information to Joel. That's my plan. It feels like a good one.

Just as I predicted, after what feels like a brief nap, Trent throws open my bedroom door with such force that the handle slams into the inside wall, leaving a fresh divot in its place. *Seriously, Trent?* Sometimes his dramatic ways annoy me. Especially when they result in unnecessary holes in my drywall.

"Geez, Trent. Good morning to you, too," I groan, rolling over so my back is to him, walling him off with my body. If I'm pretending to be sick, I need to play the part and attempt to be somewhat believable. That's easier to do when we're not face-to-face.

"Tessa! Get out of bed! You are going to make us *so* late! *Come on!*" Trent bounds into the room and tugs at the corner of the quilt I have pulled over my head. "Seriously, we have to leave. Like *now.*"

"Trent, I'm really not feeling good. I'm going to stay home today," I moan. "I think I caught that flu that Caden had last week. I'm feeling pretty miserable." I force out a somewhat realistic cough and bring my hand up to my forehead, as though checking for a sign of fever.

"Yuck, stay away from me! We've got a big game tomorrow and the *last* thing I need is to get sick."

Nice one, Trent. Way to show some compassion. His lack of concern irritates me, even if I'm not actually ill.

"Tell Joel that I'm not going to be there today, okay?" Trent's backed his way out of the room and is shielding himself from my nonexistent germs with the door, a barricade.

"Yeah, sure, no prob. What's going on with you two anyway? He hasn't stopped talking about you since Wednesday. I've never seen him act like this about a girl before."

My stomach rolls. Maybe I won't really have to fake being sick, because at this moment, I feel as though I might actually throw up. But not out of disgust or fear. Just more of those ever-present butterflies that swarm in at the mention of Joel's name.

"Just tell him, okay?" I really don't feel like explaining things to Trent. I had a hard enough time deciding whether or not to let Bailey in on the recent turn of events. Trent is even further down on that list of confidants. No, he's not even on the list at all.

"Whatever. Oh, Mom's at work today and Dad's at the firehouse. So if you need anything, you're on your own." I hope that whatever Sector Trent joins, it doesn't involve any immediate contact with those in need. He definitely isn't cut out to be a caregiver of any kind. Uncle Mark's compassionate genes must have skipped right by him.

I hadn't thought about having the house entirely to myself today, but I like the idea of the solitude. Aunt Cathy was recently hired on as a teller at the local bank in her Commerce and Industry Sector and this is her first week working full-time.

I'm not quite sure why she decided to get a job; I know that Uncle Mark makes a decent living as a firefighter. Maybe she needs something to occupy her time now that all the kids are in school. I'm sure that her role as a homemaker has greatly changed the older her children have grown. And from what I've heard, the Hub has started making it known that they expect all able-bodied citizens to fully commit to a Sector. Homemakers were permitted to take an indefinite sabbatical from their Sectors during their childrearing years, but now it's starting to be looked down upon if you don't rejoin your Sector once your children reach adolescence. Maybe that's what prompted Aunt Cathy to recently seek reemployment.

But in the back of my mind, I can't help wonder if I have anything to do with her decision. I'm sure I am an added living expense that they hadn't accounted for, and it makes me feel guilty that she will be clocking her hours at the bank while I take advantage of their hospitality at home. Now that the ranch has sold, I figure I have some money coming to me, even after the Hub takes their portion of the earnings. It's time I started paying for myself. I know they won't allow it—that it might even offend Uncle Mark in some way—but the last thing I want is to appear ungrateful for everything they have done for me. I owe them for that.

I start my morning off leisurely, taking my time as I shower, adjusting the temperature so that the water is so hot it nearly burns my skin. The beads sting as they land on me, like embers jumping from a flame, but the steam the shower produces reminds me of my own fog again and I welcome it. It makes me feel less alone. Like I'm not the only one in a bleary haze, even though I've completely created the murkiness in the bathroom all on my own. For once, I finish showering before the water has a chance to automatically shut off. I smile a little to myself, feeling like I've silently one-upped the Hub.

I peruse my wardrobe and try to find something to wear. If I'm supposed to be sick, what should I lounge around in? I land on a pair of black yoga pants that Aunt Cathy gave me after two failed attempts at maintaining a gym membership. I match that with one of Trent's freshman football sweatshirts that's somehow ended up in my dresser drawer. He'll have something to say about it, I'm sure, but after the lack of compassion demonstrated this morning, letting me borrow his shirt is the least he can do to make up for his nonexistent concern.

There's a stack of buttermilk pancakes Bailey prepared earlier still sitting on a plate on the counter. I grab one and toss it in the microwave. The timer buzzes and I retrieve my hotcakes, thankful for Bailey's domesticity. They're dry and bland, but all I need to fill the emptiness in my stomach and satiate my appetite.

Uncle Mark's recliner is posted next to the wall of French doors leading out to the backyard, and I slide in and rest my head on its pillow top. Cologne emanates from it, a familiar and comforting scent, but not one that reminds me of home, just of Uncle Mark. I wonder if that will ever happen—if the smells of the Buchman house will become the smells of home to me. Maybe they never will. Every time I open the front door the scent that greets me, though calming in nature, isn't a reminder of home. It just smells like the Buchman residence, but not my home.

I'm not sure what time it is; I know I'm moving much slower this morning than any other, and I haven't bothered to check the clock after getting ready. In fact, I haven't been aware of the time since last night before I went to bed. I momentarily freeze, trying to recall the last time I was aware of the minutes in the day, but I can't remember. And then it hits me—I didn't wake up at all in the middle of the night.

And when I finally did awake, I didn't look at the clock to check the hour. For the first time in two years, I don't feel bound by time; I don't feel as though numbers have any ownership over me. It's a strange sensation.

The wind howls against the windows, rattling their panes as they shake under the forceful gusts. I walk over to the couch, slip the scratchy wool blanket off of the ottoman, and carry it back to the recliner.

It is quiet. With two adults and three teenagers, the Buchman home is rarely quiet. I start to regret my decision to stay home. Instead of reveling in the time to myself, I'm unexpectedly lonely. I am used to being on my own, used to fending for myself in some way, but the small taste of companionship with Joel makes being alone seem so much more solitary than ever before. I wish he was here with me.

I shut my eyes and imagine the amount of work I will have to make up on Monday. Fridays are never good days to skip school. Thursday would have been the better option, and then I would at least have the weekend to complete my missed assignments. But now I won't be able to get my makeup work until Monday, and then I'll have double the amount to complete that night. I should have thought things through a bit more. But then again, I didn't actually plan on ditching. And had I skipped yesterday instead, I would have missed out on the opportunity to partner with Liam in journalism. That would have taken away any chance of me visiting the ranch tomorrow. And Liam won't be there either, so it does make more sense to skip school today.

Slow down those thoughts, Tessa. What on earth does Liam have to do with anything? He hasn't gone to East Valley for nearly the whole first quarter, so why does it matter that he won't be in attendance today? It shouldn't have any effect on my decisions, but for some strange reason, it does.

I thumb through the pages of Aunt Cathy's paperback book draped over the armrest of the chair. I begin reading right where it's opened to, somewhere around page 100, and don't bother starting from the beginning. I'm not interested in the story, I just need something to fill my mind and temporarily occupy my thoughts. I have too many of my own floating around in there, and they are becoming a jumbled mess of blonde wavy hair and truck bed confessions.

The story on the page reads like any other romance novel. The protagonist faced with the dire situation of choosing between two lovers, one who is clearly better suited for her than the other. Annoyed and aggravated, I swiftly close the book shut, so forcefully that a gust of air emerges from the pages. I toss the book to the floor with a thud. *So not my kind of story.*

The jagged, finger-like tree branch that Aunt Cathy's been nagging Uncle Mark to trim back all autumn, claws against the French door. It makes an awful, high-pitched, screeching noise as its uneven edge slides along the glass like fingernails on a chalkboard. I shiver.

A fire. That's what might make this rainy day a little less stormy and a bit more comfortable. Uncle Mark keeps the firewood lined up alongside the garage exterior under an old gray plastic tarp, so I trudge to my room to locate my rain boots before heading out into the elements. I rummage through my dark closet, sitting down on the floor and shoving my sandals and tennis shoes out of the way in an attempt to recover my boots. I vaguely remember Bailey borrowing them during the last storm, so I head upstairs to her room in an effort to find them.

After two minutes of searching through the mess of dresses, shirts, and pants piled high on her closet floor I descend back downstairs, empty handed. Funny, she's so organized in some aspects of her life. Her closet must not be one of those.

The house is even colder, and emptier, than before. A chill raises the hairs on the back of my neck, a cool whisper floating across my skin. I shudder and flip the switch on the thermostat in the hall. From the back of the house the heater rattles and vibrates to life, and hot air floats down from the vent directly above, warming me instantly like a heavy blanket wrapped around me. I soak up all the warmth it offers.

I stop back by my room on my way to the garage and stand in front of my open closet. My tennis shoes will need to do and my feet are just going to have to get wet if I am determined to create this fire of mine. But I've never made a fire, nor ever had one at the ranch. My dad wasn't big on fires. Hopefully I'll be able to figure it out on my own.

From my corner of the house everything is eerily quiet, aside from the rhythmic sound of the rain that steadily pours outside and the lulling hum of the heating system. Bending down to retrieve my sneakers, my eyes catch the metal latch on my dad's war box resting unobtrusively on the top shelf. Practically a permanent fixture, it's layered with gray dust and hasn't been touched since I unpacked it and placed it there two years ago. I've always thought of it as a time capsule or some type of memory bank. But today it feels like a secret keeper, and betrayal spikes through me as I contemplate opening it.

If he had wanted you to know about his role in the war, he would have told you. I've harbored two years worth of guilt for just keeping the thing in my room. Dad didn't want me to have this and I know it. He had tried to keep it hidden in the back of his closet, but I saw him too many times late at night, perched at the edge of his bed, with just the light from the nightstand lamp on him as he thumbed through its contents. Mom was always asleep and he thought he was alone, so I never interrupted him nor asked for that drink of water that I'd awoken for. He was different when he had that box in front of him. His expression gave it all away. Furrowed brow pushing back the tears that threatened, his lips a thin line that fastened back any words he might have had.

I saw what those contents did to him, and I didn't want them in the possession of anyone else. That's why, as soon at the officers left after giving me the news of my parents' death, the first thing I did was race to his closet to retrieve his box and stash it away in my own. I knew the Hub would rummage through my parents' belongings and I would lose any chance of ever unlocking that part of Dad's history once they obtained it. So the box was one of the few things I packed in my two suitcases bound for Madison.

But today my inquiring mind is stronger than my weak will. Dragging the piano bench across the floor, I raise myself up to eye level with the tattered wooden vessel. *You shouldn't do this. This box isn't yours. These memories don't belong to you.* I think the words, but don't heed them. I thrust open the lid and close my eyes, as if by doing so I can deflect any fault I may have in this personal intrusion.

A rectangular, manila envelope fills the entire frame of the wooden container. I have to use the edge of my fingernail to free it from where it's wedged, but I manage to peel it out. The brads on the underneath side of the envelope are completely broken off. My dad must have opened this thing a thousand times. I fold back the flap and sit on the bench. A stack of newspaper articles fall from the envelope onto my lap but I can't make out the words; everything is so blurry. I push my thumb and index finger into my eyes to halt the tears. Funny, my dad had the same reaction when looking at these contents years ago.

I blink. The headline on the first article comes into view.

RISING STRIFE SUBDUED AGAIN BY

Underneath the title is a black and white picture of three men dressed in camouflage fatigues. They stand in front of a dilapidated, crumbled stone structure. Another man outfitted in a smart looking, dark uniform holds out a medal to present to the officer closest to him. I read the caption.

Intelligence and Prediction Officer Patrick O'Donnell (pictured here along with Security Officer Marty Sardoni and Medical Officer Rick Cordella) receives a Superior Defense Informant Medal, his fourth in this his first tour.

I scan the article, pulling out words like foresaw, strategized, and executed, but my eyes keep flitting back to the photograph at the top of the page. He looked so young. And so proud. I don't know that I ever saw that gleam in his eyes before. It's an appreciation for the recognition of a job well done. I doubt that the man in the dark uniform was part of the Hub. Dad wouldn't have had that same response to a government official. I remember my dad saying that the Hub was born out of the war—that the transition of government resulted from the loss. That man must just be another military officer. But maybe Dad *did* respect authority at one time. From the looks of this article and picture, he may have even been a part of it.

The news story is short but gives Dad accolades for providing officials with predictive and analytical information as to the whereabouts of hostile troops during one of the U.S. raids. Apparently Dad was an Intelligence and Prediction Officer in the war; his job to discover, evaluate, and critique opposition plans and tactics. Judging by the fact that he'd already received three medals before this most recent one, I guess he must have been pretty good at what he did.

I rest the first newspaper clipping on the bench and lift the second article up to my face when I first hear it. The click is faint and familiar and I know immediately what it means. The increased volume of the rain beating down on the pavement outside only confirms my suspicions. And the final resonance of the door slamming back into its frame clues me in on one important fact.

I am no longer alone in the house.

I thrust the papers back into their original envelope, drop it in the box, secure the latch, and place it back on the shelf. My heart isn't in my chest anymore as I try to swallow the hard lump that's forming in my much-too-tight throat. Both Bailey and Trent are at school all day. Uncle Mark or Aunt Cathy would have entered through the garage. I instantly regret not checking the lock on the front door earlier this morning—something Uncle Mark has trained me to do. "This isn't the ranch, Tessa. We aren't safely tucked away out in the country. Real crime exists here and we have to live like we know it."

There have been reports of burglaries in the area recently. Usually done on weekdays, like today, when all members of the family are away. Last month, a house two blocks down was robbed at gunpoint, taking only jewelry and electronics with them, but leaving a lifetime of fear and panic behind for the home's inhabitants. Four days later the house went on the market and they left Madison for good.

But the idea of a burglar is more welcoming than my original thought—that somehow the Hub knows of my disobedience. It's farfetched, I know. It's not like they have security cameras keeping tabs on us at all times or anything. At least I don't think they do. But the coincidental timing with my own betrayal stings. Maybe I should be found out. I *deserve* to be found out. I took something that wasn't my own, and the Hub doesn't take things like this lightly.

I scan the room, looking for an object that can come to my defense, something to protect me. But it isn't something I want right now, it is someone. *Dang it, Tess! Why couldn't you have just locked the front door? Or gone to school like an obedient citizen? Or minded your own business and not looked at something that wasn't meant for your own eyes?*

My searching gaze lands on a candlestick on my dresser. It isn't much, but at least I won't be completely vulnerable. I hold my breath and tiptoe across the room as though by not breathing I can actually weigh less and minimize the sound of my footfalls. Just as quietly, I lift the lavender scented candle from its perch on top of the silver holder. I wrap my trembling fingers around its cold base.

Now what? Can I honestly use this thing? And what will I do with it? I decide my best strategy—if you can even call it one—is to aim for the head; that is always what they do in movies. I slide my way back across my room and slip into the narrow space between the wall and the door, brushing against the freshly made hole in the drywall. For as annoyed with Trent as I was earlier this morning, I would give anything to have him, or anyone for that matter, here with me right now.

From my new vantage point I can peer out into the hallway through the one-inch gap near the hinges on the door. At least that will take away the element of surprise. From here I can see the invader before he physically enters my room, and that gives me a little confidence, a little bit of hope that I might actually stand a small chance.

Run. Maybe I should run. Or hide. Why hadn't that occurred to me? Wouldn't any sane person be crouched down in their closet or tucked away under their bed? Who in their right mind scans the room for a weapon when they could possibly escape? Where do these crazy instincts come from? Why aren't I fleeing like any normal person would in my situation?

Whatever the reason, I am certain I'm turning out to be more of a danger to myself than an actual defender.

My drifting mind stops suddenly at the echo of two heavy footsteps making their way down the hall. They sound so very different from Bailey's sprite-like pitter-patter earlier this morning. If the intruder is searching for jewelry as Uncle Mark says is common, I am certain they will head straight for the bedrooms. And mine is the first one on that path.

I steady myself and slowly raise my left hand up, holding the candlestick firmly within its grasp. This will have to be a two-handed attack—I'm fairly strong for a girl, but not nearly enough to bludgeon with one hand. I wrap my right one around the bottom portion of cold stick as though I am gripping a baseball bat above my head, ready to swing at any given moment. I rotate it in invisible circles in the air.

The steps grow in volume and quickness, matching my racing heartbeat and increased breathing note for note.

He's here.

I can see his outline through the gap in the door, though the tears that steadily well up in my eyes blur it. I blink hard, clench my jaw, and try to shake off the fear that fills me. If I am planning to face him, I need to have all of my senses about me. They were so present this morning. Where are they now?

He pauses, less than a foot away, and is completely unaware that I am waiting for him on the other side of the door. He's standing under the same vent that I brought to life moments earlier. What a thief—that warmth was meant for me. He has no right to it.

I see his right hand make a fist. He lifts it up to his mouth and breathes hot air into the tight ball it creates. Maybe the cold will work to my advantage; maybe his fingers are frozen under the chill, unable to function. But the candlestick is slippery under my damp palms. Who am I kidding? I doubt I have any real advantage over him at all.

I try to anticipate his next move. I can smell the fresh rain on his shirt and hear his own rapid breathing echo through my room. And he's holding something in his left hand, though I can't quite tell what it is. This stranger is now in the most intimate place in my home—my very room. I'm violated by the notion that he's intruded into such a personal space of mine; the only space that actually belongs to me anymore. I pray this violation stops with just my room.

The floorboards creak and crack under the firm pressure of his foot as he takes one slow, steady step further into my room. *Now's your chance, Tessa.* I can either wait for him to pull back the door and discover me, or I can jump out and make myself known to him. Wait for the kill or ready for the strike. I pause, a luxury that isn't mine to have, and in the brief second of doing so it's over. He suddenly spins around on his heel, his wet soles squealing under the weight, and faces the wall so we are physically eye to eye, just a two-inch, solid piece of plywood separating us.

Crap! He knows I am here. I've given up my element of surprise. I'm completely in his hands now. How did everything change in just a matter of seconds? How had I given away my upper hand so quickly? How could I have been so wrong in thinking I could face him and win?

He seizes the door handle and flings it to the side. My eyes instinctively close forcefully, refusing to acknowledge what's happening. I let out a blood-curdling scream that burns my raw throat as it emerges from my lungs, like millions of tiny razorblades catching in my gullet as they rise up into my mouth. I feel a warm liquid soak my sweatshirt and cover my chest, run down my arms, and drip off my fingertips onto the floor. *This is it.* I crumple to the floor, certain I'm bathed in blood, and brace myself for the final blow. He's got to finish me off, unless he has other plans for me before doing so.

Just as quickly as I melt to the ground, he is crouched down at my level, eye to eye with me once again, though I continue to keep mine firmly closed. His two hands grab my shoulders and shake me hard, thrusting me side to side in a dizzying, disorienting motion. I turn my face and bury it in the hood of my sweatshirt. *Please just let this be quick. And please don't leave me here for the others to find me.*

Before I can make another move, my stomach twists inside of me, like a drenched towel being wrung to dry, and I retch, vomiting my breakfast all over him and onto the floor. I heave again, doubling over, placing both of my hands on the hardwood, projecting the wet, acidic contents of my stomach onto its surface. It splatters on contact. I'm covered in my own throw up.

My eyes, though still shut, begin to go completely black at the thought of the mix of blood and vomit around me. Head dizzy and ears ringing, I know within a moment I'll be out cold. At least if I pass out I won't be able to feel the pain that's sure to come. I will myself to faint, but I remain reluctantly coherent.

I try to take a deep breath in and regain my bearings in a last ditch effort to save myself. His strong hands are no longer clutching my shoulders, but have moved toward my hair, wrapping their fingers around their strands to form a handheld ponytail at the base of my skull. I envision him dragging me through the house by this hold and vomit again as I imagine my blood smeared throughout the halls for my family to discover later this evening. As I throw up, his grasp becomes even tighter on my hair, and I quake under his control over me. I'm so feeble. The retching only adds to this weakness. I'm literally spitting out every ounce of strength I have left.

But something isn't right. Why hasn't he ended this already? I must be bleeding quite a bit from whatever caused the original injury. The near fainting is likely a result of that. But I'm too terrified to open my eyes to see how much blood I've actually lost. Thoughts race through my mind as though a myriad of different voices are telling me what to do—to run, to play dead, to fight back. But none of them are clear enough to help me make an ultimate decision. They are all jumbled into one deafening chorus of chaos, confusion, and panic.

Then one voice separates itself from the rest. It's louder than the others and immediately silences them, like a conductor instructing his orchestra to cease playing. It's powerful, commanding, and warm.

It's my protector.

It's Joel.

TEN

"Tessa, it's okay. You're going to be alright." That Joel might be the last sound I hear is comforting to no end. And the clarity of it reminds me of my earlier recalling of Liam's voice this morning. It amazes me how my mind can so easily record their voices in my head for me to replay at any given moment.

"Tess, I'm here. It's okay." My closed eyes relax, no longer clenching under the fear of what is to come, and I surrender to the sounds in my head, however fabricated they might be.

"Tessa, open your eyes. I'm right here. It's going to be okay, I promise." The fictional voice is so realistic, so lifelike, that I instinctually force my eyelids apart, ready to face my attacker with a new will to fight.

His eyes meet mine. Those rich, deep chestnut eyes lock my gaze and I slam into his hard chest, his hands still holding my hair away from my vomit covered face. I am an absolute mess. The blood I'd envisioned soaking me is actually the contents of some cup that now rests on the floor amidst my own bile. I wipe my mouth with the sleeve of Trent's sweatshirt and push the remaining water from my eyes with the back of my hand.

"Oh Tess, you are *so* much worse than Trent said! I had no idea—I would have gotten here sooner but I had a quiz in calculus so I had to wait until lunch to leave. And I stopped by Java Café to grab you some tea, but now that's all part of this." Joel waves his hands over the floor at the putrid mess of vomit and the hot drink he had picked up for me. I'm instantly light headed again, this time from utter embarrassment.

"Come on," Joel says. He takes me by the elbow and raises me slowly to my shaky feet. "Let's get you cleaned up and back in bed. You must be really weak. Have you been able to keep anything down at all today?"

I haven't opened my mouth to do anything other than scream and retch, so when I try to force the words out, my voice cracks under the strain. My throat and nose still burn from the acid. I'm certain I smell even worse than I feel.

"Yeah, I had a pancake this morning, but that's it." The hot tea that covers my shirt starts to cool and I shiver at the clammy chill of it against my skin.

"Okay, well, let's get you out of this first," Joel instructs, tugging at the drawstring of my hood. "Do you have something on under it?"

I nod. I'm wearing a black sports bra. But I guess that isn't exactly what he means by the look on his face as he slides my vomit-soaked sweatshirt over my head, trying to keep the stained areas away from me as he lifts it off. Joel grins at the sight of me and nervously turns his head to the side, though I can still see his dark brown eyes sneak my direction, trying not to make contact with mine, but attempting to steal a peek of me in my state of near undress.

I probably should be embarrassed that I wasn't clear; I assume he was expecting to find me in a t-shirt or tank top. But it's good to get the soiled clothing off, and I don't mind the feeling of Joel's eyes on me. That any part of me can be attractive in this moment seems an impossibility, so the idea of Joel blushing at the sight of my practically bare skin is a welcome thought. At this point, I just hope I don't appear completely repulsive and revolting. *Oh Tessa, this is definitely not one of your better days.*

"Um, alright….so….is it hot in here?" Joel stammers nervously, pulling at his own t-shirt, billowing to let air in and fan himself with its fabric. "Oh." He draws his fingers away and rubs them together, my vomit sliding in between them.

Tessa, what have you done?

"Oh Joel, I'm so sorry. That's so disgusting," I groan, covering my mouth and face in humiliation. His own shirt is in even worse shape than mine.

"Tess, seriously, it's no biggie. Please don't apologize. I just feel awful that you are so sick." Joel crosses his arms over in front of him at his waist, pulls on the hem of his shirt, and lifts it off of his body in one smooth motion. It lands in a twisted ball of cotton on the floor next to my soiled sweatshirt.

Without intending to, I let out a slight gasp at the sight of him. He's strong, his shoulders rounded, his chest and stomach defined—every detail of every muscle is perfectly outlined on his tall frame. I stare at him—at his sculpted form—in awe of the fact that someone can be made the way he is. And how that someone is standing half-naked in the middle of my bedroom.

All of Joel's physical features are so solid. Is it possible he can be any more flawless than I had previously thought? Staring at him as he stands there just feet away from me, dressed in only his blue jeans and rain-soaked sneakers, I'm sure there isn't anything imperfect about him.

I reach out for him, a movement that isn't my own, coming from some other space, and wrap my arms around his waist, my fingers finding the muscular curve above his hip. I want to feel the heat radiating from his body against my cold skin. He reciprocates my advance and envelops his arms around me, his fingers combing through my hair, just as delicately as they had a few nights before under the stars. For as tough and strong as he appears physically, I am amazed at his ability to be so incredibly tender at the same time. The perfect balance.

Joel's fingers slide under my chin and tilt it up so I'm staring straight into his eyes. He cups my jawline with his palm and rests his fingers at the back of my neck with both hands, cradling my face. Hot breath strokes my cheek, sending chills up and down my spine. It strikes me that something so warm and welcome can evoke the same chilled sensation the cool hallway air did earlier. That chills rise in both circumstances. But in this case, I don't take any action to make them go away. I yearn for more of them, for my entire body to be covered with them.

Every hair on me stands on end. I'm grateful he's holding onto me so firmly because my legs have given out, rendering themselves completely useless.

"Wait, okay?" I blurt, pull away, and pivot on heel to rush to the bathroom. I pick up my toothbrush and squirt a dollop of paste onto the bristles. I'm not about to have my first kiss like that. Joel is practically perfect in every way. The least I can do is attempt to mask my current state with minty freshness.

Joel laughs audibly from the other room. "Are you brushing your teeth?"

"Yeah, just hold on one sec," I mutter almost unintelligibly around my toothbrush, my mouth filled with suds.

"You're being silly," he reassures as I step back into the room.

"I'm also sick," I lie. I can't have him telling Trent that I ditched. Trent would likely blab all over school and then I'd really have the Ed Sector breathing down my neck. "I don't want you to get sick—you have a game coming up and you can't afford to—"

"Tessa, I could care less if I get sick. Vomit doesn't bother me, seriously. Is it okay if I kiss you?" It's not as though he needs to ask. I'm sure everything about my body language is beckoning him to, but I physically melt at his question.

I nod, several quick nods in a row, breathing in deep, filling my senses with everything about him. His hand at the small of my back gently draws me in closer to him, to the point where I'm arched backward as he presses his body against mine. I use the little bit of feeling left in my legs to raise myself up on tiptoe to bring my face closer to his, but he still towers over me. Joel leans in, bending to bring his mouth down to mine. My eyes are open, absorbing all I can of him in this moment, worried that if I blink I might wake up. I don't want this to be another dream like before.

Then his lips, full and warm, meet mine. For years I've been so worried that I wouldn't know what to do in this moment, that I would make an utter and complete fool of myself, and that my first kiss would likely be my last. But right here with Joel all of my apprehension is gone. His mouth moves soft and rhythmically against mine, so entirely different from the intensity of the vision I had nights before, but so much more fitting and expected from the Joel I've recently discovered.

My lips follow his lead, giving in and molding to his. I trace the outline of his jaw with my finger, and pull him down to me as I stumble three steps backward toward my bed. My knees buckle at its edge. I need to lay down before I quite literally faint. I slowly ease myself backward, keeping my lips locked with his, and slide onto the mattress. Joel follows, bringing himself to my level so he's nearly on top of me, pushing himself up with his hands to create space between our bodies. His biceps are strong and hold his entire frame just above mine.

Though I want nothing more than to feel his heavy weight crushing on top of me, I know by the fact that he asked if he can kiss me it means things will probably stop at that. And I'm good with that for now. Just kissing Joel is more than enough for me. It's more than enough to reassure me of his affection. Immeasurably more considering the state I am in.

I place a trembling hand on his chest—his heart races under the pressure of my palm meeting his bare skin. My breathing, fast and deep up to this point, begins to slow as he gradually pulls himself away, our lips the last to part.

Joel flips over onto his back and throws his hands up to his forehead. "Geez, Tessa! What are you trying to do to me?"

That Joel thinks I have any power in the situation makes me laugh. I bite down on my bottom lip, hoping the pressure will make them miss the firmness of his against mine a little less, but I'm not successful. They ache, as though they need their counterpart to function. Although until just a few short minutes ago, they didn't even know it existed.

"Seriously, I wasn't expecting that today," he says, rolling onto his side so that we are parallel with one another. His hand meets the curve of my exposed hip.

"I thought I'd find you here asleep in bed—the reason I just used my key and let myself in."

"Your key?" I stammer. So Joel has a key. Of course he does. Now it makes sense why there was no knock at the door, why he walked straight toward my room, and why he didn't call out my name. He was trying to be quiet, trying not to wake me from my slumber. And I had planned to kill him. Or at least seriously maim him in some way. Luckily, neither of which I succeeded in. The only thing I have been successful at is making an utter mess of my room, myself, and our clothes. Although I'm a little grateful for that last success given that he's shirtless on my bed. I can't take my eyes off of him.

"I'm going to clean up your floor and take these clothes to the laundry room. I just want you to lay here and rest. When I come back I'll help you wash your hair, okay?" I nod and gasp at the same time, hoping the nod is more noticeable. *Joel's going to wash my hair?* He fetches a towel from the adjoining bathroom and begins to wipe up the vomit from the hardwood.

"Uh, sure. Sounds good. Can I at least help you clean this up?" I motion to the floor with my hands. I'm perched at the end of my bed and he's crouched on the floor, cleaning. It doesn't seem right to make him do that when I'm the one that caused the mess in the first place.

"No, absolutely not—you don't need to overdo it. I've got it taken care of. Seriously, just lay there. I'll be back in just a few." He wads the towel up and disappears through the door.

I hear the rush of water fill the porcelain basket of the washing machine in the laundry room and close my eyes. *What just happened?* One minute I'm vomiting all over my room, the next I'm in my yoga pants and sports bra, kissing a shirtless Joel? Who is this guy that all he wants to do is take care of me, even after I not only made an utter fool of myself, but also pretty much ruined his shirt. Not to mention the mood. It's difficult to comprehend how the recent turn of events fit together in any way.

The metal slam of the washer lid notifies me that Joel will quickly be returning to my bedroom. I jump down from the bed and pull out a clean t-shirt from the armoire to cover myself up. Although I have completely ruined any chance at maintaining my dignity, modesty is something I still have control over.

"Hey, I borrowed a shirt from Trent's closet. You don't think he'll care, do you?" Joel says as he enters the room, wearing a blue t-shirt that's obviously at least one size too small for him. It clings tightly to his body and I can still make out the outline of his strong, muscular form. I'm gawking, my eyes glued to him. This must be what it means to undress someone with your eyes. I kind of feel like a creep for doing so, but I'm still completely in awe of him and can't help myself.

"No, he won't care. Especially once he finds out that I vomited all over his sweatshirt—I think everything else will pale in comparison to that."

Joel laughs. "Oh, Tessa. That was his? That's pretty funny."

"I wasn't trying to be funny. I was trying to be brave and heroic, but failed hopelessly."

"You're sick. You can't help it."

It feels a bit deceitful that I'm trying to keep up this whole sick façade, but Joel is buying it and I figure as long as he's fooled, I won't have to fess up to my fear-induced vomiting. Seriously, I must have an unusually weak stomach and super-strong gag reflex.

"Okay—let's get your hair washed. I think you'll feel a lot better after that." Joel reaches out and takes me by the hand, leading me to the bathroom. He twists the sink faucet and holds his hand under the stream of running water to gauge its degree. "That feels warm enough—is that too hot?"

I place my fingers in the water and shake my head. "Nope, that's perfect." That he's able to decipher the perfect temperature brings a smile to my face. Is there anything he's not perfect at?

Joel retrieves the piano bench from outside my closet and places it in front of the sink. He reaches for the towel on the wall immediately behind him and folds it in thirds, setting it on the tile counter as a pillow to cushion my head. "Here, lean back," Joel instructs as he cradles my head in his hands, slowly lowering my hair into the sink basin. *This hulking, handsome football player is about to wash my hair.* His compassion knows no end.

"So, what was the deal with the candle stick?" He twists his fingers though my hair and squeezes shampoo into the palm of his free hand. Its apricot scent is a welcome change from my hair's current acidic odor.

"I thought you were a burglar or government official or something. I was trying to defend myself," I say, closing my eyes in an effort to block the droplets of water that spray off of the sink.

"And you were going to do that with a candlestick? That's pretty cute."

"I wasn't trying to be cute. I was trying to protect myself. But then you came along and did it for me," I explain. I'm a little frustrated that I didn't appear as threatening as I'd hoped.

"Technically, I didn't protect you from anything except myself. You can't really call that protecting." Joel cups his hand to collect a palmful of water and gently pours it over my hair. The streams rush through my strands, collecting at the base of my neck, and he takes a free towel to dab them dry.

"Yeah, I guess. Either way—I was pretty certain I was either dead or dying, so when I opened my eyes and saw you there, it sure felt like you were sent to protect me."

"I just feel bad that I threw that entire cup of tea on you. I really wasn't expecting you to be hiding out behind your door. You totally startled me."

"I was just relieved to find out I wasn't actually covered in blood," I pause. I sound completely crazy.

"Blood? So is that what you thought it was?" Joel stifles a laugh but fails to keep it in. He turns the water off with his left hand. "Don't you think if you were bleeding you would have felt something?"

"Yeah, I guess. I don't know. I figured I was in shock."

"I'm figuring you were delirious," he smiles. "I'm going to check around here to see if I can find a thermometer, because I'm pretty sure you have an incredibly high fever."

That or an incredibly overactive imagination.

"Here." He hands me the towel from the counter and I wrap it around my freshly washed hair. "Want me to help you dry it?"

"Nah—I'll just let it air dry. Thanks for all of your help. Don't feel like you have to stay. You can head back to school if you want to." I motion to the door, hoping he will decline, knowing I have taken more than my fair share from him already.

"Tess, I'm not going back to school. It's past two o'clock and Coach cancelled practice due to the storm. I'm staying here with you until you kick me out."

It's 2:00 p.m.

I haven't bothered to check the time all day, and though my afternoon isn't turning out entirely as I had planned, it does feel good to not be tethered to the clock for once.

"I'm serious, you need to get some rest," he instructs. "Do you think you could eat something? Maybe a piece of toast?" Joel's concerned over my made-up illness.

"Yeah. I could probably keep that down," I reply. My empty stomach rumbles at the thought of being filled. I am quite hungry. I could eat an entire steak dinner, but I figure I should pretend to ease back into the whole eating thing if I am going to keep up my act. So far so good.

"Alright then. I'm off to the kitchen to whip up some toast and get a glass of water. I think even I can handle that." He winks, turns around, and heads out the door. "I'll be right back."

The sound of his shoes—that same echo that just a moment earlier signaled the end of everything for me—now brings comfort. It makes the once empty house feel full. It makes me feel less alone. It's a sound of protection and security. Each resonating footfall calms my nerves, warms my heart, and draws me closer to Joel.

When he returns, I consciously try to slow down my chewing, to act as though I really have to work to choke back the slice of bread. I take a few sips of water and set the glass on my nightstand. Joel comes to the edge of the bed and pulls back the covers so I can slide in, then walks around to the other side.

"I'm going to stay here with you until you fall asleep, okay? Do you want me to get you a bucket or anything in case you get sick again?"

I shake my head. "No, I'll be fine. And I can make it to the bathroom if I need to. It's just a few feet away."

I yank the quilt up under my arms and punch my pillow with my fist to fluff it up. I actually am exhausted from the afternoon's events and know it will be good to rest for a while. And the fact that Joel will be here with me makes relaxation seem even more attainable.

Joel draws up the sheets on the opposite side and lies down on the bed on top of them. It's funny that earlier we were both half undressed, kissing on top of the mattress, and now he's settling in above my comforter while I am tucked down underneath it.

"I'm right here if you need me, okay?" He folds his arms behind his head, elbows protruding, and slides down onto the pillow. I roll over, lift myself up a bit, and bring myself over to his chest to rest my head on it. His heartbeat pulses in my ear, a methodic drone that steadily lulls me toward sleep. Within minutes I'm out, but still very aware of his presence in my room and in my bed. As I sleep, I feel his warm lips against my forehead and know that this isn't part of a dream. I no longer need to dream about Joel—everything he has already said and done is far greater than any fantasy I could possibility create on my own.

***

At some point in the evening Joel must have slipped from my room to head home, though my sleep wasn't disturbed by his leaving. It's still dark out when I wake. In fact I'm not sure that the sun ever came out at all, but I know it is likely after dinner by the familiar sounds of dishes clanging in the kitchen sink and the cupboard doors opening and closing.

I rise up on my elbow, which tingles under the weight of my body, and I tuck my hair behind my ear. It's completely dry. I must have been asleep for at least a few hours. *Shoot, Tessa. Why did you have to waste all of that precious time with Joel by sleeping through it?*

Though the room is dim, the sheet of white paper, folded in half neatly and propped on the pillow next to me like a little paper tent, catches my eye. I retrieve it and open it, smoothing it flat between my hands.

> *Sorry Tessa—I didn't want to wake you, but both of my parents are actually home for dinner tonight so I thought I should join them. I felt your forehead before I left and it was cool, so I'm thinking your fever must be gone. Call me if you need anything and I'll come right over. Tomorrow's the big game. Since you're sick, I'll understand if you can't make it. Wish me luck! I'll stop by after to see how you're doing if that's okay. Feel better.*
> *- Joel*
>
> *P.S. Tell Trent thanks for letting me borrow the shirt.*

The knock on the door makes me jump. I hastily fold the letter up so I can shove it under my pillow.

"Yeah? Come in."

Trent props open the door with one hand, a tray of food in the other.

"Here. Mom wanted me to bring this to you. Have you seriously not left your room all day?" Trent walks the tray to my bed and sets it up on its wooden legs. Grilled cheese and tomato soup. Aunt Cathy's go-to meal for anyone under the weather. "Oh, and what was my frosh football sweatshirt doing in the dryer?"

Oops. I brace myself for the wrath of Trent.

"Yeah, that…I borrowed it today and spilled something on it. I wanted to make sure it got washed before I gave it back to you." Not entirely a lie, not entirely the truth.

"Uh—*okay*," he huffs. "Just ask first next time before you borrow and ruin my stuff, alright?" I snicker, figuring had he really known what happened he would be even less gracious.

Uncle Mark's low voice booms down the hall.

"Hey now, what's mine is yours, what's yours is mine, remember guys? We're all family here." Uncle Mark's in my room and plops down at the foot of my bed. I lift the spoon to my mouth to take a sip from the steaming bowl. *Mmm.* Aunt Cathy sure does know how to whip up some yummy comfort food. Trent's backed a good ten feet away, practically standing in the doorframe again like this morning, trying hard not to breathe in my "germs" I'm sure.

"In that case, can I borrow the SUV after the game tomorrow night, Dad?" His carrot-colored eyebrows jump up. "A bunch of us want to go to the lake for a bonfire, and we can't all fit in my truck." Trent leaps at the chance to take advantage of Uncle Mark's generosity. So very Trent of him.

"Aren't you technically still 'borrowing' my truck?" Uncle Mark makes air quotes with his fingers and winks in my direction. We all recognize the same things about Trent.

"Well, *technically* I guess I am. So can I *technically* swap out vehicles with you for tomorrow night?" Trent is lucky Uncle Mark lets him get away with pushing his luck.

"Let's talk about that in a bit, Son. I want to chat with Tess for a minute if you'll excuse us."

"Yeah, of course—I don't want that plague of hers anyway." Trent retreats and Uncle Mark rotates to face me, resignation on his face. We both know there isn't any changing Trent.

"So, Tess. I want to talk to you about something." My heart quickens. What *is* this? I pray he isn't going to talk about the birds and the bees or whatever old people call it. I am certain I've learned all I need to know in our sex education class freshman year and don't care to hear any other details, especially from my uncle.

Maybe it's about the sale of the ranch and the money that will be wired to my account. That's probably it. I breathe a sigh of relief.

"So, about you and Joel."

Cue the birds.

"I know that you guys are seeing each other, or dating, or whatever you call it."

Cue the bees.

"So listen—he's been around here a long time. I'm close with his family and I really like the kid. I mean, I practically consider him another son, he's here so often." Uncle Mark pauses, smoothing his dark moustache with his finger. He rests his thumb on the divot in his chin, deep in contemplation. "And for as long as I can remember he's had a thing for you."

Insert record scratch sound effect.

For as long as he can remember? How long was that exactly? I want to interject and ask Uncle Mark to clarify, but he continues before I can breathe a word.

"Basically, what I'm trying to say is, be good to him, okay? I don't want to see him get hurt—I mean, he has it bad for you. If for some reason you don't feel the same, just tell him. Don't string him along—he's too good of a guy and doesn't deserve that."

Uncle Mark pats me on the leg, both a warm gesture and a warning, and rises from his place at the edge of the bed.

"Now I've got to go talk some reason into that son of mine."

"Good luck with that." I tease and tear apart a piece of my grilled cheese sandwich. It's cold, but I still pop it in my mouth.

The door swings shut behind him. His presence is gone, but his words still linger in the air. I sit in the near-dark and finish my dinner, playing his lecture over in my head. It's crazy for him to concern himself with matters of Joel's heart. I would never intentionally do anything to someone who has shown me nothing but respect, compassion, and concern. It's completely out of the realm of possibility.

For years I've wanted someone like Joel in my life—someone who understands me, and even if he doesn't completely, cares for me in spite of it. I'm really beginning to think Joel is that person. I'm not about to do anything to jeopardize our relationship. He is exactly what I need, exactly what I've been craving.

I walk my tray back to the kitchen and find Aunt Cathy sitting at the table, sorting out the mail into two piles in front of her. She's lost in her work and it takes her a minute to notice my silent presence.

"Hey you. Feeling any better?" She eyes me over her reading glasses.

The counter is littered with pots and pans stacked high from tonight's dinner. All the fixings for a make-your-own taco night are still left out on the counter. I sink. Aunt Cathy's obviously gone to quite a bit of trouble to cook me a completely separate meal, and here I am giving Joel all the credit for any ounce of kindheartedness shown to me. Maybe I'm making up just how perfect he seems to be.

"Thanks for dinner, Aunt Cathy. It was just what I needed," I say, hoping she can detect the sincerity.

"Oh, I didn't cook that for you, Sweetie. I just told Trent to take it down to you." Aunt Cathy takes her letter opener and slices open the rectangular envelope in her hand.

"You didn't? I just assumed because—"

"No, Joel made that for you before he left. He stayed with you until his parents called for the third time telling him he needed to come home for dinner. That kid has it bad for you, you know."

No, I don't.

I don't actually know how much he cares for me, and I'm not sure it's possible to fully comprehend the extent to which he does.

I just offer her an unreadable nod.

I walk back to my room in a trance to get myself ready for bed, even though I've already spent the majority of the day in it. After brushing my hair and teeth, I slip into my pajamas and lie down again. My sheets are still warm from my prolonged presence this afternoon.

Why is it so hard for me to understand just how much Joel likes me? Isn't he everything I've been wishing and hoping for? And now that he's here, why does it still seem so unreal? Staring up at the ceiling of the pitch-black room, I vow to myself that I won't hurt Joel. Why had Uncle Mark been so adamant about that? Why on earth would I want to hurt him? Everything about Joel is the perfect fit for everything I have been longing for in my life. I am beyond lucky that I've found him—or that he's found me. *That we have found each other.*

I close my eyes again for the umpteenth time today. From behind my eyelids I can see the bright light of my phone on my nightstand illuminate the room as it buzzes upon receiving a message. I roll over and yank it off the table, blinking hard, and I squint at the intensity of the light pouring from it. It takes my eyes a while to adjust, the shapes are fuzzy and blended together, but once they do, the letters come into being, like a camera lens grabbing focus on its subject.

Message from: 234-1112

The ranch is ready for you,
but are you ready for the ranch?
See you bright and early, Sunshine!

I exhale deeply, a sigh that comes from the very depths of me.

And with that releasing breath, a bit of the promise I've just made slips out from me, too.

ELEVEN

"Wake up sleepy head." Her chirping is birdlike, a morning song filling my room. I'm so not a bird person. Nor a morning person. Bailey tosses open the curtains that drape my window, though the hour is so early that even the sun hasn't made its debut. I groan into my pillow.

"You're supposed to be there by 6:00 a.m., remember! Time to get moving!" She yanks the quilt off of me and I draw my exposed legs up to my chest. The warm barrier between Bailey's overly chipper voice and me is gone. I curl up tighter into a ball. "Everyone is going to love this feature! I can see it now—*There's a New Cowboy in Town*! It's going to be amazing—even better than a *Day in the Life* with Joel, if that's possible!"

She tosses a pair of ripped jeans and a plaid, lavender, long-sleeved, button-up shirt toward me. "Here, wear these. That will make you seem a little less city and a little more country." She throws a pair of worn cowboy boots onto the bed, too. They belong to my Aunt Cathy, a token from her teenage years, but they've recently found their new home on the floor of Bailey's closet. And now, more recently at the foot of my bed.

"Bail—I used to live there, remember? And I never dressed like *this* when I was there." I hold up the boots by their back strap and chuck them back onto the floor. Bailey retrieves them immediately and shoves them toward me, ignoring my attempt to discard them.

"Trust me. These will make you so much more believable."

Believable? Why on earth would I need to be believable? Didn't I spend the first fourteen years of my life at the ranch? If anything, it is Liam that is the one who needs to do the convincing. I will be just fine. I don't need to prove myself to anyone.

"Just wear them, okay? I've heard he's like an actual cowboy. Like he knows how to rope and ride and everything." I try hard not to let them, but my eyes roll in their sockets.

"Oh come on, you don't even know what that means."

"Maybe not, but I do know that every girl in school was talking about him yesterday. I can't tell you how many of them freaked out because he wasn't there." Bailey lifts up her fingers and examines her perfectly polished nails. "There were countless rumors going around that his transfer wasn't accepted and he was heading back to Superior. Something about the Education Sector not approving his referral." She pushes back a cuticle and speaks without looking my direction. "Better not be true because there goes our feature if that happens." Bailey floats into my bathroom and returns, hairbrush in hand. She looks like she's ready to do some serious primping. "Why aren't you out of bed already? Didn't you spend enough time in there yesterday?" She pauses. "By the way, how are you feeling?"

"I'm fine—I mean, I'm better—thanks." Who needs a shot of espresso when you have fully-caffeinated Bailey? "And he's not going back to Superior. He said he had to get a few final letters from his old teachers to complete the transfer."

"Well, that'll sure make everyone at East Valley breathe a sigh of relief. He's become an overnight sensation."

Overnight sensation? By doing what? Just by having long hair and looking different than all the other boys? Is that really all it takes to stand out at East Valley? On second thought, those analytical assumptions about the shallowness of our entire class population probably aren't too far from the truth.

"I don't get what the big deal is. I mean—he seems nice and all, but what's the fuss?" I hope I'm playing it off okay. I've sure put my freshman drama class skills to use in the past two days. First to fain illness, now to fake disinterest. "What is everyone saying?"

"That he's unlike any other guy at school. He's hot. He's got his own style. He doesn't seem to care what others think of him—"

"And you get that all from just two days attendance. Seriously, Bailey? I think that's reaching quite a bit, don't you?" I follow her orders and dress in the outfit selected for me, reluctantly pulling on the boots, hoping they will be too small so I have an excuse to leave them behind.

"Look! They're perfect!" She's right. They are an exact fit. "And say what you will about Liam. Just wait. He'll be the next big thing on campus in no time. May even pass Joel up for that title if he doesn't watch out."

I hesitate at the mention of Joel's name. For as hard as I try to keep any thoughts of Liam and Joel separate, Bailey's statement is a clear indicator that I might not be able to keep that going for long.

"Seriously, don't screw things up today, okay? I don't want him banning our family from the ranch. I'd like to go out there sometime, too, you know." Bailey holds me by the shoulders, turning me slightly from side to side, studying my appearance before giving me a nod of approval. "There. You look great."

So that explains it. Bailey's interested in Liam, or at least interested in the idea of him. And her sudden preoccupation with my own attire is an attempt to keep me from making a fool of our family. An effort to help me get in good with the Hollanders so she can have her own opportunity to spend time with Liam. The whole premeditated plan stirs up emotions in me that I haven't experienced since our Chris Fenton era back in junior high.

"I hate to break it to you Bail, but Liam doesn't date. *Like he doesn't date anyone.* He has these impossibly high standards. Pass *that* info on to the other girls." I hope the generic way I phrase my statement will soften the blow a bit. It isn't often that Bailey develops a crush. I don't want to completely squash any hopes she might have of getting to know Liam. But at the same time, the thought of her alone with him at the ranch seems very unlikely to ever occur. I'm not sure I know exactly what Liam's type is, but I'm pretty certain Bailey doesn't fit his near unattainable criteria. Even in her peacock splendor, I doubt that she's a match for his terms and conditions.

I hurriedly twist my hair back in two braids, grab a bagel from the counter, and pick up the keys to Aunt Cathy's sedan that she's loaned me for the day.

Alright, Tess. This is it. Here we go.

I exit the house, get in the car, and breathe in deep through my nose, out through my mouth. With eyes still closed, the key finds its groove in the ignition and the engine sounds under the hood. I've waited for this moment for two years, and now that it's here, it scares me to death. And yet, at the same time I feel an exhilaration that borders on indescribable. This juxtaposition of two entirely different reactions makes my head hurt and my fingers tingle all in one sensation.

I grip the steering wheel until the whites of my knuckles show in an effort to take control over my body's involuntary responses. I need to get my emotions in check. I have a job to do—to spend a *Day in the Life* with Liam. Neither falling apart at the seams, nor bursting with excitement, are options. Go with the flow. Cool and collected. I've had years of practice trying to be all of these things. If there was ever a time that I needed to exercise this learned restraint, it is now.

My mind's memorized the roads from all of the times my parents drove it. The way each turn feels under the tires, the stop and go jolt of each intersection. I'm certain I could have made the twenty-minute drive in my sleep, and in a way, it almost feels as though I am in a dreamlike state of mind, the car as though it's on autopilot.

And suddenly, before I know it, I'm here.

Though the sedan moved effortlessly through town—turning, braking, and accelerating on cue—it comes to a sudden stop just as the gravel meets the dirt at the entrance to the ranch.

Hollander Ranch. The carved wooden sign stands twelve feet above the ground, staking claim on the property immediately behind it.

I strangely feel like I am an intruder.

Why wouldn't I? What did I honestly expect? Did I really think that I could come back to the ranch and everything would pick up where it left off two years prior? Like it would be a homecoming of sorts—some type of joyful reunion? I scold myself for ever thinking things can be as they once were. I'm not a Hollander. I'm not a part of their family. And this definitely isn't my home anymore. For goodness sake, someone else's name is mounted at the entrance.

For the first time during my drive, it's as though I physically have to press the pedal down to the floor to command the car to move. And it hesitates—like a stubborn mule disobeying its owner—the car lurches forward and stops suddenly, as though it won't possibly go an inch further. I push my foot hard against the floorboards and it bolts through the entrance, stirring up a brown cloud of dust behind the vehicle.

I finally roll to a stop just in front of the house and I put the car in park, glad to be done with the obstinate piece of metal. My bag containing a notebook and digital camera lies on the seat beside me and I snatch it up, sling it over my shoulder, and open the car door.

"Morning, Sunshine!" Liam bounds down the porch steps toward me and grabs my tote from my arm before it has a chance to settle there. "Welcome home! Mom made breakfast—you haven't eaten yet, have you? We're just about ready to head to the coop to get the eggs, but we gotta do our breakfast routine first. Mom's pretty particular about her family time." He leans in as he speaks and tucks his golden hair behind his right ear. *Why does he always do that? And why does it always make me feel this way?* My stomach flutters on cue.

"Come on in—no need to really show you around, but we can do a tour at lunchtime if you want to see how we've decorated the house."

I nod. I haven't opened my mouth to speak since stepping out of the car. "Yeah—yeah, sure. That would be great. I'd love to see it."

The smell of pancakes and sausage wafts from the kitchen, literally hitting me as I walk into the entryway, so hard that it stops me in my tracks. The oil from the polished stair rails, the faint must from the aged wallpaper, the coffee brewing in the pot on the counter. All of the familiar smells of home. Of my home—my childhood, my memories—all reminders of the love and comfort the ranch provided me. It's a crazy sensation, but I'm more at home in the entry of this near stranger's house than I am in my own bed at the Buchman's.

"So this must be Tessa. My goodness, you *are* beautiful." Mrs. Hollander cups my chin in her hands and pulls me into a hug, pressing my face into her long, blonde curls which smell of honeysuckle. I breathe it in. "It's so nice to finally have another girl around here. Come, sit down for breakfast. The boys have lots of chores to do today, but I'm a stickler about spending mealtime together as a family. Speaking of— Liam, will you run upstairs and get Joshua out of bed?" She pulls out a chair from the long, planked wood dining table, and motions for me to sit.

"Thank you, Mrs. Hollander. It's nice to be back here. I'm excited to see how Liam spends his days."

She walks over to the stove, retrieves two hotcakes with her metal tongs, and sets them on a plate. The way she moves about the kitchen is so elegant; it's as though she's skating across the room. "Please, call me

Rebecca. Mrs. Hollander is my mother-in-law." She smirks, a smile that reaches up to her eyes, and places the dish on the table in front of me. "And I'm sure his days look a bit different than the ones you spent here. Was your family a part of the Ag Sector, too?"

I reach out for the glass jar of syrup and douse the pancakes in molasses. I shake my head. "No, Transportation. This was just more of a home than a working ranch for us."

Rebecca's eyes gleam. So this is where all of Liam's charm comes from. And his good looks. Rebecca is stunning—her long, wavy, golden hair and pale green eyes are an exact replica of her son's. Or rather his are a reproduction of hers. And when she smiles, two defined dimples crease her cheeks and her eyes crinkle at the corners, revealing character and kindness.

"I'm up, Ma. I'm up." Another teenage boy stumbles into the room. I assume it must be Joshua. He seats himself at the spot immediately to my right, taking no notice of my presence.

"Eh hem." Rebecca forcefully clears her throat. "Josh, we have a guest in our home. Don't you think you should introduce yourself?" Joshua glances my way at the request of his mother. He's a freshman, just two years younger than Liam, but nearly the same in size and stature. His hair, darker and sandier than his brother's, is cropped tighter on the sides, leaving just an inch or so of curls on the top.

"Hey. I'm Josh. Can you pass me the syrup?" He barely looks up from his plate to make the introduction and following request. Apparently charm doesn't run in *all* of the family members.

"Hi Josh, I'm Tessa." I exchange both a handshake and the syrup jar.

"Tessa used to live here. She's interviewing me for our journalism class so she'll be spending the day here." Liam—who had left the room for a brief moment—returns, holding the hands of two, tow-headed boys whose ringlets are even tighter than their mother's. "Tessa, this is Sammy and this is Tyler. Boys, say hi to Tessa."

"Hi Tessa," they chime in unison, releasing their hands from Liam's, running to the table to claim their breakfast.

"Hi guys. Tyler, how old are you?"

"I'm six and Sammy is two," Tyler says, clearly the spokesman for the two.

"I am not! I'm three, *bemember*?" Sammy frowns, visibly unhappy with Tyler's misrepresentation of his age.

"Okay, soooorry. Sammy is three. He just had his birthday last week."

"Well, nice to meet you both. I'm excited to get to know you guys." I pick my fork up and bring it to my mouth. "Maybe you can show me around later. I'd love to see your rooms."

"Yeahhh!" Sammy screams with excitement. "And you can push me on the tire swing out front!"

My eyes immediately go to the window that overlooks the front landscape. It's like a frame around a painted picture. There, right within view, is the same swing my dad pushed me on for hours when I was a little girl. I picture Sammy perched on top of it and the vision I'd had before of curly-headed children doesn't quite seem so farfetched anymore.

"I'd love to. That is, after Liam and I do all of our work. I'm writing a story about him for school, so I have to follow him around today."

"Will your story have pictures?" Tyler's eyes light up. "I'm *really* good at drawing if you need pictures."

"Well, I did bring my camera, but I bet a drawing or two from you will be sure to get me that A+ I'm hoping for." I flash a wink at Tyler. His chubby cheeks blush in response.

"Where's Dad?" Joshua interjects, a mouthful of sausage mumbling his words.

"Don't talk with your mouth full." A voice, deeper than all the others, commands from around the corner. "Hi Tessa—we're so glad to have you here. I'm Chris, otherwise known as Dad. So you'll be spending the day with this troublemaker, huh?" He places Liam in a headlock and ruffles his hair with his fist.

"Hi Chris." Liam's tousled hair is incredibly distracting. "Thanks for having me. And thanks for breakfast—this food is amazing."

"Mom *is* the best cook, you know. Just wait for dinner; she's got something really great planned." Liam bats at his dad's hands to push them away, and smoothes out the stray curls on top of his head. I sort of wish he hadn't.

"I love that you all eat every meal as a family. My mom used to be really big on that, too. It got harder as

I got older, but she was very protective of family time. It's rare to see families do that anymore." I take one last bite of sausage and set my fork back on my plate with a metal clink.

"Nothing is more important to us than family. We work together, play together. It's sort of an Ag Sector thing. But eating together is about the only time we have to actually relax and just enjoy one another's company." Liam's dad finds his place at the head of the table. Though the family resemblance is strong in all of them, he looks most like Joshua with his darker, shorter hair and hazel eyes.

"And although eating together is *so* important— Tessa and I need to get out and gather the eggs so this family has *money* to put food on that table." Liam pushes himself back with his palms and rises to his feet. He walks around to my side and collects my plate, bringing it to the sink for me.

"Good luck. They aren't laying like they used to. I think the move might have affected them a bit. They'll settle back into their routine, but yesterday I only got seventeen from the whole bunch. Parker's not going to be too happy with that count." Chris speaks directly to Liam, who obviously knows what he is referring to. He nods. I, on the other hand, know absolutely nothing about chickens, let alone their egg-laying habits. I have a feeling this day is going to be even more interesting than I'd originally thought.

"Come on, Tess. We've got lots to do." Liam grabs me by the hand and leads me through the kitchen to the mudroom at the east side of the house.

He drops down on the top step with a thud and yanks on his boots. They don't look very different from the ones on my own feet. "Look at you, cowgirl. You have those from before?"

"Yeah, um…kinda," I stutter, wanting to change the subject before I start fabricating stories about my ranch-living days that I can't live up to. "So, that's the coop?" I point to a freestanding structure at the base of the hill surrounded by a flock of hens. They peck at the ground, rummaging for their morning feed.

"You got it. That's it. Ever stole an egg from a chicken?" Liam pops up quickly from the step as though there are springs in his legs, takes me by the hand again, and tugs me down the stairs onto the dirt pathway.

"I can honestly say that I haven't. Is it hard?"

"Only with the territorial ones, and those are only a few of them. Most of them aren't even in the coop, which makes it easier. It's the ones that are still sitting on them that you have to look out for. Those mama hens can get pretty nasty." His eyes sparkle when he speaks. "Don't worry. You're safe with me—I won't let any of them peck you to death." His lips spread into a deeper grin. "That only happened once with this one guy and we've implemented some necessary precautions since that unfortunate event." How he can maintain his charm even when speaking of made up, fatal chicken peckings is hard to believe, but somehow he manages it effortlessly.

I follow him down to the coop, dodging the array of hens that gather at my feet. A medium-sized, rusty brown one that looks like she is wearing fluffy, feathered leg warmers, gets a little too close for comfort. I jerk my knee up to my stomach and let out a loud squeal. Liam whips around to see what's caused my distressing yelp and he snickers, bringing his finger to his nose to control his laughter. But he only snorts louder as a result.

"Oh no. Seriously, Tess? This is going to be a long day if you can't even get past the entrance to the coop." He squeezes my hand firmly and a chill shoots from my palm all the way up my arm, causing the fine hairs to rise on my flesh. "Trust me—they are much more afraid of you than you should be of them."

Liam retrieves two wire egg baskets from the side of the pen and hands one to me. Its handle is corroded, and the original chipped, white paint flakes off at the slightest rustle. It strikes me that they have been in the egg laying business for quite some time by the looks of things.

"Um…I'm not sure that's actually possible. I think it's okay to have a healthy fear of farm animals." I swing the basket back and forth and watch the paint flakes fall to the ground like pieces of drifting snow.

"I agree—a healthy respect for horses, *yes*. But a healthy fear of chickens, not necessary. Come on, let's go in." The roof to the structure is only five feet high and we both have to bend down in an effort to fit under its awning. "So first I go around and gather all the eggs that are exposed. Those gals are out in the pen enjoying their morning meal. They won't bother me for taking them." He gathers three eggs with one hand.

"But it's ladies like Sally here that I have to sweet talk a bit. Most of these gals don't sit on their eggs—we've got a good routine and they know what's coming. But Sally wants to rest on each egg to try to make it hatch, poor girl. She doesn't like it when I reach under her to pull it out, so I have to charm her a bit."

Of course he does. Why did I assume that his charisma is limited to just the human variety. Apparently he can work his magic on any species, so long as they are female.

"Good morning, Sally. You are looking stunning as usual today. Love what you've done with your hair." Sally cocks her head to the side, the plume of feathers at the top moving with her quick, jerky motions. Liam pats her gently on her crest and slides his right hand under her, retrieving a light brown egg in one smooth motion. "There you go, girl. See you again tomorrow."

He sets the egg into the basket on top of the others he's already collected. "See? Nothing to it. Your turn."

"Oh no, I don't think so." I shake my head back and forth so furiously that the ends of my braids whip my cheeks. It stings.

"Come on. How are you supposed to do a *Day in the Life* if you don't actually participate? I've heard all the great writers study the subjects they write about. Now seriously, it's your turn."

But I *have* been studying my subject. I have been studying everything about him. In fact, I find it hard to focus on anything else. The way he sweet talks poultry makes *me* blush, even though none of his playful banter is even directed my way. I feel like I've learned more about Liam in the last five minutes than I have in all of our conversations combined over the past couple of days.

I think I've figured him out. He's a tease. That's it—that is why he doesn't need a girlfriend or try to pursue a relationship of any kind. He is a natural-born Casanova and he knows it. He can have his way with anyone, but doesn't want the commitment typically tied to it. So he teases, he flirts, and he charms. I guess the attention and swooning he receives in return is enough to make him satisfied with perpetually being alone. And really, when you can have the devotion of hundreds versus the loyalty of one, why would you tie yourself down?

Because maybe that one person is worth abandoning all others' affection...

My thoughts trail off, only to be completely interrupted by Liam's prodding voice. "Come on, Sunshine. Seriously, have at it—it's your turn."

I roll my eyes so far back in my head I worry for a brief moment they might get stuck. *Okay Tess, what have you got to lose?* I sidle up to a hen two boxes down from Sally. She's similar in color and feathering, but much smaller in size. *Here goes nothing.*

"Hey there pretty lady, don't mind me." Liam's grinning from ear to ear, thoroughly enjoying my humiliating introduction to the chicken. I make a mental note not to have anything to do with the Agricultural Sector. I can't imagine a lifetime of egg gathering and hen sweet-talking. "Liam, how do I even know if there is an egg under there?"

"Oh there is. Bertha is one of our regular one-a-day gals. Seriously, don't be shy. You're doing great." He waves me forward with his hand, pushing the air between us, encouraging me to continue.

"Okay…um, so I'm just going to see what you have here." Timidly, I slide my hand forward into the box, hoping Bertha won't notice my intrusion. I breathe in deep—not the smartest thing to do in a chicken coop—and the smell that enters my nostrils makes the whole scenario even more unpleasant.

Bertha tilts her head almost to a ninety-degree angle and looks straight at me with her beady, black eyes. Before I can react to her warning, she thrusts her razor pointed beak into the top of my hand, pulling it out quickly, only to reinsert it back into my fresh wound again. A shriek bursts from my lips and I grab my bleeding hand with the other to squeeze it tightly to my chest.

Liam, who has been just a foot away up to this point, pushes me aside and backhands Bertha across the face, so powerfully that she slams into the side of the coop. Her wings thrust open as her feathers hit the wood. Shaken and disgruntled, her entire body shivers and she ruffles her plumes, settling back into her roost to claim her territory once again.

The gash on my hand pulses under the pain, and I bite my lip hard to suppress the tears that are quickly brimming. I'm not sure if it is the throbbing or the utter embarrassment that brings them on, but I know that I don't want to cry in front of Liam. Not over a stupid bird.

"Seriously, Bertha? You've got to learn to control your jealousy!"

I guffaw at his ability to bring it all back to him. Maybe this is a common trait among all smooth-talkers. "So, you think Bertha pecked me because she's jealous of *me* being here with *you*?" The blood from my hand begins to drip onto the dirt ground. I clench my fist in an effort to stop its flow.

"Of course I do. Come on—*these are my girls.* This is our routine. They're not too big on sharing."

"Oh, okay. Sure." I roll my eyes again. "Well, they won't have to share much longer because I'm pretty sure this is the first, and last, egg gathering I'll be participating in."

His hand finds mine and turns it over in front of his face, examining the extent to which I've been maimed. "She got you pretty good. Come on, let's go up to the house and get this cleaned up. Joshua can finish here and I think we have *more* than enough for this section of our interview."

"You wouldn't dare! We can't include this in our assignment. This—," I lift up my bloody hand so it's within an inch of his face and continue, "—this will not be repeated to *anyone*. I'm serious Liam. If you breathe a word of this, I'll—"

"You'll what?" He pokes my ribs with his index finger and smirks, clearly trying to get a rise out of me. It works.

"Ughh! I don't know—but I promise you it won't be pretty." I hate that at the time when a good comeback is a necessity, my mind is completely void of anything remotely resembling an actual threat.

"I doubt it's possible for you to do anything and not be pretty." The way he construes my words and twists them into a ludicrous compliment kills me. "I mean, look at you. You're definitely the best looking gal out here." He spins around and motions toward the hens, now sitting quietly in their boxes, listening intently.

"Gee, Liam. How flattering."

"Hey now, I'm serious. Joyce over there is quite a looker."

I punch him square in the gut and he grabs his side, bending in half in what I hope is an attempt to ease the pain, but turns out to be just the act of doubling over in laughter.

"Oh, Tess. We are going to have so much fun today." He wraps his arm coolly around my shoulder and draws me in, pulling my head so close to his that our cheeks touch. "Now let's go get that all washed up. We need to make sure you have at least one good hand since you likely just broke your other against my rock solid abs."

"Just like you injured your finger a few minutes ago when you poked at my ribs. You're not the only tough one here, Liam."

An open invitation, I know, but I'm not about to let Liam do all the trash-talking.

"Oh yeah? So you're pretty tough, huh?" He grabs me playfully and pinches the skin on my side right above my hip. I swat his hand away with my only remaining good one, and he rests his palm on my other side, lingering—warm and welcome on the curve of my body. When his hand meets the small of my back, though never having touched it right there before, it's at home where it rests.

Liam is significantly taller than me, probably close to 5'9" or 5'10", but it's as though we are nearly eye-to-eye as we stand facing each other. I can feel the heat radiating from his flushed cheeks on my face without even touching them, like warmth from a flame. This close proximity makes it all the more difficult to break my gaze with him. I don't want to. His green eyes, which have been playful and mischievous, soften the longer we stare at each other. Unwilling and unable to stop myself, I press into him and rest my head firmly against his jawbone. It's as though he draws me to him like a moth to that same flame I felt earlier. Even if I want to turn and run, I'm completely powerless to do so. Everything about him calls me, lures me, and charms me.

Liam literally responds to my advances with open arms, encircling me and bringing me tightly into his chest as I all but push myself on him. And once there in his firm embrace, I lose all sense to stop myself. I want to just rest in this hold—something about it is oddly familiar; as though it isn't the first time we have been in each other's arms. As crazy as it sounds, especially knowing that we only met just a few days earlier, everything about Liam feels like a not-so-distant memory. Like I have been here before, like his arms have been waiting patiently for my return, and once I found them again, the pieces just fit.

"Buc-buc, bu-CUUUUCK!" Bertha belts out a squawk, so ear piercing that it nearly sends me through the shabby tin roof. I push off of Liam with unexpected force and bind my arms across my chest, as if to shield myself from any responsibility I might have in our lingering moment. I'm caught, even if it is just by a ridiculous bird. This is no longer just an innocent day of interviews and assignments. I've changed all that. The incessant flirting, the charm—it all transformed into something more when I took that initial step toward Liam.

Oh, Tessa. You've ruined everything.

"See, I told you they were the jealous type." He pushes his hands, both of them this time, through his blonde hair and interlocks his fingers at the base of his skull, his elbows protruding out on either side of him.

"Liam—I'm so sorry. I didn't mean to do that. I don't know what I was thinking to shove myself on you in that way. I mean, I'm with Joel—"

"What?" He freezes, then jerks his head back. "You're with McBrayer?"

"Um…yeah." I chomp down on the inside of my cheek, drawing blood, and the bitter taste of iron quickly fills my mouth. "Yeah, I mean…I guess. I don't really know what we are. But anyway, I had no right to do that or to think that's what you wanted. Just forget it ever happened, okay?"

"You're asking me to forget an awful lot today, Sunshine. First the hen versus girl incident. Better yet, chick versus chick." A smile creeps across his face, proud of his clever play on words. "And now the near kiss—"

"Wait a second! *That* wasn't a near kiss. *That* was just an innocent hug." My teeth find the side of my cheek again, now swollen from the original bite.

"Sure it wasn't, Tess." His tone is laced with sarcasm. "You mean to tell me if Bertha over there hadn't interrupted us that we wouldn't be making out in this chicken coop right now?"

No of course we wouldn't! Would we?

But my lips won't allow my mouth to utter the words; they don't give permission for that lie to pass straight through them. And though I might be a traitor in this moment, I'm not about to be a liar. "Whatever, Liam. It doesn't matter—it didn't happen so let's just move on."

"Sure, Tessa. If you think you're capable of that." His coy grin says it all. He and I both know the truth. That in all honesty, I probably am not capable of it, of just moving on like nothing has happened. Especially after discovering how comforting those arms of his are. Why would any girl in her right mind willingly give that up?

But then again, I'm beginning to think I can't even stake claim on being in my right mind at all. And one thing is becoming certain, I apparently am capable of feeling much more than I ever knew possible. The problem is that all those feelings aren't directed toward the same person.

And that is where things begin to fall apart.

I desperately need something to weave it back together—to make sense of it all, some reason for why things are happening the way they are with Joel *and* with Liam. I need an answer.

"Come on Sunshine, into the house you go." We trek up to the house and Liam props the screen door open, motioning me forward. I stare at his red, full lips and wonder what it would feel like if mine were pressed to them. "Let's get that cut taken care of." He pulls his mouth into a smile, and tugs at my heart at the same time.

TWELVE

The fluorescent green and blue dinosaur band-aid begins to peel at the corner and I pick at its edge with my jagged fingernail, lifting it with the tip. Nearly all the adhesive's gone from the underside, taking with it any functionality it might have once possessed. I yank it off with a quick jerk and wince. I hadn't anticipated the leftover sticky grip from the other side, still firmly adhered to my hand. I crumple it between my fingers.

"Since when do you wear little boy band-aids?" Joel slides a can of soda across his kitchen table and it stops when it makes contact with my hand. He pops the tab open on the one cradled in his own palm, sending a small spray of carbonation into the air.

Since I started hanging out with families that include little boys, I suppose.

After yesterday's mortifying chicken pecking/boy seducing activities I wanted to forget that any of it actually happened. But the used bandage and fresh scab on the back of my hand are two tangible reminders of those very real events.

It wasn't all as bad as it originally seemed. Though *I* had been completely taken aback with my forward advances toward Liam, *he* brushed them off as no big deal. I'm not sure if I should be relieved or insulted. Either way, I'm grateful that he didn't appear nearly as traumatized as I did. After laughing it all off as he so characteristically does with everything else in life, he took me back up to the house to clean the chicken-inflicted wound.

Rebecca had been in the kitchen and immediately rushed to my aid. It almost felt silly, especially in comparison with the day before when I actually needed someone to care for me given the helpless state I had been in. But even though my cut was small, her compassion was overwhelming—so motherly that I couldn't deny her the opportunity to help. She had led me to the downstairs bathroom and sat me down at the edge of the tub as she washed my hand delicately, applied ointment, and rummaged through the boys' first aid kit to find something to cover it.

"There you go, sweetie. Good as new. You know, sometimes I think I'd fit in the Med Sector better than Ag," she'd winked.

I'd half expected her to 'kiss it and make it all better,' and truth be told, had she done so, it probably wouldn't have even seemed entirely out of place. She's a mom to four boys. I am sure she has had more than her share of tending to bumps and bruises. And though she is Liam's mom, in that moment she felt like she was mine. Or at least the closest thing I'd had to one in a very long time. I don't know if it was the atmosphere of it all—the familiar smells of the house, the motherly care—whatever it was, it felt like home.

"You okay? How did you get that anyway?" Joel attempts to engage me in conversation, abruptly bringing me out of my replay of yesterday, pulling me back to reality.

"Oh, yesterday. That new kid, Liam—you know, from biology?" Of course he knows. "We're partners for our journalism class. I had to interview him at the ranch. I guess I got a little too close for comfort with a chicken." I hadn't planned to tell Joel my whereabouts. In fact, I was originally content to let him think I was in bed recovering all day from the stomach flu. But something about him makes me want to be forthcoming about my activities. At least most of them.

"You went to the ranch yesterday?" His eyes are wide. "Tess, that's a pretty big deal—how was it? Were you okay?" His questioning eyes only show concern for me and don't demand details regarding my time there. Why does he have to be so good?

"Yeah, it was fine. Really. It was actually nice to be back there, to see it full of life again."

And full of life it was. I doubt there are ever any dull moments at the Hollander house. That seemed apparent after just one morning there. When Rebecca had finished tending to my injury, Liam opted for "safer" chores, as he termed them. Apparently, that just meant duties that didn't involve animals. Bringing the hay to the horses, feed to the chickens, and even dog washing, were off limits until I had proven myself as a farmhand. So instead we were charged with keeping up the house, which I was actually perfectly satisfied to do.

I helped Rebecca finish up with the dishes from breakfast. She washed, I dried. She told me stories of Liam as a child while he and Joshua helped their dad rearrange the furniture in the adjoining room, still settling in to their new home. She spoke of Liam's first pony ride at the county fair. How he had begged and pleaded for "just one more," which resulted in an additional two hours on the poor pony until the owner told a crying, towheaded Liam that they had to pack up and leave for the night. How the pony's name was Blaze, and how when Liam turned thirteen and got an actual horse of his own as a gift from his grandfather, he—without hesitation—decided upon Blaze as his steed's handle.

"Come on, Mom. Are you telling embarrassing stories about me to Tess?" Liam questioned when he'd entered the kitchen as I set the last dish into the drying rack.

"No, Liam, nothing embarrassing. Just about Blaze and how his name came to be. You should take Tessa down to the barn to meet him. I'm sure he'd love a ride today."

"We'll have to ease into that. I have a few embarrassing stories of my own about Tessa involving animals that I could share if you like." I'd shot a look across the room toward Liam, daggers flying from my eyes. *You wouldn't, Liam—I warned you.*

"I kid, I kid." He'd shrugged off my glare. "Come on, Sunshine. You think I would do that to you?"

Rebecca laughed at our exchange and untied the apron fastened around her neck, folded it neatly, and placed it on the counter next to her. "Oh Liam, if you're referring to that small cut on the top of her hand, I'd watch yourself. I'm sure I don't need to remind you about that scar above your right eye, now do I?"

Liam's hand instinctively flew up to his eyebrow, his fingers tracing over the thin, bare line that intersected the middle of it. "Whatever, Ma. I was little and outnumbered. No one told me how hungry they would be."

"You mean you got *that* from feeding a chicken? Geez Liam, I thought you were tougher than that. At least I got mine from a protective mama that was just trying to save her young." Exaggerating the truth a bit, I was aware, but the banter was just too easy with Liam.

"Technically it wasn't really her 'young' but whatever. And yes, I was feeding them. But we were at my grandpa's ranch and he had like thousands—"

"Fifty, Liam. He had fifty." Rebecca smirked my direction.

"Okay—whatever—numbers don't matter. Anyway, I was five and small and they were big. Much bigger than the ones we have here. And I wasn't pecked, I was scratched." As soon as the words had left his mouth it was evident that he wanted to pull them back in.

"So that manly scar is from a chicken claw? Impressive, Liam, impressive," I teased, nodding my head in false admiration.

"Whatever. I'm not sure I like this ganging up on me that you two are doing here."

Rebecca had slid to my side to put her arm around my shoulder. "Oh I do. I like having another girl around. You can invite Tessa over whenever you like."

And as it turned out, I would have to take her up on that offer. Just as we were about to mark our next Saturday chore off the list, Liam's grandpa came driving up the road. Though they had all pleaded with me to stay—even Liam's grandpa, Henry—I knew that I was already intruding on their family time. And as much as I felt like I was a part of theirs' while I was there, it seemed like the right time to take a step (or drive) back and regroup.

So we planned for Tuesday afternoon to continue our interview. And whether intentional or not, I've already started counting down the hours.

"I wish I would have known. I'd have liked to go with—to see the place where you grew up." Joel gulps down the last sip from his soda can and sets it on the table with a hollow clink. "Too bad I had that game yesterday."

"Joel, by the sound of it, that game was amazing!" I say. "You pretty much single-handedly put our team in the running for the championships." He suppresses a smile. "Can you imagine how pleased the Media and Entertainment Sector is with you right about now?" I offer him encouragement, not that he needs any. Every household in Madison is surely talking about Joel's epic game yesterday over their Sunday brunch. It makes me feel guilty that I missed something nearly the entire town's population experienced together—something that was such a turning point for Joel and his football career, likely even his future. He had a huge day yesterday and I wasn't there for it. Though he doesn't let it show, he's got to have some feelings about that.

At least I'll be able to catch up on the game's events by working on his *Day in the Life* spread for Bailey. She emailed me the mock layout and a file folder containing images from the game, requesting that I work with Joel to compose captions for them. I can handle that. Plus, it will be nice to hear about it in Joel's own words. Maybe then I won't feel like the only outsider in Madison looking in.

"It *was* a pretty amazing game, I'll give you that." Joel's eyes twinkle with a hint of pride. "So, you said that Bailey emailed you some pictures?"

"Yeah, they're right here." A steady hum pours out of the laptop as it powers up. I guide the mouse under my fingers and push down on the folder labeled: *Joel_Feature*. My nails click across the glass tabletop as I wait impatiently for the computer to respond to my command. This old laptop is a dinosaur. I briefly hope to be recruited into the Tech Sector one day; they're always the first to benefit from the new technologies they develop and discover. I'd be happy to trade this in for something fancier and faster. "Sorry, it's running slow." The folder finally maximizes. "Okay, here's the first one."

Joel scoots his chair around the table so we are both facing the computer. The first image file pops up on the screen.

"What is this?" I ask, magnifying the photograph to get a closer view. I squint my eyes. "Is that a bird? A mascot? What's the Viking doing?"

East Valley's mascot is the Viking. Greg Markison, a senior, has played the role for the past two years. But the bird costume is new, so I assume it belongs to the opposing team. I don't think we've ever played them before.

"Here, let me see." Joel angles the screen on the laptop back to get a better view by reducing the glare. "We played the Hawks yesterday. That's their mascot." He outlines the bird with his index finger. "I was attempting to make a twenty-yard pass to Brian Reilly when this was shot. That stupid bird was on the field, about to get trampled. Markison shoved him out of the way."

My eyes narrow and I study the image intently. "Okay. Seems like a kinda goofy picture to include, but whatever Bailey says goes."

"It was a pretty big moment in the game. Everyone will remember it when they see this. That stupid bird was seriously in the way and it could have cost us. I guess you kinda had to be there."

My heart sinks in my chest, so hard it hits bottom. There's a slight dissatisfaction in Joel's tone.

I've never heard it before, but I think I've let him down.

"Joel, I'm really sorry I wasn't there. I should have been—"

"Oh Tess, that's not what I meant at all. I just mean some of these pictures won't make sense to you because you didn't see the events happen." He covers my hand with his. "It's not a big deal. That's why I'm here, remember? To help explain them to you." He leans over and plants a quick, heartfelt kiss on my cheek. "Let's look at the rest of them before we write any captions, okay? We might get a better sense of how everything fits together that way."

I follow his request and hover the mouse over the second file, pressing down to open it. "Alright, this one's easy. That's the school marching band. What's special about this?"

Joel peers over my shoulder and laughs.

"Okay," he says, pointing to the screen. "A flag had just been called on the play and the referee was about to announce a penalty. The marching band actually started walking onto the field right then. It was crazy—everyone in the stands was waving them off—but no one in the band seemed to notice. They had already played the first few notes before the other team literally pushed them off the turf."

Bailey's pictures are becoming more and more obscure with each one I open. "Another big moment in the game?"

"Pretty much. There were a lot of weird things that happened yesterday. This was definitely one of them." Joel takes the computer mouse from my hand and glides the cursor over to the next photograph. No description is necessary for this one. Obviously taken post game, it is of a handful of East Valley football players hoisting a large drink jug over a soaking wet Joel, still dressed in his football gear.

"A little victory celebration?" I smile at Joel.

"You got it. And seriously, that stuff was so sticky. I had to shower like three times just to get it out of my hair. I feel like it's still pink from all that dye." He tousles his cropped hair with his fingers.

Joel moves to the last file in the email document. It's of him again, slightly less juice-stained, standing next to Herb Nicholson, the local sports television anchor for the Media Sector. Herb's microphone is angled toward Joel, and I think he's questioning him about their big win against the Hawks.

"Okay, so tell me what was going on here," I say, my fingers tracing the static covered screen. It sparks under my touch.

"Herb was interviewing me for the evening sports segment. He was asking how I stayed so focused during the game with all the random interruptions and distractions."

"What did you tell him?" I reach for the notepad lying on the table next to me. Now is as good a time as any to start writing the captions.

"I told him that they weren't distractions," he says. "They were all pieces of the game that fit together to make things turn out the way they did. If they hadn't occurred, the game could have had an entirely different ending, and I might not be the one that he'd be interviewing right then. He seemed pretty pleased with my answer." I guess by the slight smile edging onto Joel's lips that he is just as pleased, too.

"Here, can I have that for a second?" I wave toward the mouse and Joel slides it my way. "I want to open up all four pictures at once so we can write up something that ties them all together then, too."

I click the four separate files and wait for the computer to react, but it's sluggish and hesitant. I'm losing patience with it. After a few seconds of whirring and humming, the photographs maximize, one in each quadrant of the screen.

First the Hawk. Then the marching band. Under that the spilled juice. Next to that the interview.

My eyes scan from image to image, and my pulse begins to pick up speed.

Hawk. Band. Juice. Interview.

Without warning, my heart leaps within me, catches as it hangs for an instant—just long enough that I worry it won't start back up—then thunders to life sharply against my ribs. Now that it's working again, it keeps an impossibly fast double-time tempo. My breathing adopts that same pace.

A wave of dizziness, combined with the rapid ticking, produces an entirely different sensation than the palpitation-induced rhythm alone. All of my senses spiral together, twisting vision, sound, and touch, into a whirlpool of deep steel and charcoal gray. I can hear the room swirling around me, tumultuous waves flooding into my ears. I reach for the wooden edge of the table to support me, but the sweat from my fingers slides off the surface, my knees give like jelly, and I drop to the floor. My head cracks against the tile. Everything around me—the mouse, the computer, even the kitchen itself—recedes, replaced by slightly less distinct, less tangible, versions of themselves.

Then it all goes black.

***

Seconds that feel like hours tick by.
"Tessa! Tessa, wake up!"
We're outside now because there's fog everywhere. It coats every surface, making it impossible to see. I flutter my eyelids and the haze diminishes. No, we're still in the kitchen. My head feels fuzzy.

Joel raises me up at the shoulders and slides his knees under my back. He rotates my head side to side, checking for injury. He doesn't find one. He presses my face to his chest and kisses the top of my head fervently. The warmth pulls me back into the present, and assures me that the earth hasn't completely spun off its axis. "My God, Tessa. Are you okay?"

"Yeah, I think so." I blink again. "I don't know. I just had the weirdest sensation." I close my eyes and try to take a cleansing breath through my nose, hoping the lingering unsteadiness will flow out with the subsequent exhale. "I just feel a little lightheaded now, but I'm fine. Maybe I need to eat something."

"Tessa, you just passed out," Joel says.

"Did I?" I've never fainted before. Joel pulls me up to the kitchen chair. The laptop hums on the table in front of me and it matches the ringing in my ears.

I see the four images again and my heart surges and shuts off briefly within my chest. I involuntarily clutch it, as though I can manually start it pumping again to send blood to the rest of my chilled body. I double over at the waist and wait for this second palpitation to pass.

"Seriously, Tessa. What's going on?" Joel strokes my arms with his palms. I feel the damp beads of sweat secreted from them. "You've got goose bumps all over! Something's not right. You should lie down. You *were* sick just a couple of days ago."

Robotically, I follow his lead and unsteadily limp toward the couch in his family room. My head throbs and I grit my teeth to endure the pain. Soft, worn leather and brocade pillows envelope me as I slide down onto the sofa's surface. They feel much better against my head than the cold tile floor. "Here, close your eyes for a minute. I'm going to get you a glass of water."

Obeying his instruction, I force my eyes shut.

It all flashes before me again, like slides in a projector. A series of four, separate events, yet all strung together in one cohesive vision.

The hawk scavenging for food in the middle of the street as Joel's car comes to a sudden, unexpected stop at 2:34 p.m. The school band taking to the field after practice, interrupting conversation with Liam at 4:47 p.m. The orange juice that slips out of my hand at the sound of Trent's voice at 7:36 a.m. And Mr. Crawford holding up our latest journalism project— our assignment to interview a fellow classmate at 11:12 a.m.

My eyelids, though still closed, squeeze hard. I try to physically push the nonsensical visualization from my head. But it's as though my closed lids have a series of red digital clock numbers etched on them. I shudder, trying to shake them from my mind.

A second set of visions materialize.

The mascot. The marching band. The drink. The sports broadcast interview. All of the random, isolated occurrences from my week merged together into one single incident. Like Joel had described to Herb Nicholson, all the pieces put together to result in one, distinct culmination.

But there is more to the sensation than what the images evoke as they flash before me. Their interconnectedness runs deeper than that.

"Joel. What time was kick off?" My voice is shaky, trembling as I ask the question that I already know the answer to.

"Let me think." He taps the pad of his index finger against his lips, trying to draw the answer out of them. "It was a strange time, not like on the hour or anything. It was 2:34 p.m., I think. Kick off was supposed to be at 2:30 p.m., but things were held up for some reason. I remember thinking it was a funny time to start the game, but liked how it was 2, 3, 4, you know?"

Yeah, I know.

Although I, on the other hand, haven't found much to like about those numbers until recently. But now their meaning is starting to take on a whole new, separate significance. And though I still am not completely certain what that is, I figure it is about to change my life forever.

For the second time.

THIRTEEN

The pacing. The constant pacing. As though repeatedly traveling over the same path will somehow produce an answer. Like it will rise up out of the trampled floorboards. Choosing a new direction, a different way to navigate the room makes more sense to me. Maybe then something that was overlooked will make itself known.

But Joel seems so close that I'm not about to interrupt him or ask him to embark on an alternate route, even if the pacing is making me crazy. Or crazier—I think it's fair to say that I reached crazy status a while back. And even if he didn't keep reciting, *"It's right there. It's right on the tip of my tongue,"* I would know it to be the case by the way he keeps pushing his fist to his forehead, physically wracking his brain for the answer.

He slides his fingers across the dusty bindings, tracing the embossed lettering on each spine. I'm not sure exactly how long we have been at this. I can tell by the way the shadows on the wall stretch almost horizontally that it's near sundown. I contemplate rising to my feet to turn on the lights, but I worry any slight disruption will send Joel into a tailspin and we'll be back to square one. And he really does seem so close. Maybe I just want to illuminate the room because it is the only way I can contribute to literally making the light bulb turn on, to putting the pieces together.

I'd exhausted all of my usefulness when I scribbled the four phrases on the notepad in front of me, originally meant to brainstorm captions for the layout. Now its purpose is to aid in my diagnosis.

Light headed. Rapid heart rate. Flashing visions. Fainting. Déjà vu like sensation.

That last description is the one that Joel keeps honing in on. When he asked me earlier to explain as accurately as I could the feelings I experienced when everything started to culminate, I used those words. *Déjà vu: the uncanny sensation of experiencing something again.* Something familiar. Something that has already happened.

That description sent Joel nearly flying into his parents' study to retrieve the answer. At the time I was certain he knew exactly where to find it, and was immediately relieved that I would have a reason for feeling the way I did. But his epiphany moment stopped right there. And that's when the pacing ensued.

I play with the fringe on the Afghan rug that spans the entire library, looping the fibers over and under my fingers. The act is pointless, but it helps to focus on something, especially when the matter at hand requires all of Joel's concentration. I don't want to do anything that might distract from that. So I sit and I twist and I let him do his thing.

It dawns on me the number of times I've counted on Joel to rescue me in biology, to provide me with answers. But those answers seem so trivial now. All they could afford me were letter grades and possibly a teacher's praise. Now I rely on Joel for so much more. I need him to put together the pieces of my last two years of life. I need him to diagnose me, and provide me with the cure.

I knot a loose thread around my finger. It makes me think of those illustrations where someone ties a bow around their finger to help them remember something. It's a fitting comparison, considering what Joel's trying to do right now.

"Describe it one more time." His voice cuts through the silence. I startle at the sound of it. I pull my knees up to my chest and bury my face into them, pressing my eye sockets firmly against my kneecaps. The pressure on my eyes makes everything go black, isolating my vision so the images clearly appear.

"It was all at one moment, right before I fainted," I say. "When we were going over each picture, they didn't really mean much at first. But the second it clicked, each set of visions flashed before my eyes—each one grouped with its counterpart. The two hawks, the marching band, the juice, the interviews. Just like déjà vu—that sensation you experience when it feels like you've done something before."

"Okay." He continues to pace. Recounting it for a sixth time doesn't seem to help Joel, but I'd gladly have it tattooed across my forehead if I think it will draw out the answer I know is buried somewhere in his brain. "Like déjà vu. *I know what this is, Tessa.* I swear I do." He bites down hard on his full bottom lip and I think it's an act of frustration, but something about it makes my heart skip. My heart's been doing a lot of that today, for all kinds of reasons.

"I remember sitting in here with my dad when he was studying for the Medical Sector Chair position," says Joel. "He was reviewing for the exam. It had to do with immunizations or war intelligence or something. It changed every year, but that much I remember." His eyes rove across the study, like he's playing out the scenario in his head. "I held the flashcards and Dad walked the room—back and forth, back and forth." Joel acts it out as he speaks, trampling the same beaten path. "He knew the answers to each one before I even finished reading it. He didn't even look up—he just knew them off the top of his head." How his dad wasn't appointed Medical Sector Chair, I'll never know. He is by far the brightest man I've ever met. And his son is a close second.

That also explains the pacing. It is as though Joel is attempting to channel that moment years ago to produce the answer. I never doubted he had a vault of medical terminology locked away. He's always so quick to label our fetal pig parts and diagnose classmate ailments. But this is much more complex, so it shouldn't come as any surprise to either of us that the route to finding its meaning might be equally as complex.

"I know it's in there, Tess." He taps on his forehead. "I know it's in my memory." Joel's face goes white, like some plug has been pulled and all the color drains straight out of it.

"What is it Joel?" I slowly rise to my feet, pushing myself up steadily, so as not to startle him and cause everything to slip away as suddenly as it came on.

"Memory Tracing. That's what it is, Tessa!" He's breathing more rapidly now. "*Memory Tracing*—or Tracing as my dad called it for short." He bounces on the balls of his feet as though he's suddenly loaded with springs.

Joel flips around to face the wall of books. His hand lands on a maroon covered one. There's an illustration of a head with an open skull revealing a brain embossed in gold leafing on the front. "I remember my dad reading this book when he studied for the exam. It's somewhere in here."

He earnestly scans the pages like he knows right where he'll find it. He's completely dedicated to figuring out my condition. I wonder if he will ever get tired of constantly coming to my aid.

"Joel, I almost feel stupid asking this, but is there a reason why we haven't looked on the internet yet?" I'm certain there is, knowing that Joel wouldn't have wasted the past several hours when the answers could be right under our fingertips on a keyboard.

"You're not going to find it on there, Tess." Joel shakes his head. "This is one of those things that isn't really documented anymore. I remember Dad saying it's something the Hub likes to keep under wraps."

"Then why was it part of his exam?" I ask.

He cocks his head to the side, thinks for a moment as if to give value to my question, then answers. "Dad said Chair exams were always based on things like that—things that were difficult to study. If you were able to ace a test where the material was that much harder to come by, then you were a shoe in for the position."

"Well that just seems weird."

"I know, but I'm sure they have their reasons for doing it that way," Joel explains. "The Chair has to be someone who knows all there is to know about everything medical."

"Even stuff they don't want the rest of us to know about?"

"*Especially* stuff like that." Joel skims a page as he speaks. He's quite the multi-tasker. "Think about it, the Chair is the highest position in a Sector, right?" I nod. "Shouldn't the person whose appointed to it know everything that specifically relates to that Sector?"

"Yes…probably." I've continued twisting a stray fringe from the rug around my fingers without realizing it. I look down at my thumb. It's completely purple, like a swollen grape. I unwind the string, unwrapping it counter-clockwise, and massage the circulation back into my finger. I didn't realize I was so tense.

"Your dad didn't know enough then?" I infer.

Joel waggles his head back and forth. "I don't know. Maybe not." He shuts the book and particles of dust spring into the air. "I guess maybe I should be glad about that."

"I would be. I wouldn't want that much knowledge." I wring my hands together. My fingers are now all the same pink color again. "I think the more you know in our society, the more of a threat you are."

"I think that's why they try to appoint those people as Chairs." Joel takes me by the hand and leads me to the two high-back chairs at the opposite side of the room. A chain dangles from an old, freestanding lamp next to him. He pulls down on it to turn it on, but it reminds me too much of a spotlight in an interrogation room and my eyes squint in response. "Yes, they want the best and the brightest representing them at the Hub, but they also want to monitor them since they know so much. Dad must not have made the cut."

I take a seat on the velvet-covered chair. "That or he didn't want to pass. You said he'd studied a lot for it? Maybe he threw the exam."

Joel shifts in his own chair, the heels of his hands pushing against the worn armrests. His chest fills with air and his shoulders tighten and pull upward, like he still has the hanger inside his shirt. He lets out his breath with a huff. "I honestly don't know, Tessa." I don't think Joel likes not having all the answers. "There are a lot of other ailments out there that the Hub doesn't talk about. Dad really focused on Tracing. Maybe there were others in the exam that he didn't know as much about."

I don't like that he calls what I have an ailment, even though that's what it feels like. I wonder how intentional he was in choosing that word.

"I don't have all the answers," he surrenders.

"But you have all the answers *I* need." My eyes offer him some confidence. "All I want to know about is Tracing," I say. "You helped your dad study. Tell me what you know."

"Okay…let me think of where to start." He rests his elbows onto his knees and twists his hands in circles, one around the another. "You already said it was like déjà vu. I think most doctors just dismissed it as that at first." He interlocks his fingers and rests them under his chin. "But others thought it was something totally different. Déjà vu is when you feel like you've experienced an exact moment before. Tracing's different." He unlocks his index fingers and touches them together at the tips, steepling them. He presses them to his lips. "Remember how all of those things—the hawk, the marching band—all of those separate details turned into one event?" I bob my head to say yes. "Tracing happens when you experience that event and it triggers something in your mind to recall the moments that led up to it. Your mind literally *traces* your memory and pulls the details out. Then it flashes them before you. That's the déjà vu feeling—that instant when everything culminates."

"You mean the instant when you pass out." I squirm in my seat, still embarrassed by my earlier episode.

"I don't know if that always happens." Joel attempts to camouflage a smile, but it's given away in his eyes. "But I can imagine it would be an intense sensation, to feel like you're reliving so many separate moments, but all in one instant. That's gotta be crazy. Especially the first time."

"Intense doesn't even begin to describe it." I rub the base of my skull and wince, pain shooting from the bottom of my head to the back of my eyes. I feel the crack of the tile all over again. Joel extends his hand and carefully begins to rub my neck where it stings. "So I have this thing that causes me to pass out and nearly get a concussion. What good is having something like that?" I think his fingers are meant to relax me, but having Joel's hands on any part of me does just the opposite. I slowly slide out from under them to keep from being completely distracted. He picks up on my body language and pulls his hand back, folding it across his chest.

"I'm pretty sure Tracing used to be common. I think it was used in the military way back when. Some soldiers were Tracers." Joel opens up the maroon book again and stops on a page toward the back. The title of the chapter reads: *Military Utilization*. "It says here that they were called Intelligence and Predictions Officers. They used this ability to string events together to provide information on the strategies and plans of the opposition." His fingers move so fast across the pages that I worry he'll slice them on the edges. "I'm pretty sure they played a huge part in battle for a time."

Three soldiers standing in front of a rubble wall flash across my mind. I know what this has to mean.

My dad was a Tracer.

"Somewhere along the way I think something went wrong," Joel says.

I snatch the book out of his hand, eager to know exactly what that is. The chapter is only five pages long. Aggravation settles deep into my stomach and water collects behind my eyes.

"You're not going to find it in there. And I don't know much more, either," Joel explains as I deflate. I'd hoped this would be easier, that I'd have some type of manual at my disposal to reference. But of course I don't. That would be too simple, too straightforward. That would make too much sense. And why on earth should I expect things in my life to make any sense?

"I only know what I overhead my parents discuss at night when they thought I wasn't listening," Joel continues, "but I think Tracing got the military in a lot of trouble." The room is completely dark, the sun fully set, but the bulb next to Joel illuminates his face just enough that I can still make out every detail of it. His brows crease as he remembers, the shadows folding into his strong features. "I didn't know it was called Tracing when I was listening in, but now it kinda makes sense. Dad said something about officers misinterpreting details or providing information that wasn't in our favor during the war. I don't know. I just know that Dad said the government blamed those officers for the losses in battle that began to stack up."

My dad had been a Tracer.

He had been an Intelligence and Prediction Officer.

And then at some point he became a Reallocate. What role did he play in all of this?

"I'm guessing that's probably when Tracing started to be viewed as a curse rather than a gift—"

"Right," I interrupt, weakly. "You called it an ailment earlier."

"I did?" Joel's stunned. "Well, that's not what I meant." He's so sincere that I have no choice but to believe every word he says. "I think in medical terms a lot, Tess." He grins, the ambient light highlighting his cheekbones. "*I* think it's a gift. The Hub doesn't. And if you have something that the government doesn't like, then they'll look for ways to get rid of it."

Joel stares intently into my eyes. I wonder how clearly he can see them. I hope the black of the room swallows up any emotion they might be emitting. I don't want him to know how rattled I am by all of this.

"Like with déjà vu, there's a group of thought that this is some type of disorder." Joel's voice is deep and there's so much certainty and authority in it. "I remember one night Dad came home from work and was really shook up. Something about being required to diagnose a group of retired Prediction Officers as schizophrenics. It forced them out of their military positions permanently and stripped them of any honor they once had in their post. Thinking of it now, they were probably all Tracers."

Yes, Tracers, I'm sure. *And Reallocates.* I wonder if my own dad was in that mix of the diagnosed. I can easily see how anything that might show something, or someone, in control other than the Hub could pose a huge threat to them and they'd want it eradicated. Dubbing those who possessed such a thing as crazy would likely do the trick.

Joel pauses, lending me a moment for things to sink in. But instead of sinking in, it feels like they're swallowing me whole. "Okay," I breathe. "So how do *I* get rid of it?"

"Get rid of it?" The words fly so fast out of Joel's mouth I feel the rush of air behind them hit me. "Why would you want to get rid of this?"

"Because it sounds like I'm a freak, right? Or even some kind of threat. That's essentially what you're saying, isn't it?" I don't tell him just yet that I think my dad was a Tracer. That will only certify my craziness. The apple doesn't fall far from the tree.

"Tessa, it's just the opposite." He closes the distance between us and clutches my hand, pulling me close so the back of it is pushed up against his solid chest. His eyes pierce fiercely into my own. "Tess, you've experienced firsthand that everything isn't as random as it appears." Joel hesitates, choosing his words carefully this time. "Think about it. Each of those four events that occurred show that life isn't

202

haphazard—that there's more meaning to what we just see on the surface. Don't you think that everyone wants that?" His eyes, round and wide, plead with me. "Wouldn't we all like to have something else controlling our lives other than the authority of the Hub?"

Maybe. Maybe not. To admit that there is some type of tie, some kind of interconnectedness, to the events of my life doesn't produce the warm, reassuring, fuzzy feelings in me that they evoke in Joel. Because admitting that there is something more means that there is a reason for the clock numbers, a reason for the sleepless nights, a reason for every daily interaction.

And a reason for my parents' death.

Honestly, I think it *is* easier to pretend it's all random chance and let the Hub be in control of everything.

"So let's say you're right—though I'm not 100 percent sure you actually are." I play the devil's advocate. "If this was once common, how come there aren't more people our age with it? Why is this the first I've ever heard of it?" Words and phrases muddle in my brain, becoming one big jumbled mass of confusion.

"My guess is that we were immunized against it." His words are so direct, so matter of fact, that I shudder upon hearing them, like each individual syllable creeps up my spine, clawing and scratching at my back. "Think about Tracing in relation to the war. It's seems like it's kinda blamed for the loss. And if all these soldiers suddenly became Reallocates and

Discards, they probably wouldn't want their own children to be Tracers, would they?" He pauses briefly. I wonder if he's made the connection about my own dad yet. "You'd want your kid to start out in the best possible standing before the Hub."

"So you'd get them vaccinated."

"Exactly." He's still holding my hands and I hope he can't feel them tremble. I lace my fingers tighter through his so the shaking isn't so obvious. "We were immunized against all sorts of things as infants."

I keep my hands in his and slide into the chair with him. I can feel my entire body shivering. Maybe curling into his will mask that. "And we can't know for sure until we get our immunization records." As youth, we're not allowed access to our medical files until our eighteenth birthday, a policy put in place by the Medical Sector. It never mattered to me before; I'd had no use for them. But with all of this talk of vaccines and immunizations, I feel like there is some secret, locked up file that contains much more information than I'd ever imagined. It reminds me of the wooden box sitting on my closet shelf.

"Right, we get them when we're eighteen...when we're recruited."

I swallow, pushing hard on the knot rising in my throat, and it tightens as my muscles constrict around it. I hadn't counted on this. A virus maybe, or low blood sugar, or something. But definitely not being part of something that the Hub has tried to erase from existence. It just doesn't make sense. If the government has taken precautions to make Tracing essentially extinct, then why am I experiencing it?

Joel tosses the maroon book on the hard floor with a thud and wraps me in his protective arms. "So you know what this means?"

No. I have absolutely no clue.

"One of two things, Tess." He pushes back a lock of hair that's slipped onto my forehead. "Maybe your vaccine didn't take. Like you know how we learned about outliers in Statistics? Maybe you're the piece of data that doesn't fit the mold." Joel has an effortless ability to make things seem so cut and dry, so black and white. It makes the idea of him possibly being trapped in a football career seem unjust. It's evident he was made for so much more.

"And what's option two?" I bend my entire body around his and rest my head on his firm chest, hoping the steady beating of his heart will echo in my ear and mine might slow to match its rhythmic pulse.

"That you were never vaccinated," he asserts. "That your parents somehow got around it. That they took a quiet stance against the Hub."

"That they were silently disobedient." I press on Joel's chest with the heel of my palm to lift myself up to eye level. Knowing my dad's character, along with what I've recently discovered about his past, it seems as though the only option is the latter. "But why would they want me to have this thing that sets me apart so much?"

"Because obviously they saw some value in it," Joel replies. "Maybe it was their way of rebelling against authority. Giving you the freedom to be controlled by something other than the Hub."

But my dad was a Reallocate. Maybe he'd even been diagnosed a schizophrenic. He had paid his price for being a Tracer. Why would he want me to carry around that same burden?

"He was a Tracer." The words slip from me.

"Who was, Tess?" Joel's body tightens and his shoulders lift.

"My dad. He was a Tracer and an Intelligence and Prediction Officer. And he became a Reallocate when they moved him to the Transportation Sector," I say. "I found his war box. I shouldn't have opened it, but I had to know. That's what I was looking at when I nearly bludgeoned you the other day."

Joel steadily nods his understanding. "No wonder you were so out of sorts. I've never seen a war box before. I thought the Hub maintained control of all wartime artifacts."

"I thought so, too. And they would have if I hadn't taken it with me when I left the ranch. Dad never talked much about his time as an officer. But I used to see him flipping through the box at night and he always looked so sad. Maybe he was upset about the role he'd played." My voice lowers. I probably shouldn't be talking about the war. It's not my information to know.

Joel's forearms squeeze around me. It's a warm reassurance that he's not going to reject me for the things I've said. I exhale a loud sigh of relief.

"Maybe that's not what he was sad about, Tess." He fingers the ends of the strands of my hair. "Maybe he was upset that something so essential to his existence was taken from him. Maybe he was sad because the Hub had won."

"Maybe. But they always win in the end, right?" I surrender.

Joel waves his head back and forth. "No they don't, Tessa. You're proof of that." His encircling arms pull me in tighter to him. "You don't fit into any of the molds they try to stuff us into, Tessa. You're the outlier."

FOURTEEN

"Happy birthday to you! Happy birthday to you! Happy birthday, dear Tessa, Happy birthday to you!" My eyes aren't open, but I sense their presence—likely all four of them by the sound of their voices in unison—soprano, tenor, and baritone all blending as one.

"Seventeen and you don't look a day over sixteen," chimes Uncle Mark, always a jokester. It's much too early for a comedy routine. My eyes still burn with sleep.

I've never wished away my teenage years, but after last week's discovery, I'd hoped to miraculously wake up and have it be my eighteenth birthday. Instead, I'll have to wait one more year. One more year until I'll receive my medical records at my Sector Expo. One more year until I know exactly what I've been immunized against. One more year until I know for sure what society deems useless or threatening.

Did my parents really get away with not vaccinating me? I wish I could somehow magically fast-forward the next 365 days to speed up to that point in time, or somehow convince the Medical Chair to give them to me early. But the Sector Chairs are pretty set in their ways. I kind of wish Joel's dad had been appointed—maybe then I'd have some pull.

"Rise and shine, sleepyhead! We want to hear all about your plans for your big day." Probably just a courtesy; I doubt Aunt Cathy truly cares about what I'll be doing today. She's taking Trent and Joel to an Entertainment Sector football game this weekend in Monarch to watch the pros, and they won't be returning until late tomorrow night. And Uncle Mark has another 48-hour shift at the station. With Bailey planning to spend the afternoon in the yearbook room and then over at her friend Julia's house to slumber, I'll be on my own for my 'big day.'

"No plans, just homework."

"You can't do homework on your birthday, Tess." It's ironic that Bailey says such a thing. I know full well that she's spent the past two birthdays locked away editing. "You have to do something fun, something crazy! You're only seventeen once!"

"Alright, alright. Let's give Tess a chance to wake up," Aunt Cathy interjects. "And I don't think she needs any ideas planted in her pretty little head. You don't want to be responsible for messing up seventeen years of a good thing, do you?"

Not that it is likely to happen. Bailey and I both know I'm not a daredevil, that I've never really done anything foolish up to this point. I don't plan to start now. After all, the craziest things to happen in my life have all occurred in the past few weeks: opening up my dad's box and discovering I have some type of government frowned upon ailment.

If I'm completely honest, though they might be crazy, I'm glad for both recent discoveries. In a way, they've recreated a sort of relationship with my dad that I've longed for since his death. A type of beyond-the-grave connection. So call me a schizophrenic. Psychotic. Pick any name from a lengthy list of words found in a psychiatric textbook. I think I'm fine with it because Dad probably heard those same names whispered regarding him, cursed to him, or written about him. If he was actually a Tracer and the government did something to take that away, then I'm sure he endured an onslaught of labeling, persecution, and oppression. Maybe his silent disobedience ran deeper than what I'd seen on the surface. Maybe it boiled in his blood. And since he and I share the same blood, maybe that passion should fester inside me, too. I think it's slowly starting to.

But I'm still wrapping my brain around what all of this means in my own life. Dad somehow used his gift at an advanced level. I feel like such an amateur, still learning the rules of the game; a game in which I'm the key player and Joel is my teammate. A game that my dad knew I would one day play. Like he left the pieces out for me to take his turn. There's something comforting in that.

It's still a rush when that minute strikes, when I know that whatever is occurring has some purpose, some hidden significance for my future. I no longer faint when it happens—that I've gained some control over. I'm still overcome by that falling, dizzying déjà vu response, but knowing that I'm not going to hit the floor each time is reassuring and takes the edge off a bit.

Joel's even been trying his hand at Tracing. Though we both think he's been immunized against it, if I tell him the minute it's going to happen based on the time I woke up the night before, he's gotten pretty good at actually being able to figure out the clues.

Like two weeks ago in biology. I knew the time would be 8:23 a.m—biology class. I've begun writing the time on the inside of my wrist, just low enough that my shirtsleeve conceals it, but quick and easy to glance at if I forget the time. Not that it's likely to happen. But every morning it's the first thing Joel does; slyly rolls my sleeve back to make a mental note of the etching. It's a secret that just we share and I think he likes it. I know I do. Even if it does mean that I'm crazy or a threat to the Hub. At least he doesn't seem to think I am, and I guess that's worth something.

The clue that day was when Mr. Harrisburg sneezed. Joel and I actually laughed out loud when it happened, because it was so startling, yet so glaringly obvious at the same time. I'd sent a thank you up to whoever orchestrated these clues, because it couldn't have been clearer, and I was thankful for that. Even though Joel thinks being a Tracer is something I should be proud of, the fact that I'd be seen as a menace to society in some way still makes me leery of anyone discovering it just yet. It has to be on my own terms, and I'm not entirely sure what those are. All I know is that I'd prefer to have the upper hand in choosing when to make it public. It has to be my decision, not the Hub's. So for now, I'll keep it under wraps. The hidden, tattoo-like drawings on my wrist feel like a literal representation of that.

So when Mr. Harrisburg sneezed at the exact second the minute on the digital clock morphed from a two to a three, I knew we had our first clue. That's how it works. Down to the second. It turns out that sixty whole seconds allows for a lot of possible puzzle pieces. It helps knowing that the thing to look for will occur just as the minute changes. And since the Hub regulates all systems relating to time, it's always consistent from clock to clock. I don't like to admit it, but that does make it a little easier. I guess I'm willing to give the Hub credit where credit is due.

It turns out that the sneeze, compiled with Missy Belltroth's presentation of her strawberry pie in home economics, along with a strange, bumpy rash that Trent developed after running through the woodlands behind campus during practice, all culminated in a scene from a school play that I attended later that week. We received extra credit in our English class by supporting our fellow schoolmates, so Joel and I made a sort of date of it. But when Lola Buckmeyer took to the stage, her face drenched with counterfeit tears, acting as a young mom whose infant daughter was straddling the line between life and death due to a recently discovered strawberry allergy, I wanted to fall out of my chair. Not out of shock or dizziness this time, but more out of annoyance than anything. My eyes had rolled so far back in their sockets that my body literally felt like it was being pushed over as well.

"Seriously? All that work for *that*? For a silly scene in a school play?" I'd huffed. "No wonder all the Intelligence and Prediction Officers became Reallocates. If they provided insignificant information like that I can easily see why they'd be offed." The mood was quiet in Joel's car on the way home that evening. "Doesn't it seem like we've wasted all this time for nothing?"

He didn't look over at me—his eyes were fixed on the road in front of him—but I could sense his frustration. It was as though he breathed it out from him and it hung in the air. Tense and thick. It was the first time I'd ever experienced it. I didn't like the tightness it brought to my chest.

"What? You mean like those *whole* three minutes?"

"Three seconds, actually."

"Even better, then." He wasn't angry—I wasn't sure I'd ever seen him angry—but it was evident he was irritated by my complaining. "I don't know why you think this Tracing thing of yours has to be this big rush every time. Even when it's just something trivial like it was tonight, it's still a gift, Tessa. It doesn't always need to be monumental." He paused, collecting his words before delivering them to me. That's how it is with Joel, his words packaged neatly in one cohesive bundle, one planned out thought. It must be nice to have control over your thoughts and words. I swear I used to, but mine seem to just fly out of my mouth lately.

"That doesn't devalue what you have," he continued. "To have that sensation you experience, even if all I ever got was the stupid allergy scene from the play, it would be worth it to me," he said. "It still means that you get to see life differently than we all do—that you know for sure some deeper meaning exists. I don't think you realize what I would give to have that assurance—to not have to live it vicariously through you, but experience it for myself."

His words had shot at me like a slap in the face, forceful enough that they completely flipped my mindset around. Away from facing a skeptical, somewhat frustrated, resignation to the fact that Tracing isn't always going to be life-altering, and toward a brighter outlook on the things that I know to be real. That Joel could clarify this for me seems like almost as much of a gift as Tracing itself.

So I've begun to accept the fact that I'm not going to be Intelligence and Prediction Officer material right off the bat. I think I have to ease into it all, like any other gift or talent. You perfect your craft over time. And I slowly have been. The week after the strawberry allergy incident was filled with a myriad of different moments, ranging from being splashed by a rain puddle to scoring an 87 on my English exam, all of which culminated in two separate tracings. And after a couple of weeks of practice, I've also discovered that all of my déjà vu culminations occur after one full night's rest. Joel teases that the only way I could be able to figure out what it all means is to have a good night's sleep under my belt, that otherwise my dreary fog would inhibit any chances at interpretation. He's probably not too far off with that assumption.

***

This morning I don't have that well-rested luxury. I roll onto my side, but the act doesn't get rid of the extra bodies in my room. My family still hovers at the edge of my bed. I look at my wrist and the four black numbers written on it are instantly inscribed in my brain.

10:21.

I'll need to be near a clock then. Wake up at 10:21 p.m. the night before, clue at 10:21 a.m. the next day. I wonder if the soldiers ever got sick of constantly being woken in the dead of night during the war. I can't imagine that being this tired and foggy could have been a good thing during battle.

"What's that?" Trent grabs my hand to twist it over and I recoil, yank it out of his grip, and thrust it under the covers. That my family is still here is starting to annoy me a little. "Is that a *tattoo*?"

"No, of course it isn't. Tessa wouldn't get a tattoo. Now would you, Tessa?" Uncle Mark's brow hardens and his moustache straightens as his lips purse together.

"Of course she wouldn't," Aunt Cathy interrupts, not letting me fend for myself and I'm thankful for her interjection. It gives me time to fabricate a story. I don't want them to know I'm a Tracer yet. "Come on guys, let's give her some privacy and let her get ready for her special day."

"Love you, Tess! I'm sorry we can't be here today, but I know you're going to have the best day ever!" Bailey's the last one to trail out the door and she softly closes it behind her, the latch quietly clicking into its frame.

I shower and dress and join Aunt Cathy and Trent in the family room. They're waiting for Joel. When his truck roars into the driveway, my heart races at the sound. I rush to the entryway and the doorknob is at my fingertips before anyone else has the chance to get there first. I twist the handle and the door falls open in unison with the sigh that slips between my lips. There's a swelling inside me, a near bursting pressure in my ribs that's always present when he's near. I don't know the word for it, if there is one at all. In fact, none of the sensations I have when I'm around Joel can be bound up in words. Feelings aren't easily described, they're experienced. And being in Joel's presence is quite the experience.

He passes through the threshold and instinctively reaches out for my left hand, delicately turning it over in his, his chocolate eyes widening a little as a smile of recognition grows. 10:21 is only twenty minutes from now, but he'll be well on his way to Monarch with Trent. I'll have to be sure to record it for him. I know it will be the first thing he inquires about upon his return.

"Happy birthday, Tess." He plants a kiss squarely on my cheek. "I have something I want to give you." A brown paper package materializes from behind his back; the type of paper that looks old and worn, yet timeless still. He places it in my hands and the weight and shape reveals what's wrapped underneath. A book. I envision the rows and shelves of books from his parents' study in my mind and I wonder if it's one of those. Maybe the one on Tracing. I pull him through the house and into the backyard, not wanting my family to see what I suspect might be concealed in the brown wrapper. He follows upon my heels.

"Go ahead, open it." My finger slips under the clear tape and the flap pops open. I peel the corner back—apparently not quickly enough for Joel's liking—and he tears through the remaining paper, tossing it to the ground, discarding it.

In my hands is a soft, supple, leather-bound book. No title on the spine, no illustration on the cover. "It's a journal for you. To keep track of your tracings." He beams. "Look, I even wrote in the front of it." The book's in his hands now and he thumbs to the first page, propping it open so I can read the inscription along with him.

For my Tessa.

May you never forget the indescribable gift you've been given.

I focus on the air going in and out from my lungs because I'm certain if I don't they'll cease working altogether. Any breath I have he's taken away. Consistently. I follow the outline of the words, *'For my Tessa,'* with my fingernail and for a moment I am someone's. I am his. I belong to Joel.

And I'm not sure if the gift he's referring to is the actual ability to trace, or himself. Because right now I really can't imagine a greater gift than Joel. How could I ever forget either of those two indescribable gifts? After all, he's the one who brought the first to life. And in a way he's brought me to life, too. The two seem to go hand-in-hand, as though one can't exist without the other. And I'm starting to feel like he and I are becoming that way, too.

"Thank you, Joel. It's beautiful. And I'll never forget, how could I?" I push my mouth onto his and he flinches with surprise, then molds to meet mine with curved lips.

We're folded in each other's arms when Trent props the patio door open, only his upper body emerging through the glass, the receiver of a phone in his hand. "Tess, it's for you. It's that new kid, Liam." I hadn't heard the phone ringing, but if it did, it would have easily been swallowed up by the ringing in my own ears when I kissed Joel.

And though I'm still in his arms, still reveling in the gifts he's given me, still tasting his lips on mine, through my closed eyes it's not Joel's face I see any more, it's not his arms I feel around me, and not his scent I breathe in.

One thought surfaces as my eyes open to meet his dark russet ones.

How quickly we forget.

FIFTEEN

"Go ahead, take it. He probably wants to wish you a happy birthday. And I have to get ready to head to Monarch with Trent and Cathy." His broad hand at my back innocently nudges me forward, yet I can't shake the feeling that he is unknowingly pushing me into someone else's arms. My mouth silently forms the words 'Thank you' and Joel's eyes lift, crinkling in the corners with a smile.

'I'll see you tomorrow,' he mouths back, his hand reaching out in a half-wave as he slips back into the house and disappears.

I briefly close my eyes, a necessary act to draw Joel out of my mind and shake his voice from my head, to prepare myself for the boy on the other line. "Hello?" I sputter after a deliberate pause, but I'm only met with silence. I wait a few seconds more, about to hang up, when a voice booms through the speaker.

"Happy birthday, Sunshine!" Liam echoes through the phone. "Sorry to leave you hanging. My mom needed help getting something down from the attic."

"No problem. What's up?" It's good to hear his voice, reassuring and familiar. I've been intentionally avoiding it these past few weeks. For some reason, Liam is the last person I want to think differently of me. If he found out I was a Tracer, I don't know how he could ever see me the same. I've never met someone with whom I feel so instantly comfortable—even Joel and I had known each other for several years before we really connected. I figure that connection can be severed just as quickly as it developed, so it seems the only way to protect myself is steer clear of Liam altogether. But now after hearing his voice again, I think keeping this distance is going to become harder and harder to do.

I hadn't gone to his house that Tuesday like we'd discussed. I'd made up some lame story about taking dinner to the firehouse, and told him that I thought we had enough material to work with for our journalism assignment. He said he completely understood and offered to help me make the meal, but I was able to shake him off with some other various fabricated excuses.

But it was the first real lie I had ever told him. At the time I didn't realize that it was just the beginning of many more. Keeping something so integral to who you are—or what you have become—a secret is quite a feat. It was easy to hide from the people I didn't care

221

about; even some that I did, like Trent and Bailey. They made it natural—their own lives are too busy to bother being preoccupied with the details of mine. But with those who genuinely seem interested in you? Those who want to be a part of your life in some form? That's much harder. Façades don't work when someone knows the before, as well as the after, version of yourself. It's easier to stay in the in-between, to refuse to admit that things may have changed. It's so much safer to fall into your old ways for the sake of self-preservation. So that's what I'm doing with Liam. For all he knows, I'm the same Tessa he met on the blue bench at school. Nothing has changed. But even I can't convince myself of that lie.

"So, I know it's your birthday and I want to do something for you." There are people who love receiving gifts, and there are those who get just as much joy out of giving them. Liam is clearly the latter, as is evident by the raised inflection in his voice. I can literally hear the massive grin on his face.

"Okay, so what does all this involve?" The weight of Joel's journal tugs in my hands.

"I want you to come to the ranch today," Liam says. "I have a few things planned and I know your family's out of town. I didn't like the thought of you all alone on your birthday, so what better place to celebrate than your old house?"

"Sounds good, I should tell Joel—"

"Tess, I know Joel's your boyfriend, *okay?*" His tone harasses me, rich with mockery. I feel stupid for letting the words escape from my mouth. "I'm not trying to do anything here. It's nothing big, just a few things."

"Liam, he's not my boyfriend," I clarify. But then again, I suppose the inscription in the journal begs to differ.

"Doesn't matter—*we're* friends, right?" His voice rises into a question.

"Yes, Liam, *we're* friends," I reassure him.

"Even though you avoid me."

"I don't avoid you, Liam." I try to add impact to my statements by including his name in them. It always seemed to work when my parents did this with me as a child. "I've been busy. You know, school and stuff."

"And Joel." His words suspend in the air.

The opportunity to lie presents itself again and I almost snatch it up, a cat-like reflex. "Yes, and Joel."

"But since he's gone this weekend and your family is away, all you're left with is me. Aren't *you* lucky?"

Maybe. Or maybe he's lucky to have me. Even though all of school is abuzz with chatter regarding the 'new kid, Liam,' it turns out that people do more talking *about* him than actual talking *to* him. I wonder how that must make him feel, going from the homecoming king to the new guy. His level of popularity is the same, I'm sure, but I bet he would trade it for a few close friends given the opportunity.

I'm one of those friends. I'm close to all he's got at East Valley, one of the only real relationships he has. But how can our friendship even be considered real when he isn't aware of this one important fact about

223

me? One that is starting to change and shape the whole way I live my life. Guilt skates through me. *Some friend you are, Tessa.*

I break the discourse in my head with an answer. "So what time do you want me there?"

"How about noon? I'll have everything ready by then."

I reflexively nod in agreement, though he can't see me, tell him I'll see him in a bit, and head to the kitchen to pull together some breakfast. I get the cardboard egg carton from the refrigerator and I can see Bertha's beady little eyes. A chill rises on my spine and I determine it's the cold from the fridge hitting my skin that triggers it. Chickens shouldn't get that much credit. I get some slight satisfaction as I crack open an egg and drop it onto the sizzling pan, the edges immediately turning white, responding to the heat. Take *that*, Bertha.

"Alright, see you tomorrow night, Tessa!" Uncle Mark, clad in his firefighter attire, pulls open the door to the garage and it crashes shut behind him, the entire house rattling under the slam. I had assumed everyone was already gone, and I jump at the noise. The second egg falls from my grip and lands on the wood floor near my feet, its yolk splitting, oozing into the gelatinous goo surrounding it.

Fantastic. Another mess. I wonder why I'm even allowed in the kitchen anymore. I seem to make more messes than food in there lately. I'm struggling to sop up the broken egg and keep the one already on the stove from charring, when my eyes find the digital clock on the wall.

10:21 a.m.

I should have guessed. I pull out the journal.

November 17th
10:21 a.m.
Egg drops and cracks

My handwriting is too plain, my sentences are too simple in the keepsake journal Joel's given me. I contemplate tearing out the page and starting again, but I don't know how to fill the lines with anything other than those three facts. I won't know until later their deeper significance. Until then, they are just empty words on a page.

I'm nervous as I read them over, like a bride reciting her vows, embracing the longevity of her actions. It feels permanent to have them scribbled into the book. Now they exist outside of my brain. At least before the only other place they'd resided other than mine was Joel's mind. But now they've been documented; they've manifested themselves into physical form. They're out there for someone to see and interpret, though I know I don't have to worry about anyone deciphering their importance. Even *I* have no clue what they could mean.

Stowing the book away is the only option. Something that wasn't even in my possession thirty

225

minutes earlier is now an object I feel oddly protective over. Because if someone is ever to find it, they'll have a piece of me. Just like the war box. The only one I'm willing to share this with is Joel. I'll tell him where its hiding place is. Maybe I should even buy him his own, that way we can compare notes. Somehow the idea of gifting him with the same present steals away a bit of the intimacy his gesture offered.

Geez, Tessa, you're not being very unique. Even the two relationships with these boys are strangely morphing into one. Evidently that's the only way I know how to be. Like re-gifting the journal, I reuse my emotions and actions with both Joel and Liam, smiling at one, feeling flushed by the other and vice versa. And I strip away the intimacy from each in doing so.

This is why I can't tell Liam I'm a Tracer. I have to create one major distinction between the two by carving out a huge chasm that pushes all things Joel to one side, all things Liam to the other. And I can't stand in between them in an attempt to be the same person reaching out in both directions. Instead, it's as though there's a river that runs the length of this self-made gorge. It washes over me, transforms me from one Tessa to the other as I pass from side to side, from Joel to Liam. Like walking through a veil of some sort. I have to discard one and clothe myself with the other. Tracer versus Non-Tracer. This division must happen—it's the only way to keep my emotions separate. And it's the only way any sort of relationship with either Joel or Liam can coexist. Maybe it's cheating a bit, not allowing Liam to know the real me—or at least the newly discovered version of me—but selfishly speaking, it's the only way I can keep it up.

I stash the journal under my pillow. With the house empty until tomorrow, I don't need to waste time thoroughly concealing it immediately. Right now the ranch's call feels more pressing than the journal's.

Liam has plans for me. Even after my weeks of blatant avoidance, I must fill the corners of his mind, inhabit the purpose in his actions. He's getting the ranch ready. *For me. For my birthday.* I'm surprised he even remembers the date. Part of our follow-up interview in journalism class was to learn the mundane details of our subjects: their eye color, hair color, blood type and birthday.

"Seventeen on November 17th!" he had remarked, noting that it would be my 'golden' birthday this year. But the words funneled into my ears and tinkered in my head, distracted not by my golden birthday, but by a single, golden wave of hair that spilled onto his forehead.

Has he been planning something this whole time? I doubt it. That was weeks ago, and for just being 'friends,' that seems like an awful lot of prep time. Maybe it's a cake. Or a pie. Strawberry pie, like Missy's from home economics. *No, Tessa, that was Joel you shared that moment with.* My mind keeps interweaving—these moments with each boy—twisting them into one person. Joel and Liam. Joel. Liam. They are two distinct people. I slam my hand into my forehead. *Get it straight, Tessa. Get them straight.*

The drive to the ranch is fast and automatic. The sedan glides through the gate unlike last time when it lurched and lunged, hesitant to arrive. This time I'm eager with anticipation and the car reacts the same, coasting along, resting gently in park near the edge of the house.

A flapping clatter of paper whipping in the wind hits my ears and my eyes locate the origin of the sound. Blue, pink, yellow, and green triangles are all strung together, some bigger than the rest, held up by a white string wrapping around the banister of the porch. A handmade "Happy Birthday, Tessa!" banner is tied between the two strands of construction paper triangles, each word clearly written by a different family member. My guess is that Sammy scribbled *Tessa* with the help of Tyler. Liam kept telling me how disappointed Sammy was that day of the chicken pecking when I had to leave early and couldn't stay to play. Luckily, I made it up to him one day last week while waiting for Joel to finish football practice. Rebecca had to come to school to sign the final papers authorizing Liam's transfer, and I watched Sammy out front while they met in the counselor's office.

This energetic, towheaded boy—his matchbox cars and toy trains brought to occupy him—embodied everything I envisioned of Liam as a child. The slight stutter, the round, wide green eyes. I wondered if Liam had a twinge of that same lisp when he was little, too. We instantly became friends as we waited on the bench for Liam and Rebecca. Just like Liam and I had a few weeks prior—an immediate connection. Same setting.

Different person. Same family. Same feeling of home. Sammy and I formed a bond, like a big sister and a little brother, on that bench that afternoon.

"So, what do you think?" Liam's arms span out on either side of him as he twists back toward the pennant banner.

"I love it! Looks awesome!" I climb out of the car and stretch my legs onto the dusty ground. Liam paces toward me, takes my hand to raise me out of the car, and pushes the door shut.

"This was all the boys' idea—with the exception of Joshua. He wasn't too interested in helping, no offense."

"None taken—I wouldn't expect anything different from him." Though I'm sure Josh likes me just fine, we don't seem to share the same lovey-dovey feelings that I sense from the rest of the Hollanders. You can't win them all over.

"Right." Liam's fingers interlock hesitantly with mine. He hasn't let go of my hand since helping me out of the vehicle. I push them further together, my fingers sliding between his knuckles. He glances down at our hands, his eyes dart to mine, then he finds the words that are trapped in his throat. "So the banner was all them, but I've got something else for you. Want to see it?" His eyes enlarge and sparkle and for a moment they are innocent and full of wonder, similar to Sammy's childlike expression. "Wait, no—I take that back. I want to build up to it for a bit longer. Unless you want to see it now?" The way he vacillates

229

back and forth, a debate forming with his own words—it reminds me of my own endless wavering.

"Let's go see it now." I make the decision, figuring I should take advantage of any opportunity when clarity presents itself.

"I was hoping you'd say that." His charm is there, ever-present, but faint. As though there is a layer of nerves just over the surface of that assuredness I've come to expect from Liam. It's the first time, really. Every other interaction has been so flowing, like a song or music. Our back and forth banter just comes effortlessly. His teasing, my mocking. His charm, my wit. Like a type of dance we've learned to do. But this moment here in his front yard—this pause where he doesn't know whether to save the surprise or give it right away—it's as though he's forgotten all the steps to his own choreography.

I take the lead. "What? Liam…are you *nervous?*" My words fill in the beats that he's skipped over. "What, you think I'm not going to like it?"

"No, no. You'll like it all right." That spark is back. He's remembered the next moves in his routine. "It's just…I'd hate to show up your *boyfriend*. My gift really is *that* amazing."

"Again, he's not my boyfriend." I lie, because I think he might be. Add one more to the tally. "And he just got me a book." Not quite a lie, but not quite the truth. Maybe only half a mark for that one.

"Okay, well this is *much* better than a book. Come on, I'll show you."

His paces are quick and my arm extends almost to its full length as he nearly drags me behind him. It's like that half-walk, half-run stride that's awkward and eager. Wonder and anticipation sweep through me like the wind that whips my hair across my face. A strand falls across my eyes and Liam stops to brush it away. "Sorry, I've just been working on this for a bit. I guess I'm a little anxious for you to see it."

We reach the hangar. Or barn. Or whatever it's become. It's not the same place. The sturdy structure and shape remain, but what's inside is vastly different. Horses versus airplanes. I guess they both are means of transportation. Maybe if I grasp at straws and try to make some parallel the sting of its transformation won't be so piercing. Not like a knife through me, but more like a dull blade. But at least a sharp edge would create a clean slice. I think I'd prefer that to the blunt, jagged carving that's materializing in my chest. Underneath me my feet rock back and my heels catch like they're pushing me, pressing me toward the barn door at my front. My heart, my mind, they want to hold back, they want to turn and run, but my body thrusts me forward.

"Oh, Tessa. I'm so sorry." He shifts. "I can imagine this must be really hard. We don't have to go in if you don't want to. But I have something for you in there, and I think you'll want to see it. At least I hope you do." His words fill me, taking up the vacant space and persuade me to push forward. I'm glad he's able to do that since I obviously can't summon the motivation on my own.

Sweat slips between our fingers and I clench his hand tighter, not wanting him to fall from my grasp. Though it makes it more difficult for Liam to slide the heavy barn door open one-handed—its solid wood structure must weigh upwards of fifty pounds—he doesn't break our connection. The scraping of the caster rollers in their metal grooves as the door shoves sideways is met with a bellowing whinny from the bay immediately on the left, the first note in a chorus of neighs that echo out of the remaining five stalls. It's as though they're all saying hi, greeting Liam and I, welcoming us into their home. Warm and inviting. The very opposite sensation I anticipated from the once hangar. Cold. Lifeless. Dead. Those were the feelings in my visions and recollections. But it was once so full, so rich with passion and adventure. I never assumed it could become that way again. Funny how the snorting and chortling of a few horses instantly changes that.

"Afternoon, Blaze." Liam reaches out, his palm landing on the broad side of a massive tan horse with a blonde mane that stretches from the crest of his head to its wither. Liam releases my hand and steadies both of his on either side of Blaze's long face, draws his large, almond eyes up next to his own, and presses their foreheads together. In unison their eyes close and they exhale; Blaze's breath is followed with a vibrating sputter between his lips.

My hand is empty and aching, searching for something to occupy itself, insecure that it can't find anything. *It's been traded for a horse.* The act is much more telling than I want to admit, but it divulges a side of Liam I've never experienced. An intimacy I didn't know existed. I'm surprisingly refreshed by the reality of it. There's no cover, no charm, no pretending. It's raw and emotional, his relationship with his horse. And I think I now know my place, know my rank.

"Blaze, I have someone I want you to meet. This is Tessa, remember? The girl I've been telling you about?" The vacation Liam's charm takes is short-lived. "Blaze, Tessa. Tessa, Blaze." Motioning back and forth. Blaze nods, as though he comprehends the meaning in Liam's words, and I stretch out my own open palm toward him, not sure how to shake a horse's hand, so to speak. I gently place it on his cheek, then promptly yank it back. Horses are so not my thing.

"You guys will get to know one another a bit better later on during our ride." A ride. One of my birthday plans I suppose. The further I step into the barn, the less connected I feel to Liam.

Maybe I've dreamt up this bond we have. Maybe I've longed for it to be real and created it in my head because I somehow need there to be one. After all, he is the boy inhabiting my home and living out my future. For there not to be something between us means yielding to the fact that my life here is gone. Maybe it's been gone all along, slipping away with the last breath my parents took. That a horse ride is on the agenda somehow solidifies that for me. Liam doesn't know me. Liam isn't my family. Liam is just a boy whose parents happened to purchase my old house.

233

Maybe he is nothing more than that now. Maybe he never was.

"Okay, this is where you close your eyes." He sidles up behind me, his fingertips push gently on my eyelids, and he presses them closed. "Are you ready?"

"I don't know." I'm honest. For once today I say something truthful.

Liam guides me forward and rotates to the right. I'm thrown off, trying to envision where we might be standing, but the horse stalls and hay bales are new additions that aren't familiar. It's not a hangar anymore. In fact, there is no sign that it actually ever was.

"No peeking."

"I'm not, don't worry." I don't want to peek. I'm not certain I even want to open my eyes when he gives me the go ahead. I worry that whatever this gift is, it will just be another reminder that Liam isn't Joel, and that this made-up relationship between us is just a smokescreen.

"Three…two…one." His hands drop from my face.

My eyes unwillingly pop open.

"I made it when my dad built our sign for our gate at the entry. It's been hard to keep it a secret these past few weeks. What do you think?"

I open my mouth to speak, but the words die in my throat. A million visions, but nothing adequate to describe them. I see my parents as they walk down to the hangar that day, the sun reflecting off my mother's auburn hair, my dad in his leather jacket that was crinkled and worn with memories of flight. I see myself as a little girl seated in the cockpit, twisting and turning the knobs and controls, pretending I am on some magical space expedition. I see their smiles, hear their laughter, and feel the vibration on the land as the plane rumbles before takeoff.

All of these things I experience as I look at Liam's gift in front of me.

O'Donnell Aviation

The letters are individually carved out by hand on a long plank of wood mounted to the back wall of the barn. And below it on the plaque, in near perfect condition—not a single nick on it, no sign of wear or abrasion—is their plane's propeller.

It's difficult to see beyond the tears brimming, like trying to look through a glass of water yet expecting to see clearly through to the other side. A sheen of sweat forms on Liam's anxious brow. I know I owe him a response and that crying isn't the one he is hoping to receive.

But it's all I can do. To weep. But not over my parents like I imagine he suspects. I've done plenty of that in the past. I doubt there's anything left in that reservoir. These tears are over Liam. Over my lack of confidence in his depth. Over the fact that he probably began building this for me just days after our first encounter. Over the notion that our relationship is more authentic than I gave it credit. Over the reality that the feelings I have for him in this moment are

235

unlike anything I've experienced before. Unlike those with my own family. Unlike those with Joel. Unlike anything I've ever known.

So I cry. That heaving, trembling, ugly sob that shakes your entire body. The cry you have no control over, but it has complete control over you.

"Oh Tessa, I'm so sorry. It's too much. It wasn't my place to make this." The apologies begin to fly. "I just saw the propeller over there in the corner of the barn, virtually unharmed and I wanted to preserve it for you. A memory of your parents—kind of a symbol that even though they might be gone, a piece of them is still here with you." His head moves quickly back and forth, his golden curls flipping side to side. "I should've listened to my dad. He said it wasn't my place."

"No—no, Liam. It's amazing." My fingers find his and I squeeze them tight. If only he knew that a piece of my dad actually *is* still here with me. If only I could tell him I'm a Tracer. "I'm not crying over them. I can't do that anymore. I don't know why, but I can't." His eyes question me, not understanding my words. "It's you, Liam. I'm crying over you." I shove the tears off my face with my palm and wipe them on the front of my jeans, hoping once they absorb there'll be no evidence they ever existed.

"Tessa—why on earth would you cry over me? Am I *that* irresistible that I make you cry?" His words are awkward and clumsy. It's difficult for him to fit his charisma into the question, difficult to mask his insecurity with charm.

"Liam, you're too much. This?" I wave my hand toward the plaque. "Who does this? I don't deserve this, not from you. You're too good for me."

He freezes, and it's as though the pause button has been pressed. We just stand there in front of one another, not stirring, not moving. Barely breathing. I wait for him to push play.

"I'm not too *good* for you, Tessa. I'm too *late*." His strong, somewhat cocky shoulders drop, his guard right along with them. "I'm too late, Tessa. Someone else beat me to you."

Liam throws me an unexpected blow and I don't know how to block it. Sorting out my feelings with Joel and Liam separately is already more than I can handle. But to think that Liam is affected by Joel— that somehow the two of them have a strange connection all their own—I can't begin to wrap my brain around how to detach those emotions.

"I shouldn't have been wasting my time in here working on this for you while he slipped his way into your heart." His words are heavy and weigh down on my chest, constricting my breath. "Can we just forget all of this? Forget that I made this—forget that I just told you all of that?" My stomach squeezes as he starts to walk slowly backward. "Come on, my mom baked a cake. Let's just go back to the house and eat and then you can go home." I don't like the resignation in his tone.

He turns on his heel and I catch his elbow.

"You're asking me to forget an awful lot today, Liam."

He spins around to face me, briefly stricken, and then recovers, his mind registering his own words I've plagiarized from our first time at the ranch. "I don't want to forget. Not this. Not my past. Not you."

"Then what do you want, Tessa?" He's not calling me Sunshine like usual. I recognize the intent in his question.

I stand in the middle of the barn, exposed and vulnerable, just like he was minutes earlier. It only seems fair to switch places for the moment. "Come here."

Stray bits of hay crunch under the weight of his feet as he steadily treads toward me. His green eyes don't falter from mine.

"What do you want me to do?" He's six inches from me, his breath rushing over my skin. I'm transported back to our first meeting on that blue bench, back when his close proximity bothered me. Now I just wish he could get even closer.

"Kiss me?" It's simultaneously both a question and a command.

"Tessa," Liam sighs, frustration seeping through the way he utters my name. "I want to, believe me I do. It's literally all I think about." The pad of his thumb lightly follows the edge of my bottom lip, drawing goose bumps up on my arms. Blood rushes to and stains my cheeks a deep scarlet. "Seriously. I had this vision of showing you the plaque and you swinging your arms around my neck and planting one on me…but I can't."

The anticipation, the urgency—it's all cut off with his words. "You can't?" My eyes grow wide and wary.

"No, not when you belong to someone else." I want to scream out that I don't belong to anyone—that it's just him and me—but Joel's perfect handwriting flashes before me. *My Tessa*. He's claimed ownership over me and I let him. I wanted him to. I craved it.

But all I crave right now is this boy in front of me—the boy with the pale green eyes and the twisted, waving, golden hair that stops just above his strong jawline. This boy so full of magnetism and appeal. And full of love for me. Because if making something like that plaque—dedicating himself to creating a space for me in his barn, a memory for me made from his own hands—isn't bordering on love, then I must not know what love is. And doing it all while he watched me fall into the arms of another, sacrificing our own time together, hoping that the end result would be me in his arms instead.

There is only one way I can think to respond to something like that.

But Liam continues. "And even if you're not with him completely, even if there is a space left for me, I'm not good at this stuff." My knees nearly fall out from under me as he sweeps his hair behind his ear. "Why do you think I act the way I do, Tessa? Why all the flirting, the playing? I don't do *this*." His hands go back and forth between the two of us, the rhetorical question holding in his eyes. "I need something to hide behind. I'm awkward and new at all of this."

"Me too," I quickly interject. "The only guy I've ever kissed is Joel."

Liam's eyebrows lift, catching on his intersecting scar, and his upper half leans ever so slightly back as though examining me. "Really? Well, that's still one more person than me." Shifting in his place, Liam's eyes no longer make contact, but stare at the ground underneath him, as though he has to keep a close watch on it to make sure it doesn't fall out from under his feet. After a fleeting moment, those green eyes snap back up and lock with mine. "Okay, I'm sorry, but I can't have Joel showing me up in that category, too."

He plunges toward me, grabs me by the shoulders, and draws me to him, his lips crushing mine. They're tender, yet firm, slightly open so his breath enters my mouth, so we're breathing the same air. We instinctively know what to do, know how to read one another like this isn't our first time. The movement of our lips against each other, the pressing in and pulling back in a rhythm and beat that we seem to recognize. It's familiar. Actually feeling Liam this close to me, his body near mine, his lips mimicking my own, his hand at my back and fingers twisting in my hair. *He's* familiar.

"Tessa, I don't know what I'm doing." His words are quick, his chest heaving under his shirt as our lips briefly part.

A small bit of hesitation spikes through me and I shake my head. "Neither do I."

His lips curl up and his eyes become smaller as a smile grows, starting from the corners of his mouth.

"Um, *yes you do.*" He laughs, which makes me giggle. It's like everything he does elicits the same involuntary response from me.

His right hand tugs the hem of my shirt and he draws me further toward him. He embraces me, wrapping his arms all the way around me, his fingers gripping me tightly. He's strong—leaner than Joel— but solid and defined in his own way. I push myself as close as I can to him. My hand finds the waves of his blonde hair and entwines itself in them, one loose curl per finger. It's all I can do to keep from pulling those curls out as his mouth presses firmly into mine.

My body tenses and my breath holds then exhales, wanting to do so much more than this dance of kissing and teasing. The tightness in his brow gives away that same anticipation. Liam steadily pushes me backward toward the two bales of hay stacked at the edge of the barn, their bristles and straw tickling and scratching at my exposed arms and neck. He unbuttons his outer shirt, keeping his white tank on underneath, and drapes it over the top bale I'm up against, creating a barrier between my skin and the hay.

Our lips find each other again, bending and molding with the other. It's difficult to believe that he's never done this before—that *we've* never done this together before. My fingernail traces his collarbone to his shoulder and wraps around to the blades on his back. Liam shoves off slightly, pulls a loose piece of straw from my hair and laughs thoughtfully. "Even in a barn with a bunch of horses, you're still so beautiful."

I want to tell him that he is too, because he truly is—his defined jaw, his light emerald eyes, and his golden hair. He's rugged and gorgeous and I can't believe I didn't see how much until now. But I don't know how to form the words to tell him so. "You're pretty hot yourself," is all I can muster.

"Oh yeah?" He grins and nods repeatedly. "Yeah, you think so?" Liam laughs, a playful snicker, and he kisses me quickly again, gently pulling on my bottom lip, lightly biting it between his teeth.

"Tessa, you're going to think I'm crazy for saying this, but since I'm on a roll with firsts today, I'm just going to do it."

My heart drums inside me.

He moves back the hair that covers my ear and brings his lips to it. "I….love…"

I'm holding my breath, hoping he finishes his sentence before I pass out.

"…*birthdays*! Come on, I have one more surprise for you." He coils back, retracting from the punch that my fist tries to fire at him.

"You punk!" I attempt to hit him again, and this time my hand makes contact with his chest.

"What did you think I was going to say?" Green and wide, his eyes twinkle and entice me.

"What*ever*, Liam. You are such a tease."

"Oh, *I'm* the tease? You're the one that got me all hot and bothered against that hay stack!" He rakes his fingers through his own hair and several bits of straw fall to the ground. "You should be gentle with me—I told you I was new to this."

"I don't believe that for a second, Liam. You're such a liar—I bet you've kissed nearly every girl back at Superior." I walk to the hay bales and retrieve his shirt, twist it in to a ball, and chuck it at him.

"I'm telling the truth—scout's honor." Apparently he's not the liar I've proven myself to be. "I've never done that before, but I kinda like it." His lips push against mine again, tender and sweet, and when he pulls back, our foreheads still touch. "And I kinda like you, Sunshine."

"I like you too, Liam." It sounds so simple as it passes between my lips, but the meaning those five words carry could fill up an entire novel with paragraphs and chapters on affection and emotion. I feel the need to expand my inadequate response. "Like, a whole lot." That still doesn't seem sufficient.

"I know you do, Tessa. You don't need to assure me. You pretty much just did that."

Outside of the barn the wind beats against the siding and the sky has turned gray with cover. The clouds are ominous and looming, and I'm certain they'll open up any minute and dump on us.

"Come on, let's get inside. It's pretty threatening out here." Liam pulls me to his side.

The barn's behind us and I turn my head over my shoulder to steal a glimpse. It truly doesn't seem all that different from when it used to be the hangar. It once housed something my parents loved, and now it holds Liam's love, his horses. It seems like a fitting transformation. And the building standing in front of me houses something, or someone, I'm growing to love inside it, too. Maybe it's all the perfect fit.

Liam takes note of my falter and halts just outside the door. "Tessa, what is it?"

I answer, vague and elusive. "Nothing. I just realized something."

"And what's that?" Head cocked to one side, he tries to read between my lines.

"Maybe my life didn't stop when I left the ranch after my parents died. Maybe it was just a temporary pause." I pull on the handle to the door. "Because this—*you*—it all feels like coming home."

"Well then, happy birthday, Sunshine." He props open the door and the scent of warm vanilla cake spills out from the kitchen onto the porch. "And welcome home."

SIXTEEN

The hail cracks against the porch awning, spilling onto the wood decking, bouncing and jumping as it lands like popcorn on a stove. Over the past two hours the sky's transitioned from murky gray into deep black. The clouds billowed at first and then stretched out, spanning the entire valley, like a lid on a bowl. A few hours back would have been the best time to leave, had I been worried about driving in the rain. It's now turned completely into frozen marbles of hail. But the minutes passed by as we sat in the kitchen, decorating the cake his mom made the night before, and I was too lost in the colors of frosting, sprinkles, and birthday messages written in icing to notice the change in the color of the sky outside.

"Shoot, Tess, it's really coming down." Liam eyes the window and licks a patch of yellow frosting from his thumb, leftover traces of the sun he drew on the cake. "I don't think I feel good about you driving in these conditions."

Any other time I would have shrugged it off, said 'I'll be fine,' and headed out without caring. Mom and Dad had driven those roads a million times and I'd memorized every inch of them. Hail and ice wouldn't be too much of an obstacle. But Liam's tone, coupled with the thunderous claps outside and the luminous streaks that flash across the bowl of the valley, are warning enough for me.

A low hum mingles with thunder and Liam's phone vibrates across the kitchen counter. Rebecca's image graces the screen.

"It's Mom. Scoot over." He effortlessly slides my chair with me still in it to his side. He's much stronger than I'd given him credit. "Let's show her the cake—she'll want to see it." He presses down on the answer key with one finger, our dessert creation propped up in his other hand. Rebecca and her stunning golden curls fill up the screen.

"Hey kids!" She waves. "Happy birthday, Tessa! Love how you've decorated the cake." I smile, certain she's just being nice. I glance toward our mess of an icing covered concoction. "It looks very…sugary."

"Notice the sun, Ma? That was my special touch." Fingers tracing its outline, Liam motions to the handheld screen.

"Oh…yeah, I get it. *Sunshine.* Nice work, Liam." Humoring comes naturally for her, too. I wonder for a moment if she might actually be impressed by our decorating abilities, she's that convincing. A second look at the cake reneges that thought. "So kids, we were planning to come back from Gramps' tonight, but the weather is absolutely crazy. A warning just came over the television that everyone should stay indoors and wait it out. Gusts up to 50 mph are expected out there." A few seconds pass before she continues. Her face looks less jovial and more serious. "I don't know how long it will last and the little boys are already getting ready for bed now, so we'll stay here until tomorrow morning."

She's looking at Liam and talks directly to him as though I'm not sharing the same screen, let alone the same room. "Liam, I don't feel comfortable with Tessa driving home in a storm like this. And I don't like the idea of you driving her home any better. I want her to stay at the ranch tonight, okay?"

Liam bobs his head in agreement. "I was just going to call you and ask the same thing." Most boys, given an empty house and a girl they just made out with in the barn out back, wouldn't be asking their mother for permission for a sleepover. Then again, Liam isn't like most boys.

"Okay Liam," Rebecca says. Her eyes emote a trust that conveys the confidence she has in her son's character. "Make good choices. I trust you, you know. You've never given me any reason not to, so don't start now, alright?" Eyes lowered, Rebecca shoots a cursory look of caution through the screen.

"Don't worry, Ma. I'm the good son, remember?" His reply makes me wonder if Joshua has done something in the past to slip from Rebecca and Chris' good graces. It offers a reason for why Joshua doesn't appear to be as tightly meshed as the rest of the Hollanders.

"All of my sons are good, Liam. Just don't give me any reason to say otherwise."

"I won't, Ma," Liam assures. "Love you. Call me in the morning when you're on your way home." The screen blips and goes black. Liam and I sit together in the quiet, dark kitchen for a few seconds that feel much more like minutes. I search for something to say, contemplate shouting 'So, it's a slumber party!' but nothing is natural. I offer him a hesitant smile.

"Alright then." He finally speaks words into our silence. "So it looks like you'll be staying over." Like a twelve-year-old boy, his voice cracks with unease. "Come on, I have an idea."

Following Liam's lead is natural for me, so when he takes to the stairs my feet fall immediately behind him, just two steps back. We pass the second floor without stopping and wind up the staircase to the third. I know where we are going. My old room. His room.

My heart paces in time with my feet on the steps. His door is open so I'm offered a glimpse of its setup before I enter. The bed is on the long, windowless wall to the back. The desk sits across from it. Same arrangement as my old space, just a few random teenage-boy knick knacks thrown in like a guitar and his riding boots, propped up at the foot of his bed.

"So I doubt you're ready for bed—I think it's only around 8:30 or so—but there is one last gift I want you to have for your birthday. Since the weather didn't cooperate we'll have to take a rain check on our riding." He looks toward the bed, then timidly my direction. My heart jumps into my throat. I swallow hard to push it back down to my chest where it belongs.

My eyes search his face and I try to decipher what he means. After his sincere pledge to his mom about being good tonight, I'm sure he's not planning something that could potentially break that promise. Even though a small bit of me desires him to, I know neither he, nor I, are anywhere near ready to take that step.

"So. This is it." The room sits quietly around us. "One night's sleep in your room. The sunshine—hopefully—waking you in the morning. Just like old times."

Two gifts in one day, hundreds more if you count all of the minutes we've spent together. Each moment with Liam feels like a gift. It's almost too much. "Liam, you keep doing this to me."

"Doing what?" He shrugs, his eyebrows arched, eyes inquisitive.

"Making me speechless," I say. "I mean, seriously, I'm fine sleeping downstairs on the couch. This is *your* room now."

"Maybe it is now, but for tonight, just pretend it's still yours, okay? I want you to." As he speaks, he's stripping the bed, pulling out a clean set of sheets from the closet, and fitting them onto the mattress, re-making it for me.

"Um…so," he hesitates. "You don't have any pajamas. Let me find something for you." Ahead of him stands a blue painted dresser, and he pulls open the third drawer down to retrieve a red t-shirt and basketball shorts. The top has *Superior* written in white cursive across the chest. I snatch it out of his hands and hold it up to me.

"This will be perfect since I'm *so* superior," I mock.

"Well, you definitely are to me." His eyes are down and he fiddles with a loose thread on the shorts he's gotten out for me. I'm half full with appreciation, the other half nerves, and I yank the shorts from his grip. "I'll go downstairs while you change."

"No, it's okay. Just wait in the hall." He nods and the door falls nearly closed behind him, yet a two-inch gap remains. I slide out of my shirt and into his, breathing leftover traces of his cologne as my head slips through the neck opening. All day something in me has wanted to be as physically close to Liam as possible. Wearing his clothes here in his room—it doesn't seem like I could get any closer even if I tried.

"All done." Liam pops his head into the room, checking to make sure I'm decent before he fully enters. "So, what, you said it's like 8:30?" I take his word for it. I've spent the entire day at the ranch and my eyes haven't met the numbers on a clock once. So drastically opposite from my new routine. I'm not a Tracer here. I'm just Tessa. The ranch, Liam, being here with him—it offers a temporary escape.

My breath catches at the thought. Maybe this *is* just an escape. What if this can't actually be my reality? I push the notion out of my head and resolve to take it up again in the morning. For tonight, and even if it is only for tonight, this will be my truth. Liam and me. His home. My home. *Our* home.

"You're not ready for bed, are you? It's kinda early." He's close to me again, rubbing the thin fabric of my shirtsleeve between his index finger and thumb. "By the way, I like the way this looks on you." He tilts my chin up with his other hand so my eyes have nowhere to look but straight into his. "All of the girls back at my old school looked so ridiculous wearing anything with our school name written on it because it was clearly a lie. But you really do seem so superior to all of them. Especially in this."

"Thanks Liam. I sorta feel bad that all of us at East Valley always made fun of your school. I had no idea you had such great logos on your shirts." I wink, stealing another one of his trademark moves as my own.

"Oh yeah? You made fun of us, huh?" He pokes at my side with his finger again, like the day in the coop with the chickens when I nearly threw myself at him. At the time I couldn't have even guessed that this is how I would be spending my birthday, practically reliving all of the tension, teasing, and flirting that began on that day when we were just classmates working on an assignment together. *Liam, what are you doing to me?*

I raise myself slightly up on toe to kiss him—surprising him, surprising myself—and his mouth presses into mine in response. "Twice in one day? Seriously?" He smiles.

"Make that three times." My lips meet his again, this time I linger there for a while. Liam leans into me as I slowly draw back out of our kiss, not wanting to let go. The way he tastes, the way his lips yield to mine; everything about him is comfort. Given the option, I'm not sure I'd ever leave Liam and the ranch at all.

"You know—Josh owes me fifty bucks now." I go red, hot from the idea of his brother taking bets on if Liam would kiss me. His statement brings a sudden awkward, slightly used, feeling to my stomach.

"You had bets on me?" Wariness rises in my voice.

"Oh gosh no, Tessa. I'm sorry—that came out totally wrong." He collects his thoughts. "No, Josh has always been saying that it'd be my wedding day before I ever got kissed. That my standards are just too high. Now he owes me big time." A haughty grin spreads across his face and I kind of like it. "We should do something fun with the money I've got coming to me."

Waiting until his wedding day to be kissed. Something deep down in me flutters at the idea of Liam standing at the altar. His golden, twisting hair. His dark, formal suit. A leafy green boutonniere that's been made to match the color in his celery eyes. I can almost see myself heading down that aisle to pledge a life together. And maybe this crazy fantasy isn't too far off. Raising a family at the ranch, continuing on in this life I've projected for us, *together*. As rushed as my thoughts are, they don't seem entirely out of the realm of reality. As natural as everything is with Liam, it almost makes sense to play out how this relationship could naturally progress. *Almost.*

But I'd have to keep something from him, and when you're promising your future to someone, how can there be any secrets? My heart sinks at the realization that this is as far as things can go between us. This playing house. After all, that's what we're doing, isn't it?

"You sleepy?" He interprets my far off stare as fatigue.

No, I'm just busy picking out our wedding colors and compiling a guest list.

"Yeah, a little." I play it off.

The room's gotten darker as night falls across the clouds still looming outside. "I can leave you if you're ready for bed."

"No, don't go yet." I sit right where I am on the cold hardwood floor in the middle of the room. Liam lowers himself and slides down in front of me, pulling his knees to his chest. "I have some things I want to ask you."

"Shoot," he instructs. "I'm an open book."

What would you say if I told you I have this thing— this Tracer thing—that basically means I can see the future. Or maybe not the future, but the links in the past. The interconnectedness of life. What are your thoughts on that? Oh yeah, and you were probably immunized against it since most people view it as some sort of disease or paranoia. My dad even became a Reallocate because of it.

"So, when did you realize you liked me?" Any other time in my life this question would be weighty, could potentially be harmful, but in comparison to my alternative inquiry, it seems as safe as asking his favorite color.

"When I saw you on that bench outside of school last month."

The first day we met.

Liam continues on. "You were so familiar, Tessa. Like I'd known you forever. I kept wanting to ask you if we'd met somewhere before, but I was worried I'd freak you out." He turns his head and the light from the moon that breaks through the clouds washes over his face, illuminating him against the dark. "Seriously, Tessa. If that stupid band hadn't started up and snapped me back into reality, I probably would have kissed you goodbye, you felt so familiar to me."

I nod, knowing exactly that same feeling.

"And then one night I was lying awake in here, thinking about you, and it dawned on me. You'd probably sat awake in this very room before, too. That maybe this connection I felt with you existed because of the experiences we've shared, though not together, but the same experiences still."

It makes sense, Liam's hypothesis about our instant—and somewhat irrational—feelings for one another. I lived out life in this house before and now he's taken over. It's like there's some kind of overlap that draws us to one another.

"I had to keep reminding myself that I actually didn't *know* you, no matter how close I may have felt to you. That's why I've tried so hard this past month to put myself in your path—to sit next to you in biology, to work with you in journalism. Any excuse I could have to be around you I took."

And I understand this need to be near him, for him to be near me. I completely get it.

"Me too."

It's only two words, but it sums up so much more than just reiterating what he's said. *Me too,* to the feelings at first sight. *Me too,* to the wanting to constantly be in his presence. *Me too,* to the need to experience the ranch together. All of it. All of Liam. I've wanted it, too.

We sit and talk for at least an hour more, and with each conversation I feel myself drawn further into him.

"It's getting late and I don't trust myself with you. Especially not here in my room." Honesty drips off of his words as his eyes rove the room. "I'm going to go check on the horses before the storm gets too bad." He's on his feet, hand outstretched to pull me up. I take it.

"I trust you, Liam." I'm not at all ready for him to go.

He cracks a smile. "I'm glad you do, Tessa. But if I don't trust myself, then I don't think it matters how much you trust me. I am still a guy, you know. Don't give me more credit than I deserve." He's truthful and warm and open and I love it. "Get some sleep." He kisses me softly. "I'll see you in the morning, Sunshine. I'll be on the couch downstairs if you need anything, but I'm pretty sure you know your way around the place." Liam turns and heads toward the door. "Happy birthday, again. Happy *golden* birthday."

I climb into his bed and even though the sheets are new, his smell lingers on them and it's as though I'm wrapped up in Liam.

"Thank you, Liam," I say. "I honestly can't think of anyone I'd rather spend my day with."

And for all the little lies I'd let slide between my lips today, I'm pleased that the last words out of them are true.

More true than I'd ever suspected.

***

I jolt awake, the thunder shaking the frame of the house, rattling the pictures hanging on the wall. My eyes don't adjust immediately, and as I peer at the image the forms of four teenage boys begin to transform, their fuzzy edges gradually becoming clear. I don't own a picture like that. But this room isn't filled with my furniture. Nor my decorations. And these aren't even my own clothes on my skin.

It's a few seconds before it all rushes back. The kissing in the barn. The invitation to wait out the storm at the ranch. The bed made up for me in Liam's room. I look around and even though it's the dead of night, the room is eerily quiet. There's no low hum of electricity. No light left on in the hall. I turn to the wall with the digital clock and it's one solid block of darkness.

The power must be out.

This is a first. I don't ever remember during any of my time at the ranch when the power had shut off completely. The Technology Sector is usually on top of things like this. I remember the occasional flicker or power surge, but not minutes at a time of total outage. *Oh, I bet the Hub hates this right now. But how much would my dad love it? How much do I love it?* I giggle, my inner silent disobedient sneaking out.

I fumble around on Liam's nightstand, hoping to find his grandpa's watch, but my hands trace the form of a book, a cup of water, and a pencil. No sign of the watch and no way to know the hour. No way of recording the time. No way to be a Tracer.

Then I remember my phone downstairs. I head down the flight of stairs to the second floor, my feet having memorized the number and they guide me through the darkness. *Fourteen, fifteen, sixteen.* I'm at the landing. I continue on to the bottom floor, twelve more steps, these ones a bit wider than the previous. Light from the moon outside shines through the windows that stretch the length of the downstairs. I look for Liam's outline on the couch.

But it's not there. He's not there. An un-anticipated clap of thunder practically shoots me to the ceiling. I panic. *Where is he?*

I reach my hand out to the couch and it's still warm from his body. He hasn't been gone long. I want

257

to curl up on it, to wrap myself in the heat of Liam, but I'd rather have the real thing. I've got to find him.

The room lights up in reply to the back and forth with the thunder, lightening bolts across the sky, blanketing everything briefly in white before it returns to shadow. In the second of illumination my eyes locate the barn outside, its door slid open. He has to be in there.

I navigate my way to the mudroom, pull on a pair of Rebecca's boots, and push hard on the door to the outside. The wind whips and whirls, like the screeching of fingernails on a chalkboard, and I can't make out the barn through the black around me.

"Liam?" I call out, but the howling sucks up my voice and drowns it. "LIAM?" I scream again, my words releasing into the air, swept up in the gusts and carried into the void.

Somehow he hears me and steps out from the barn. "Tessa? What are you doing out here?" His voice is loud, growing louder, as he presses through the rain and wind toward me. I can't clearly make him out until he's practically on top of me. I collapse into his arms.

"Tessa, what are you doing out here?" he repeats, this time softer. He pushes my rain-soaked hair from my face with the back of his hand. "It's awful out. Go back inside." It's not a request, but a command. I don't follow it.

"No. I can't sleep. The power's out. I came downstairs to look for you and you weren't there," I say.

"Yeah, it's been out for a while. The horses were spooked from the storm. I heard Blaze bellowing so I came out here to try to calm them down." He shines a flashlight back toward the six stalls.

"Do you know how long it's been out for?" I try to decipher the time. "Any idea what time it is now?"

"No, not really. It's weird that it's been out so long. I don't think I've ever known the Tech Sector to drop the ball like this. I'm guessing it's been out for at least two hours, so maybe it's somewhere around 3:00 a.m."

"Gotcha." I follow him into the shelter of the barn and out of the elements. "What can I help you with down here?"

The horses are quiet now, like they're eavesdropping on our conversation. Liam's sitting on one of the hay bales from earlier. He must have unstacked them and pushed them together to create a makeshift bed. "No, I'm getting you back in the house. Come on, let's go." His hands twist my shoulders firmly, digging into my collarbone, so I'm facing the house. He nudges me forward though my heels lock in place.

"Liam—you think I'm going to be able to sleep all alone in that house knowing you're freezing to death out here? Not an option." My words are as firm as my feet planted on the ground.

"Okay." He acknowledges my stubbornness and gives in. "But *I'm* not letting *you* freeze out here, either. Take this." He pulls off his jacket and offers it to me. I probably should have planned a little better for my expedition outside; my arms and legs tingle

259

with cold. "You in no way have to, but I'm going to stay out here with them until the storm passes or morning comes—whichever happens first."

"Then I'm staying with you."

His shoulders sink and his eyes are insistent. "Tessa, you seriously don't have to do this—"

"I want to." My reply ends things.

"You pretty much have your mind made up then, don't you," he says through a growing smile.

Yes.

Yes I do.

SEVENTEEN

My gut's bruised and sore and I rub the pain out of it with my fingers. I've tried to focus on tightening my muscles like he says but it isn't doing much good. *Hold out your arms. Get ready for the catch.* The ball rotates rapidly through the air, whistling as it flies closer. But like the past dozen passes, this one ricochets off of my stomach, lands on the ground, and wobbles back and forth before rolling to a stop at the edge of a clump of grass.

"No offense, Tess, but I don't think anyone will be scouting you any time soon. No future in the sports division of the Entertainment Sector for you." Joel laughs and jogs over to my side, snatches up the football, and pushes the leather tip of it into my ribs. "Try to have your arms ready to receive it once it hits here, okay?" He's turns and jogs back to his place about twenty feet away, just far enough to make conversation difficult, and just out of range where we can talk at a normal volume. Today, this distance feels just about perfect.

I'm still searching for the words to say to him. He knows I was at the ranch yesterday. He knows that the storm kept me there overnight. The cake decorating, the horse tending to. I've told him the general gist of my birthday events. But I left out a few things: the kissing, the lack of parental supervision, the cuddling and huddling up in the barn to keep warm as we waited out the storm together, talking about our childhoods, dreaming about our future. Joel apparently trusts me. Obviously he shouldn't. Maybe he's giving me more credit than I deserve, the same credit I gave Liam last night. But Liam proved to be entirely trustworthy. Maybe I can, too.

Whirling toward me again, I ready my stance and the ball slams into my abdomen. To my shock it stays there, cradled in my arms.

"Beautiful catch, Tess! That's what I'm talking about!" Joel claps his hands and applauds my lucky break. "Okay—now toss it back to me."

The laces find their place under my fingers and I arch backward, twisting at the waist as the football releases from my hold. Bright and glimmering against the sun, the glass-coated face on my wrist catches light and a prism of colors reflects across the ground.

Liam's watch. A relic from his grandpa. Another birthday gift for me.

When I awoke in the barn this morning—the sounds of birds chirping outside as they came out from their shelters, soaking up the nearly forgotten sun,

262

starting a new day with a song—I felt it heavy on my arm. The worn leather band, the cold clasp, the round face with not only an hour and minute hand, but second as well.

"You asked me last night what time it was. I completely forgot I had Grandpa's watch." Liam spun the band around on my wrist. "I remember you commented on it the first day we met, and honestly, I don't have a lot of use for it. I thought maybe you'd get more wear out of it than me."

To say something with so much meaning without realizing the depth and power in the words is a strange phenomenon. If Liam only knew the truth in his statement. If only he actually understood how much use this watch *would* be to me.

Especially now that—even with the power back on—every clock in Madison (in all surrounding cities for that matter) is still out.

00:00

A message came across the television this morning that Tech Sector officials were working diligently to get it back up and running and that it shouldn't be too much longer until the digital clocks would sync with national standard time once again. But it's been six hours and twenty-seven minutes since that announcement, according to Liam's watch. I suppose I'm the only one who knows, and is bothered by, that.

All of Liam's gifts—the plaque with the propeller, the cake decorating in my former kitchen, the night in my room—they were all pieces from my past. Gifts that symbolized what I once was. Things I once did.

Joel's journal was such an obvious representation of my future. My recordings. My clues. My tracings. Even the notion that those clues culminate into some future event reinforces that idea.

But the watch is different. It's the first piece that crosses over between the two. Some artifact bridging the divide between my past and my present. I hadn't counted on Liam entering into this reality at all. Keeping him separate—keeping *us* separate—at the ranch seemed like a necessity. But now there's this watch, this reminder of Liam on my wrist.

There's an overlap.

"So does he know?" The football hits me the same time his words do. "Have you told Liam that you're a Tracer?" Squared in front of me, Joel rests his hands on his hips, his jeans slung low on them. His jaw is tight and his body locked as he waits for my answer.

"No. Liam doesn't know." I look at the watch.

4:13 p.m.

We've been tossing the football for the past two hours. Liam had said I probably woke up somewhere around 3:00 a.m. last night. Joel and I were still playing catch at 3:00 p.m. this afternoon. *Something having to do with playing catch then.* I mentally inscribe the words, promising to jot them down in my book later. "No one knows. Just you."

"Don't you want him to know? Don't you want *everyone* to know?" My secret to keep, he's been sworn to secrecy and has obliged. "I know it's your choice, but if I were in your shoes, I'd want to scream it from the rooftops." I snicker at his statement. *The Hub would have a field day with that, wouldn't they?*

"It's not that easy, Joel." We find the cover of shade under the awning in the back of his yard and sit on the outdoor couch next to one another. What a strange change in the weather, this hot sun on my skin compared to yesterday's wind and hail.

"What's not easy?"

"It's not easy to explain. It's not easy to live. I'm not even sure it's legal." I pause. "This Tracer thing? It's just not easy. It's changed everything. It's changed me."

"But that's a good thing, right? To be changed by something greater than you?" he asks. "And the fact that it's not easy, that doesn't mean that it's not worth it. There are plenty of things in life that are difficult, yet worth it in the end. Relationships for example."

Joel looks away, releasing the connection between us. He pretends to study something at the edge of the yard. It's only been a day, but things are different and it's evident he senses that. Maybe he's not as clueless as he pretends. Maybe he knows more about Liam and I than he cares to admit. At least more than I want to admit. *Shoot Tessa, what have you done?* I think the words, but I hear Uncle Mark's voice speak them. He'd warned me not to play with Joel's heart. I thought I'd listened. Turns out, I must not be very good at following directions.

"Joel—even if I explained it to someone, what are the chances that they would even understand, let alone *believe* me? They'd turn me in to the Medical Chair immediately and the Hub would have me locked up."

"People have believed crazier things before, Tessa." His words suspend around us.

Silence grows, not unlike that day in the car with the hawk. But now it feels forced and awkward for a different reason. Not nerves and butterflies, but disappointment and disagreement. His, not mine. Even with things the way they are with Liam, Joel could never fall from grace in my eyes.

"Especially now, especially with this whole clock outage thing," he continues. "Don't you take that as some type of sign?" He speaks as though some revelation is brewing. "Doesn't it make you think that maybe something, somewhere, is trying to stop you? Like the Hub is trying to put an end to this gift you have? Maybe you're the one to change things, bring Tracing back to the forefront and shake up the government. Don't you think that's a possibility?"

"Not really. It's more likely that it's all just a coincidence." My words are hollow and empty, void of emotion or meaning.

"Tessa, let's be honest. I think we've already learned that things don't happen by coincidence, haven't we?"

Of course he's right, but I don't know what to make of it all. It's impossible to think that someone could have found out that I'm a Tracer. It's even less likely that the Tech Sector would take any sort of action to stop me.

"I'm insignificant." It spills from my lips.

"What?" Joel catches my whisper and doesn't let me get away with it. "No you're not, Tessa. Think about it, you could be a threat. If the Med Sector's been immunizing us against this sort of thing and you're the one that slipped by—either by rejecting the vaccine or failing to get one—whatever the reason, you could be the one to spread it again."

"Spread it like it's some kind of disease," I say.

"Spread it like it's some kind of revolution," he corrects.

"That seems a bit extreme, Joel." There's a tension here, a back and forth that I'm not used to. It's not like the playful banter with Liam, and not even the nervous back and forth of emotions that I'm accustomed to with Joel. It's something new. It's a back and forth of words and meanings. He's much better at this sort of thing than I am.

"Let's say you're right for a minute. Let's just pretend that this Tracing thing has been found out. Tell me how on earth anyone, anywhere, could have any idea that I'm one?"

"You don't fear the authority of the Hub much, do you, Tessa?" He's direct in his questioning and it stuns me, though it shouldn't.

"No, of course I do," I blurt, knowing it's the right and expected thing for me to say. Everyone fears the Hub. "I respect our government. We've always been taught to, haven't we?"

Joel smiles. "Yeah, of course. But there's a difference between respecting something and fearing it. Fear comes from recognizing the ultimate authority and control that something has over you." He hesitates. "Your dad didn't fear the Hub, either."

Panic rises in my throat and I choke it back hard. It scratches on the way down. "How do you know how my dad felt about the government?" I know I'd told him my dad was a Tracer, but I didn't go into much detail about his government opposition.

"Tessa, I think everyone kinda knew." The look he gives me, it's like he's in on something I'm not. I suspect he just might be. "Your dad was well known in Madison for his disapproval of the Hub. My parents attended a meeting once at your ranch laying out some kind of plan to form an underground insurgent party. They seriously contemplated joining, but then my dad was up for the Medical Sector Chair position and everything fizzled after that."

How can Joel know so much more about my own parents' stance than me?

"Why didn't they tell me?" I shake my head, failing to understand. "I knew he was a kind of silent disobedient—"

"Tess, he was more than a silent disobedient. He was pretty outspoken from what my parents say. Which makes sense now knowing that he was a Tracer and became a Reallocate."

Some feeling—pride, maybe—increases in me. I strangely feel more connected in this moment with my dad than I ever did when he was alive.

"Fine. He was outspoken against the government. What does that have to do with me? What does this have to do with the clocks?" I ask.

"I just think you're not giving the Hub the credit they deserve. Think about it Tess—if you're a Tracer, they'd easily know. They know everything. Especially if your dad was one and you didn't get your vaccine. They'd obviously have records from that. It wouldn't take much to make those links."

I need those records.

But nobody knows what vaccines we've been issued as children. No one our age does. It's not something we see, not some document we have. It's all recorded in our medical data systems at the Medical Sector and those practices that work under them, but we don't get access to them until our Expo. They literally keep them as paper files in cabinets. Joel's just one month shy of getting his.

"You'll get your records next month, right? At the Expo?"

He rotates his head to the side. "Yeah, I guess so."

"So then you'll know if you've been vaccinated, won't you?"

Joel nods. "Yeah, I suppose. But I think it's pretty clear that I have. No way would my dad still be allowed in the Med Sector if he hadn't had his own kid immunized." His hands wring themselves and I study

269

their movement with my eyes. A plan twists in my brain the same way his hands twist over one another.

"We need to find out. We need to get our records, Joel," I say.

"We can't do that, Tessa. I don't have access to anything like that—"

"No, but your dad does."

"Yeah, he does, but we can't get them. It's totally illegal. You sound a lot like your dad right now, you know?" He's so good, all the time.

"I know, never mind. It was just a thought."

"Not a very smart one, Tess. A little fear would be healthy for you, you know?" he teases, jabbing me with his elbow.

"I don't need to be the smart one—that's your job. You're the guy that's heading off to the Med Sector or whatever you plan on doing next year."

Joel rocks into the back of the patio couch, settling into the cushions. "Maybe, maybe not. That trip yesterday to Monarch, it kinda just threw me for a loop. I thought I had this plan, this outline for my future. It kept changing, though. Football to medicine. Then back to football again. Med Sector to Entertainment, and back and forth. But either future, I had a vision for it and knew I'd be a part of some Sector, whichever one it might be."

I remember being jealous a few weeks back about Joel's plan for his life.

"I woke up this morning with this feeling of resignation. This sensation to just give up my claim on my future. To just live life and see where it takes me. Whatever Sector I'm recruited for, it's fine with me."

His words shock me a bit. All of our lives we're told we should strive for a certain Sector. I always assumed I'd end up in Transportation since that's what my parents were in. But now I don't want to be tied to anything having to do with that Sector at all, especially knowing that Dad was a Reallocate, that his original Sector didn't want him anymore. I honestly don't care where I end up, either. And now Joel is professing the same indifference.

"That's exactly how I felt up until this Tracer thing began. I'd given it all up—I just took life one minute at a time. It's all I could handle."

Joel stands up from the couch and grabs the football from the ground. He tosses it into the air and it lands in one hand. He does it again and it lands in the other. "Maybe that has something to do with it. Maybe it's all more complex than we think." The ball springs into the air again and lands in his cupped palms.

Here we go again. Diagnosing time.

"Maybe your dad's death had something to do with you becoming a Tracer. Maybe it was some kind of legacy he left behind for you."

The football hits my stomach, and I catch it in my lap—so much easier to do sitting down.

"If it was a part of me, how come I didn't know about it before he died?" I want things to make sense, but I just can't put the pieces together.

"I don't know any more than you do, Tess. But maybe you didn't have the need for it because he did it for you, you know? Once he died, it was time for you to make it your own. Do you have any memories of him as a Tracer?" Joel asks.

"No. I didn't even know what Tracing was up until you figured all of this out." I feel like he should know this already. "If something was so important to my dad, so vital to who he was, then why didn't he tell me about it?" A strange anger billows within me toward my own father. Just as quickly, I feel the sudden pang of guilt for being upset with someone who isn't even alive to defend himself.

Joel's expression is pained. "I wish I knew the answer to that, Tess. Maybe he was protecting you. Maybe he knew it would be dangerous for you to know."

"Then why didn't he just have me vaccinated?"

He slams his hand to his head, aggravated. "I honestly don't know. I wish I was better at this whole hypothesis thing. I should stick with football." I chuck the ball at him and he fumbles it. "Maybe not even that."

"Give yourself some credit. You're the one who figured out what this whole thing is. Without you I'd be a fainting mess of visions and déjà vu moments." Swelling and ebbing, I feel rushes of both gratitude and anxiety. Grateful for the fact that he's discovered I'm a Tracer. Grateful for this gift I've been chosen for. But anxious that I don't know what to do with it. Anxious that I don't feel like I know how to live my own life to its fullest potential. And anxious that somehow the Hub could be keeping tabs on me, however farfetched it seems.

"You made it easy to do. It was obvious there was something different in you, Tessa." Joel turns to toss the ball back toward me again. "I'd just love if you'd give everyone else the chance to see it in you, too."

EIGHTEEN

The ringing sounds in my dream before it registers in reality. Shrill and ripping into calm of night, like a coach screaming through a loud speaker, it hurls me out of bed and across the room to silence it. I really don't want to wake up my entire house tonight. And I'd just fallen back asleep. I couldn't have been out for more than ten minutes, yet the sudden, blaring volume in my once-quiet room shakes me.

It's Joel.

I hesitate to answer, knowing that phone calls in the dead of night are never a good thing. An accident. Or some type of tragedy. Whatever it is, it's something that can't wait until morning.

In my wavering back and forth I miss his call, the trill echoing for the final time. My breath holds and the phone rests heavy in my palm, the sound turned off completely now. Two minutes pass on my watch before the phone vibrates to life again.

"Joel, what's up?"

"Hi Tessa. We need to talk, can I come over?" His voice is clear, too alert for the hour. He's been up for a while from the sound of it.

"Joel, you know it's nearly three o'clock in the morning, right?" I crack, the night falling off of my words.

"Really? Sorry Tess, I didn't. No clocks, remember?" I'd forgotten. The Tech Sector really needs to show what they're made of and get things back on track with that.

"You can come by. You'll have to be really quiet so my aunt and uncle don't hear." My voice breaks again, but this time from nerves, the blush tangible in my speech. "And how are you going to explain why you're here in the morning?"

"Tessa, I'm not sleeping over," he replies curtly, and I embarrass at my assumption. "I just really need to talk to you."

It's less than fifteen minutes and he's standing on the front stoop.

"Hey," I whisper. "Come on in." I hold the door open, pushing it quietly shut behind him. Joel slips his shoes off and carries them in his hand, his footsteps quieted, as we make our way to my room.

I prop myself on the edge of the bed and he pulls out the bench tucked under the old piano. It creaks under his weight and he rests his elbows onto his knees. His hands are wringing again like earlier this afternoon. "So I think I've got it."

"Got what?" I ask, hanging on his words. "You've got some kind of answer?"

"No, not completely." His head shakes off my question. "But I can't stop thinking about you and your dad. And the things that my parents used to say about the war. About why he didn't tell you, Tessa."

I don't know if I want him to continue. Will knowing why my dad kept such a secret change the way I view him? The way I view being a Tracer? I've just recently started to really own my abilities. I don't know if I want any information that might jeopardize that slow-growing acceptance.

"I think it had to be a choice for you." He stops and reads my face as he says the words, looking for some sort of reaction, but I don't offer him one. "From what I remember from freshman history, soldiers weren't allowed to select their ranks. People were recruited based on their talents, like how we're recruited for the Sectors. I think it's actually part of the reason why the government transitioned into Sectors during the war. They adopted that same mentality."

Joel pauses and I stare at him, my face upholding an emotionless front.

"Your dad didn't have a choice to be anything but a Tracer, Tess. And he also didn't have a choice when it all was taken away. He became a Reallocate and he had to stop doing the very thing that once defined him. The Hub made all his decisions for him. Like they make so many of the decisions for us."

Joel's really been wracking his brain about this. And he's come up with a pretty compelling explanation.

"Maybe he wanted you to be able to choose for yourself since that wasn't something he was able to do. By not vaccinating you, he gave you the opportunity to have that choice to make one day," Joel says. "Think about it—we don't get to decide too much in this life. I mean, yeah, they say we can choose our Sector, but the truth is that we'll be recruited by one come Expo day, and our lives will be played out according to their wishes."

Despite the gravity of his words, there's a shred of hope in his tone. "If he had told you about Tracing, and you'd known what it led to in his life, would you still choose it?"

I know the answer he wants me to say because I know what he would say. *Yes, I would still choose it because it's worth every minute, no matter what the Hub may think. This ability to see that life isn't haphazard is worth any opposition I might face.* But I can't do it. And he's sitting here, with a childlike eagerness, and I feel like I'm just about to take it all away. About to tell him there's no Santa Claus or something comparatively devastating.

"I don't know if I would," I admit. "I want to say yes, but I keep seeing my dad sitting on his bed at night with tears in his eyes and his war box on his lap."

Disappointment creeps across his face. I don't know if I can ever be as confident and assured as Joel. "And that right there doesn't show you just *how* worth it all this is? The fact that he was crying over the loss of something so significant should be your answer, Tessa."

He breathes in, his chest puffing as it fills with air, and he slowly exhales.

I get where he's coming from. I do. But I'm still apprehensive because I don't know what all of this means for me. And that completely scares me.

"Tessa, you get to see life and all its details, not just the surface, or what the Hub wants you to see. And I bet your dad wanted you to have the ability to choose this life, for it to be a life you really wanted and weren't just handed down."

"To choose to become infected," I mutter.

"To choose to accept the gift you have." It's the second time he's corrected me today. His russet eyes catch mine. "I hope it's a choice you're willing to make. Because some of us don't even have the option."

***

Joel's got a way of making even the apprehension of the unknown seem thrilling. Maybe that's a trait he's learned from his parents—to be able to sugarcoat things and spin them in such a way that they don't seem so terrifying. I'm sure doctors do this with their patients all the time. And part of me thinks this might be what he's doing with me. But the other part honestly believes every word he says.

We stay up practically all night. Joel's committed to helping me grow as a Tracer. I know he wants to support me in any way he can, that he wants me to choose this for myself. And I do, but it's just so much to take in, especially in the fog of night. Maybe things will be clearer with the sunrise.

"So do you think I'll ever get as good at this as my dad? I mean, if he received four medals for his Tracing abilities in the war, he had to have been on a whole different level than I am." I'm still such a beginner. I can't fathom someone even believing me at the moment, let alone hiring me for a military operation. The opportunity for growth has to be an option.

"I'm sure it's something that you'll grow into, Tess. For now, I think we should just focus on your ability to see life through a different set of lenses. Don't you like the idea that the Hub isn't in total control like we once thought?" I nod and smirk his direction. *How silently disobedient of you, Joel.*

"Yes, of course I do. I think that's the best part," I admit. "But what if someone finds out? I really don't want to be a Reallocate."

A laugh sputters from his lips, his head tilts slightly back. "Um...Tess, you're getting ahead of yourself. You haven't even been recruited yet. First things first," he says. "You're seriously too cute, Tessa." He smiles and it's a smile that shoots through my body, causing my heart to slam against my chest. I'm not trying to be cute, but I'm glad he sees me that way. Glad that my wavering isn't completely repelling him.

"Joel, the chances of me ever being recruited will be slim to none if anyone discovers I'm a Tracer. I'll be a Discard." The thought casts chills up my back.

"No, you won't. I'll make sure of it," he promises. I don't quite know how he thinks he'll have any power to stop that from happening. But he's always been my protector, so I'm comforted in knowing that he wants to continue this role.

Joel's my safety net.

Maybe I'm the actual risk.

Because it's risky to form a relationship with someone who doesn't fully know your true self, like I've done with Liam. It's risky to hide behind a made-up exterior, trying not to let a small piece of your inner core slip through. It's risky to live in the past when your future is heading in a very different direction. No matter how natural things may seem with Liam—how much I want our relationship to bridge the gap from past to present—every ounce of what I've created with him is risky.

It's so much safer to travel down the path clearly mapped out. To know exactly what your purpose in life is and take it by the hand, no turning back. And even if it's scary, even if it's difficult, it ultimately has to be safe because it's how you were meant to live, right?

So maybe it's been Joel all along. If I'm making decisions based on the most sound, most logical choice, then it has to be. And the way he's laid it all out, I don't see how there's any other option. Joel knows my secret and shares the same perspective on my future. I'm not sure there is any other bond stronger than that. I don't even think sharing the same past trumps that.

So my voice of reason chooses him. Because if all of this is true, then Joel has to be the clear winner.

I just don't understand how something so clear-cut can be so convoluted at the same time.

NINETEEN

"Nice of you to join us, Mr. McBrayer and Ms. O'Donnell." We are forty-five minutes late and Mr. Harrisburg's annoyed. "Welcome to biology."

"I apologize for our tardiness, Mr. Harrisburg." Joel and I shift across the room to our seats. Liam's one desk over. His eyes catch mine and don't avert, even when I forcefully look away. "It's the outage. We didn't know."

"Your other classmates seemed to manage just fine." It's unusual for Mr. Harrisburg to be frustrated with Joel. The Education Sector must be breathing down his neck about tardies again. I can feel the annoyance radiating from Liam as well.

"What's the deal with you and Joel showing up together?" He leans closer, just out of earshot from our classmates. "That some sort of coincidence, I hope? Or is that just wishful thinking on my part."

I sink into my seat and my heart sinks with me. "He was at our house last night. Some sleep over with Trent or something." I lie, picking up my newly-formed habit where it left off.

"So you obviously didn't use the watch I gave you, then." The clock on the classroom wall still reads 00:00. Why isn't anyone else frustrated with the inability to tell time? Seriously, how successful has the Hub been in making us their little, fearful robots, accepting everything they do as fact? I release a huff of breath that lifts the hair off my forehead.

"No, I didn't. I completely forgot."

"Yeah, I figured," he grins. "That old thing doesn't come with an alarm, so you should probably pay a bit more attention to your internal clock, Tess. That is, unless you want to make a habit of disrupting the whole class."

"Funny, Liam." The leather strap around my wrist feels tight, bordering on constricting. "I'll be sure to pay more attention tomorrow."

"Tell Joel to listen to his, too. Unless he's planning on staying over again and will just use the watch I gave you, too." He's fishing, looking for some type of reassurance that there is nothing going on between Joel and me. I can't give it to him.

"I'll tell him." It's all I've got.

There's a murmur—a hum of noise—emanating from the students around us as we begin today's assignment: dissecting the respiratory system. Bailey's already got the lungs splayed out on our pig and is jotting down notes on our worksheet. I, myself, am

283

finding it equally difficult to breathe, as though my own lungs have been ripped from my body, too. Maybe someday I'll breathe easy again. But I'm fairly certain that won't happen so long as I continue this impossible balancing act between two different boys.

"You have plans after school today?" Liam asks. "I was thinking we could work on our homework together while Josh has football practice." It feels like an attempt at an apology for his less-than-cheerful greeting. I accept it.

"Yeah—that sounds good. I have to wait for Joel and Trent, too." Mr. Harrisburg shoots us a look of warning. I lower my voice. "I'll meet you out on the blue bench, okay?"

Liam nods. "Yep, sounds good to me."

***

I trace the peeling paint, this time careful not to splinter myself, as I wait for Liam to show up. The whistles from the field echo into the air, the clash of pads and gear as the players practice emanates in the stadium. The second hand ticks round the clock again. One more minute.

"Hey Sunshine. I'm stumped on the answers for problems three and six. What did you get?" Like our first encounter, Liam's voice draws me out of deep thought. My shoulders jump, but my eyes remain fixed on the second hand.

2:34 p.m.

My journal's at home, so I twist my sleeve up a touch and inscribe a *3* and a *6* just inside my wrist with my pen. "I don't know, let me check." The papers rustle through my fingers. "Trachea for three. Esophagus for six."

"Thanks." He pulls out a pencil that's stashed behind his ear, wrapped in his dense, golden curls, and he fills in the blanks on his sheet. "So. I didn't hear from you yesterday after you left the ranch. I'm guessing that's because Joel came home, huh?"

"Joel and Trent did come back. But that's not why I didn't call." I don't have anything better to add, so I leave it at that.

"So all of that—that whole twenty-four hour period—was that like a one-time thing?" Liam reaches for my hand like he's about to grab it, but drops his in his lap at the last second. "Because if it was—if that's all I'll ever get—then I wish I would have known so I could have soaked it up a bit more. I would have tried to make time stand still with you if I could have."

If you can find a way to make time stand still, then all of my problems will disappear.

"If you can find a way to make time stand still, then all of my problems will disappear, Liam." I'm shocked that the truth glides out of my mouth simultaneously as I think the words.

"What does that mean, Tessa?"

I can't tell him. Not now. Not after I've buried myself so far under this disguise I maintain with him. I'm not willing to risk losing this, and I know if I open up completely to him, that might become a very possible reality.

"Liam?" The green of his eyes match my envy, my jealousy over how simple everything must be for him. No choices to make, no decisions to face. Just one person. No back and forth between realities. A pang of guilt clutches me for letting him fall for a façade and not the real thing. It's not fair that I've put him in this position.

"What is it, Tessa?" Alarm and hesitation are heavy in his voice; his eyebrows lift into a cautious arch.

"Have you ever had a secret that if you ever told anyone, it would change the way they view you forever?"

His lips tighten and tension slides into his brow. "No, I haven't," he says. "But I'm guessing you have. This isn't rhetorical, is it?"

"No, it's not. I wish it was, but it's not." Silence draws out and it's louder than any noise I've ever heard. My ears almost hurt from it.

"Okay." Liam hesitantly breaks our pause. "So, is this a good secret or a bad one? You haven't killed anyone or anything, right? And your real name is Tessa, isn't it?" His humor brings relief to our conversation.

"No, Liam, I haven't killed anyone. And yes, my name is Tessa." I don't need to answer these questions, but it helps to lighten the mood and lift the heaviness. "And I think it's good. But it's something that will change the way people see me. I don't think everyone will accept me, or even believe me."

The bench is hot underneath me, radiating the heat it's trapped from hours out in the direct sunlight. It surges through my body; sweat builds on my upper lip.

"And I'm guessing you're not going to tell me what this is, right?" Liam says.

"I can't—not yet. I don't know how. And even if I did, I'm not sure it's entirely my own story to tell." I think about my dad and his Sector reallocation.

Bracing for the blow, I'm surprised by the contentedness Liam displays. "Okay, I get that." He shrugs. "Let me just make one thing clear."

Here it comes. The part where he says he could never be with a liar. The part where he says trust is the most important thing in a relationship. The part where he says he never knew me and wants nothing to do with me. The part where he rejects me and I fall apart.

"This secret you have?" Liam bends toward me, filling up the gap between us with his presence and his words. "You're obviously keeping it for some reason, right? I mean, you're clearly trying to protect someone, whether that's you or me." He pushes his hair out of his eyes. "So there's gotta be some honesty in that, right?"

I hold in all my air as he continues. My lungs start to sting.

"And you're worried people won't accept it? Or accept you? Let me tell you something, Tessa." We're close, only a few inches between our faces, as he speaks. "There is nothing you can do that will change the way I feel about you, nothing you can ever do to make me reject you. So if you're keeping this secret because you're worried about my response...don't." Liam stops. "But if you're keeping this secret because you can't tell it yet—because you're not ready to make that step on your own, or because it could get you into trouble—then who am I to push you into it?"

I release the air from my lungs.

Liam's words are freeing. Freeing me to be a Tracer, but also freeing me to keep it to myself at the same time. He's given me permission to be two different Tessas. Like it makes everything I've been doing, this back and forth between the two, okay. But it's not. And just because he's freed me from the accountability, I'm still at fault. There is still a thick cloud of guilt and lies that looms over me. I want the truth to come to light.

It's my responsibility to force that truth out. It's up to me to live up to my name that Liam's given me. It's my job to let the sun shine in and push this cloud of darkness away. I don't think I want to keep up this façade any longer, even though he claims it's justifiable. It just isn't.

"Hey, Liam? Can I ask you something?"

"Of course."

"*Sunshine*. How did you come up with that nickname for me?" I ask.

"Oh, sure." He smiles. "You remember that day when we first met about a month ago on this bench?" How could I forget? I nod my head to say yes. "Well,

I'd had a really stressful day—the Ed Sector was making me jump through hoops to get things transferred from Superior. I just felt really out of place."

"Yeah, I remember."

He looks straight ahead, squinting as he recollects, like there's some kind of screen in the distance replaying our memory as a movie. "There was so much going on, so many distractions, so many students and new faces. And then I saw you on this bench." His hand skims the seat underneath us.

"And you were familiar. Like you'd always been there. There was just something about you that set you apart." He pauses. "I'm so not good at describing things, but having two little brothers around the house, we do our fair share of singing. Mom's favorite song has always been *'You Are My Sunshine'* and the moment I saw you, it played in the back of my head. *'You make me happy when skies are gray.'* I know that sounds completely cheesy, but everything else felt so cloudy and foggy and you were like sunshine to me," Liam explains. "And you felt just as familiar as the song."

"I was familiar." I nod and echo. *Just as you were so familiar to me, Liam.*

Behind us the track team races by, their rubber tread bouncing like the clip-clop of horses on the gray concrete. Not too unlike the faint tick-tock of the watch on my wrist. I look down at it.

"But what if I tell you this thing and all of that changes? What if I'm not familiar anymore?" Leaves above us rustle on their branches and a wind blows through that pulls up the fine hairs on my skin. "If I tell you this thing, it'll change who I am in your eyes. What if I'm no longer your sunshine? What if I cloud everything up between us?"

When the words come out they don't sound familiar. It's like my voice belongs to someone else, all crackly and on the verge of breaking. On the verge of telling him the truth.

"Like I said before, there's nothing you can say or do to change the way I feel about you." Liam's fingers etch the glass face on my wrist. "There are other verses to that song, you know."

"What are they?" I rack my brain, trying to bring back the words to the song but can't place the lyrics.

"They're not nearly as happy, Tess. It's actually a really sad song about some guy's true love leaving him. It's not some cute little nursery rhyme. It's basically a plea for her to stay with him."

I pause for a moment. "And what does that mean? Does that part mean something to you?"

"Of course it does, Tess." Liam's fingers slip from the watch into my own, a light squeeze as they intertwine, and his vulnerable eyes peek out from under a canopy of blonde waves. "I hear it in the back of my head every time I see you with Joel, like a mantra over and over," he says. "*Please don't take my sunshine away.*"

TWENTY

Open to just a few pages in, the journal Joel gave me sits empty, waiting for our latest entry.

"So what's the verdict?" He forces back my shirtsleeve to inspect the area and reads my chicken scratch. "Three and six?" His eyes light up and my room takes on some sort of energy as recognition, excitement, and anticipation spills out of Joel and into the air. I grab on to a bit of it, too.

"Tessa, that's really is incredible that you can do this." He pushes my sleeve back down.

And it kind of is. Tracing is a rush, and having Joel to support me is so much better than doing it on my own. Experiencing this with him adds validity to everything and confirms that this isn't some accident, some cosmic coincidence that can't be accounted for or explained. It appears we're much stronger in twos.

The journal is in his hands and he writes:

I pull the notebook from his grasp. "Do you think this is how it was in the war? I mean, do you think they talked about it and kept notes and wrote things down?"

"I'm sure they did. They had to, right?" Joel chews on the cap of the pen. "Just think about all the Tracers there must have been in the Intelligence and Prediction division of the military. I'm sure they worked together to provide the government with information," Joel replies and picks up his biology textbook, flipping to our assigned homework page. Though he's here in my room with me, there's a distance between us.

"I would love to know what became of all their notes," I utter. "And what became of all those Tracers."

Joel's eyes glint as he turns to stare out the window, some far off place. "Me too, Tess. I'm sure they're still out there. They're probably just Reallocates like your dad."

Or diagnosed as crazy.

"We've got to find them," he announces suddenly. "We have to figure out a way to get more information about what happened to the Tracers after the war. There's got to be some way for us to find out, right?"

Joel's developing a plan for us. It's not the first time he's talked like this, but this time I hear it in a whole new way. Before, whenever Joel said 'we,' I interpreted it to be the two of us as a couple. And I'm sure that's what he'd intended, and even wanted, at the time. But now the two don't seem so tightly intertwined. Maybe Tracing defines our relationship, not necessarily romance. We're obviously some sort of team, but I don't know where it begins and ends. The uncertainty surges a wave of nauseous doubt through me.

"Tess, I gotta go. I promised Mom and Dad I'd be home for dinner tonight."

He stuffs the biology book back into his bag and gathers his things to leave. I'm not ready for him to go, because even though we've connected on such a deeper level with this whole Tracing, silent disobedient thing, he still feels like he's slipping from my grasp. And I haven't answered his question yet.

"Joel—wait." He doesn't look at me when I speak his name. He busies his hands and his eyes with the contents of his bag instead. "Joel, what's going on with us?"

All evening I've oscillated between wanting Joel to kiss me, and wishing he would break up with me. It's a strange sensation, to equally desire two opposite things from the same person. One act could bind me to him; the other could free me from him. To not know which one I want more is suffocating.

Still avoiding my eyes, Joel answers. "It depends, Tess. What's going on with you and him?" He's hurt and I've done it to him. I've inflicted this pain.

"I don't know. Honestly, I don't know," I confess. "And I'm a terrible person for not knowing."

Joel can't continue evading me and angles his head up. "You're not a terrible person, Tessa," he says. "Liam can just offer you more than I can. I can't give you back your past. I don't have a ranch I can take you to and relive all of your childhood memories. All I have is me and your secret. Maybe that's not enough." If the pain I'm feeling right now is in any way similar to the pain registered on his face a moment ago, I wonder how he's still standing, because this pain is crippling.

"Joel, that's an awful thing to say." Hot and wet, the tears involuntarily spill from my eyes. Just as instinctively, Joel's hand reaches to wipe them away. The back of his knuckles graze my cheek.

"Tess. Don't cry." For two years I hadn't cried. Only at first after they died. But now within two days I've cried just as many times. And I'm beginning to realize that the feelings aren't much different. After they passed, I cried because my future was uncertain. And now, two years later, I'm crying for that same reason. "I'm not trying to hurt you, Tess. I'm just trying to keep myself from getting hurt."

Joel the protector. But now it's not me he's protecting, but himself. Protecting himself *from* me. The irony stings.

"I don't want to hurt you." I want them to be deep, but the words can't help but sound shallow. "And you can offer me just as much as he can."

"And what's that?" Joel gathers me in his arms and I lean my head into his chest, lulled by the steady beat of his heart. It's nearly impossible for me not to feel utterly secure when I'm here. It also seems impossible for Joel to just stand by and not be the hero again, even if he hadn't intentionally wanted to. He just can't help himself.

"You can offer me a future, Joel." I don't want to admit the thought that comes next, but I speak it still. "And I can't live in the past."

His weight shifts at the same time his feelings do. "No, you can't." Chin resting on the top of my head, he continues, "But you can make the past part of your future." I feel his breath push through my hair as he sighs. "And between the two of us, Liam's the only one capable of playing both of those parts."

***

5:37.

I've inscribed it on my wrist, but figure I won't need to reference it.

The day passes quickly. It always helps when the time is set for after school so I'm not distracted throughout classes by constantly looking at my watch. It's become harder to be so secretive about checking my wrist. I'm pretty sure Mr. Harrisburg caught me snatching a glimpse today in biology. Once winter turns into spring it's going to be even more difficult to keep it under wraps. I can only wear sweatshirts and long sleeves for so long without drawing unwanted attention. But with warmer weather I'll have to figure something else out. Luckily that's still months away—who knows what my life will look like then? Who knows what it will even look like tomorrow?

I'm at home and it's five o'clock when Uncle Mark phones. "Tessa, I completely forgot it's my night to cook for the guys at the firehouse. There's a bunch of meat in the fridge and some tomatoes. Would you mind bringing that, and the pasta in the pantry, down to the firehouse for me?"

"Yeah, no problem Uncle Mark. I'll leave here soon, okay?" I say.

"Sounds great, Tess. I owe you one." But of course he doesn't owe me anything—if anyone is indebted it is me. Taking his ingredients to the firehouse is the least I can do.

As I gather up the food and place it into one of Aunt Cathy's reusable grocery bags, I actually contemplate just whipping up the whole dinner first to deliver to him ready to eat. But with only a half an hour or so until 5:37 p.m., I know I can't afford to make that thought a reality.

Joel shows up just as I'm about to leave. "I'd rather be with you just so you don't miss it." It's a good idea, I guess, but I also like the idea of him receiving his own clue apart from mine. It was pretty amazing to see how we both had two completely different experiences yesterday, but both led us to the numbers three and six. Separate lives, same outcome. I wonder how many of my dad's fellow Intelligence and Prediction Officers were actual Tracers. Maybe not all of them were, maybe they were just helpful accomplices like Joel has become.

"Tessa, you are a lifesaver." Uncle Mark kisses me on the cheek when he greets us at the firehouse door. "Come on in. It's been a slow night."

Captain Nolan, and a few other firefighters I don't recognize, gather around an oblong table next to the kitchen. I look up at the clock in the wall and it still reads 00:00. Uncle Mark's eyes shadow mine. "It's made it a bear to get anything done, not knowing the time. It's always been relatively easy to forget exactly who is in control, but with blatant reminders like that coming from the Hub, it's evident they're making a statement about who's really in charge."

Joel shoots a look my way and my entire body freezes, chilled by the truth in Uncle Mark's statement. I unpack the groceries methodically in an effort to shake off my rising fear.

"Uncle Mark, we can stay and help make this if you want. I don't have anything else going on." I slip my sleeve up. 5:29 p.m.

If we leave now, I'll be in the middle of driving when it's time. And if we wait it out at the station, it'll be easier than if I'm driving, a myriad of things passing by my window that could be what I'm supposed to be looking for.

"That would be great, Tessa!" Uncle Mark slaps me upside my back, gentle but firm enough that I stumble forward. "Hey boys—have you all met my niece, Tessa, and her boyfriend, Joel?"

Joel's visibly uncomfortable with our introduction. He shifts his stance from left foot to right. I am a bit, too, because it's as though I'm taking something from him that isn't rightfully mine with that title. Like I'm claiming him as my own and I'm not sure that's what he wants anymore. I'm not sure it's what I want either. I honestly don't know what I want.

"Hey kids," Uncle Mark's coworkers echo. We nod and play the game of being respectful by shaking hands and introducing ourselves. Each free minute I push up my sleeve and either Joel or I make note of the time. *Just five more minutes.*

We're at the stove; I sauté the tomatoes and ground beef while he puts a large pot of hot water on the ignited burner. "So, what are you thinking?" he whispers in my ear. "Burned spaghetti? Rotten tomatoes? I'm not good at anticipating what's going to come next yet."

"Me neither," I murmur back. "I think it works better when I don't try to analyze it and just let it happen."

The minutes sluggishly tick by. My sleeve's rolled up into a cuff on my arm and the watch is in full view. I keep my back to the rest of the room, hoping to conceal and hide it from the others.

"Sixty seconds," I whisper.

Joel's lips form silent outlines as he mouths, 'Sixty, fifty-nine, fifty-eight…'

I don't look at him. Anxiety, though exciting and suspenseful, charges through me and it increases with each number counted down.

'Eight, seven, six…'

Five, four, three, two…

One.

The wooden spoon, once in my right hand stirring the bubbling mixture of meat and diced tomatoes, flies into the air and I trap it against my shirt with my other palm before it plummets to the floor. I seem to be the only one startled by the high-pitched ringing; the firemen glance at each other as they casually rise from their seats and briskly head toward the door to the garage that houses the huge red trucks.

"Sorry, Tessa!" Uncle Mark shouts, taking note of my stained clothing. "I should have warned you—that siren can be pretty jolting if you're not used to it."

Joel's startled as well, but it's hard to see past his heaving shoulders, racked with laughter he's unable to contain. "I'm sorry, Tess. I don't mean to laugh at you, but you're a mess."

"I always seem to be a mess when I'm around you." I recount the vomiting scene from weeks earlier. "Anyway, it's your fault. All of that counting got me all nervous."

"I know, I'm sorry." He's still laughing. "Okay, so I guess maybe something to do with a siren then?"

"Yeah, that or a spaghetti-sauce-covered girl." Joel hands me a damp dishrag to clean myself up. "But I'm betting on the former."

"Me too. I don't see how the other could fit into anything. But then again, we've seen stranger things before." I like how he's saying 'we' again. "So, the noodles have eight minutes to go. I don't think they'll be back from their call before then, do you?"

Sticks of spaghetti tumble out of the cardboard container into the boiling water in the pot and Joel drops the lid on. I kind of like watching him be domestic.

"I don't think they'll be back either. We shouldn't let it go to waste."

"And there's plenty here for all of us." He's hungry and so am I. This Tracing thing can work up quite an appetite.

We wait twenty minutes before deciding to dive in and help ourselves. I store some spaghetti in the fridge for Uncle Mark and his colleagues so they'll have a meal when they come back from the call.

"So I've been thinking a lot about these vaccinations." Joel says around a mouth full of noodles.

"Yeah...and?"

"I'm really interested to see your records." He scoops another helping of pasta from the oblong, ceramic serving dish in front of us. "To see if Tracing was the only thing your parents managed to avoid vaccinating against."

"I guess I won't know for another year."

There are theories about why you have to wait to see them. Most circle around the idea that it is to protect your parents—that if they managed to avoid immunizing against certain things, you couldn't hold them accountable for either allowing or not allowing your exposure to certain illnesses. It never made any sense to me; why would anyone fault their parents for protecting them against disease? But never before had I realized we were vaccinated against much more controversial things, things they hid under the label of infection.

But maybe it has more to do with protecting the Hub than our parents after all. Who knows what else was on that list of required immunizations? And once you're eighteen and recruited for a Sector, the likelihood that you would speak out against any of the information your records provide is slim. No one wants to be discarded.

Another idea is that they wait until just before your Sector Expo so the individual Sectors have full access to your records and can arrange interest accordingly. That theory always seemed so obscure, practically implausible. Why would any Sector other than Medical care about vaccinations and immunizations? But now viewing things from a Tracing perspective, I can see how they would want to segregate us, how they could position us in such a way that certain students were corralled one direction, encouraging them into one Sector over another. After all, it would seem crazy to have a Tracer in the Technology Sector—especially now with all the games they've been playing with the clocks.

"You have to show me yours the day of the Expo."

"You'll be the first to see it, Tessa," Joel assures me.

"The second—*you'll* be the first." The garage fills with the sound of voices. Uncle Mark's back from the call.

"No." Joel takes his plate to the sink and rinses it under the faucet, sauce swirling down the drain like a red whirlpool. "You can be the first. It doesn't change who I am, Tess. I can't change the decision that my parents made for me back when I was a baby." He loads his plate into the dishwasher. "You're the only one who can change, Tess. I don't think you realize what a gift your parents gave you by letting you have that choice."

***

"What time did you wake up last night?" Hushed and quiet, Joel whispers over his right shoulder. Liam's at the table next to us, eyes glued.

Someone a few seats up shushes us and I reply, almost inaudibly, "I didn't. Slept until morning."

No waking in the middle of the night. Last time I had a full night's sleep, the next day was when all of the pieces fit together. That's how it's been working lately. A break before déjà vu. A calm before the storm.

"Got it." Joel turns back to his paper.

"Mr. McBrayer?" Peering over his spectacles, Mr. Harrisburg shoots a stern warning our direction. I go red. I really don't like getting caught. "Eyes on your own papers class."

Liam rotates toward me and mouths, 'What's going on?' and I shrug, 'Nothing,' back at him.

I'm going to fail this test. And then likely this class. Maybe I'll even flunk out of high school altogether. I wonder if I'll still be recruited if I'm kicked out. It doesn't seem like an entirely unattractive option at the moment.

"Five minutes left, students." The timer on Mr. Harrisburg's desk counts down. All teachers at East Valley have been given these sleek, metal, digital timers to set once the commencement bell sounds, signifying the beginning of class. A Tech Sector representative came by the school yesterday to equip each classroom with one. You'd think it would be just as easy to get the clocks back up and working, but no one's argued. They're all robots. Obedient, content little robots. Sometimes I wonder if Joel and I are the only two people in town who are bothered by the inability to know the exact time.

Half of my answers are still blank when the bell tolls and classmates shuffle toward the front to hand in their papers. What a fitting representation of my own life, this half-certain, half-cluelessness.

"What's with you talking during a test, Sunshine?" Liam's voice catches up to me in the midst of a sea of students and chatter in the hall. "You've become quite the rebel lately. Showing up late to class, cheating…what's next? Grand theft auto?"

His stomach begs to be jabbed. "I wasn't cheating, Liam. Joel asked me something."

"I seriously doubt that Dr. McBrayer needed any help with that biology quiz."

This eye rolling, wanting-to-punch-him, sensation I get with Liam is starting to feel routine. "It wasn't about biology. It's nothing." I change the subject. "So, what have you got going on today?"

Luckily, Liam takes my bait. "Not much. School of course. Then I'm watching my littlest brothers tonight while Mom and Dad go to Joshua's game. Wanna come over?"

I do, of course I do, but I can't. "I wish I could. I'd love to see Sammy again; I miss that little guy. But I've already got plans."

"With Joel?"

"Yeah, but it's not what you think." The first warning bell rings. Two minutes until class. "Things have gotten weird between us. I'm not sure what's going on."

"I hope I'm not the reason for that." Liam stops and turns to face me, his thumbs hooked under the straps on his backpack. "Wait, I take that back—*yes I do.*" He's cocky again and it helps take the edge off.

"You would, Liam." I don't want to give him the satisfaction. "It's not all about you. It's complicated."

"Isn't everything?" He's walking backward now, still facing me, as I make my way to second period. "I mean, we're teenagers, Tessa. Our lives are the very definition of complicated."

Mine certainly is. Though for some reason, Tracing makes it a little less so. Challenging, definitely. Confusing, sometimes. But not necessarily complicated.

Complicated was not knowing why I woke up when I did for two years. Complicated was not understanding why things happened the way they did. Complicated was trying to come up with a reason for the patterns in life. Complicated was not knowing anything about my dad's past, yet sensing his dissatisfaction with our government. Tracing takes away that complication and provides me with an answer, even if just a hint of one.

"I'll call you tonight after I put the boys to bed, okay?" Loud and piercing, the final bell blares. Liam skips back in response. "See you later, Sunshine."

"Bye Liam!" My voice falls flat in the now empty hallway. I feel like there should be more words to follow, but he's gone and I'm late. I'd rather spend the evening with Liam and his brothers at the ranch, but I can't. There's no way I could do this with Liam around—that would take some serious explaining I'm not ready for. I'll just call him once it's over, when things go back to normal. That brief moment after the déjà vu. The in-between. The time when I don't belong to Liam, or Joel, or even my gift. When I'm just Tessa.

Though I'm not even sure that she still exists.

And if she does, I'm not sure I want her to.

TWENTY-ONE

"It's late, right? It feels late."

8:41 pm.

I don't remember waiting this long the last few times. "It is late. It's like it should have happened by now."

Joel's pacing, treading across his family room floor, back and forth. "Could we have missed it? Maybe it's not going to happen today."

This is all still so hard to figure out.

"Maybe not."

It's black out. The sun's been down for nearly three hours, but we have yet to turn on any lights in the house. A glow from the streetlamps outside reflects through the windows, sliding a white coating across the furniture, spilling onto the floor. Joel steps out of the shadows and into the streaks of light as he paces.

Illuminated then darkened. Darkened then illuminated.

"I should go," I say. He's frustrated. He wants so badly for it to happen tonight.

"Just wait a bit longer. We might still have time."

Two headlights pierce the black, one shining on each of us through the big bay windows at the front of the house.

"Who's that? Is that your Uncle Mark?" Joel steps toward the glass, squinting to examine the truck outside. "What's he doing here? Do they know you're here?"

He's panicking, afraid he's done something wrong, that he's kept me out past curfew or some other offense. "Yeah, they do. I called and left a message on my way over this afternoon." I'm at his side, peering around his broad shoulder. "I don't know why he wouldn't just call, though."

The engine to his truck cuts off in the drive and Uncle Mark's door pushes open. My heart quickens, that feeling that I'm about to get caught that I can't tolerate, especially coming from Uncle Mark. I really don't want to disappoint him.

Maybe this is the same fear people have for the Hub. I recognize the feeling because I used to have it, too, but it was for three numbers that woke me up each night. Recently that fear has been replaced by a sensation I can't quite put into words.

As far as I'm aware, Joel and I haven't done anything wrong. And Uncle Mark admittedly loves Joel like a son. I doubt he'd even have a problem if I

307

ran away with him. This current scenario doesn't make much sense.

Joel's at the door before the knock echoes through its solid wood core. "Hey Mark, how's it going?" It's forced and overly welcoming, as though he's masking some underlying guilt. "What's up?"

"Hey Joel, can I come in?" Solemnity trickles off of his voice. He looks around Joel to meet my eyes. We're not in trouble, but something's not right.

"Yeah, of course, Mark. Please come in." No one breathes as the three of use make our way to the leather couches at the center of the room. "Is everything okay?"

"I need to talk to you two about something." I've come to realize that when someone doesn't directly answer the question 'Is everything okay' with either a firm 'yes' or a 'no,' that it always means everything is definitely not okay. The officers never answered me, either, when I'd asked that same question two years back.

"Of course, what is it?" Joel takes the reins to the conversation. My mind is still a few minutes back—trying to process the vision of Uncle Mark's truck driving up the street to Joel's house—and can't seem to catch up to the current conversation. Uncle Mark seldom tracks me down.

"I just finished my shift at the station." His eyes are hollow, and though his dark mustache nearly covers his mouth completely, the tension is still detectable underneath. "It's the ranch."

My heart burns within me, his words like an arsonist setting it on fire, blood searing deep into my veins with each forceful pump. "The ranch? There's been a fire?" They shake and tremble as they come out of me.

"No, the ranch is fine, Tessa." I breathe a cooling sigh of relief and the tightness in my chest wanes. "But we *have* been at the ranch."

Liam.

"What happened? Is everyone okay?" Joel's waiting for Uncle Mark's response, too, but his eyes don't move from me. His hand extends and rests solidly on my knee.

"Tessa—I don't know how to say this." His words float into the dark of the room and are swallowed up. "I just don't know how to put it."

"Uncle Mark, just tell me." I'm pleading, begging to know what happened, because surely whatever he says will be better than the feeling I have right now. This feeling of knowing something terrible has occurred, but not knowing what. Even when my parents died and I saw the officers walking up the drive, I knew what they were going to say. I hadn't expected them to actually answer my question. But now, this not knowing, not having any clue what has happened at the ranch is unbearable, constricting and suffocating.

"Liam?"

Uncle Mark shakes his head and that slight movement releases the breath I've been trapping in my lungs. "No, it's not Liam."

"Then what happened?" Joel's leaning in now, too, and pleads for an answer for me. I'm glad because I don't have any more words.

"It's Sammy, Tessa." Uncle Mark's frame drops, giving way to a sigh. "There's been an accident, Tessa." He pauses once more. "Sammy's dead."

The room is spinning, memories flashing as he recounts the accident.

"Sammy and Tyler were out in the front yard playing catch. Liam was helping Mr. Parker load up the eggs from the coop for delivery. They said it all happened so quickly—that Mr. Parker was backing up his truck at just the same time Sammy came bounding around the corner—that there was no way he could have possibly seen him," Uncle Mark says. "Tyler's badly hurt, too. He tried to throw himself in front of Sammy, but it was too late. He's been admitted to your mom's hospital, Joel."

The waves rushing over me fill up my ears with a blaring whooshing that drowns out the rest of his sentence. I'm going to faint. "The egg cracking," I murmur.

"And playing catch," Joel continues.

"Three and six. Sammy was three. Tyler's six." I'm like a robot as I process the words.

"And the siren from the station," Joel continues.

"What are you two talking about?" Bewildered at our exchange, Uncle Mark interjects.

"Nothing, it's nothing." Joel covers for us. "So Tyler? He's going to be okay?"

Uncle Mark nods, his hands twisting each other, the white of his knuckles pushing to the surface of his skin. "Yes. A few broken ribs, but he'll be okay."

"Where's Liam?" My voice is loud, near shouting, and I try to bring it down to a normal level. "Where's Liam? Is he okay?" I say again.

"Yes, he's at the hospital with his parents. He's fine physically, but that's all I can say. I'm sure he feels a huge responsibility—I guess he was watching the boys tonight."

No, we *were supposed to be watching the boys*. Had I been there, this might not have happened. I might have been able to stop it. I might have been able to process everything and predict what was going to happen. That's what a Tracer's supposed to do, right? Sammy might still be alive if I'd just gone to Liam's house like I'd wanted. Instead I spent my evening sitting in a lightless, lonely house waiting for some type of revelation.

Uncle Mark stands to go but places a warm hand on my shoulder. "He's going to need a good friend, Tessa. He's in a very dark place." The irony in his words is chilling as I feel myself being devoured by the blackness around me. "And don't worry about curfew tonight. Come home whenever you are ready. I completely understand."

Joel sees him off, thanking him for coming to give us the news. How he can thank him for such life-altering, horrific news sickens me. I bite back the bile that seeps into my mouth. I won't be thanking Uncle

Mark. I hate him. Or at least I want to. I need to project the hate I have for myself onto someone else.

"I should have been there." It spills out.

"You couldn't have known." Joel's trying to protect me from my own attack on myself. "This is in no way your fault. This was an accident."

My eyes are still blank, unable to produce any tears. Apparently anger is stronger than sorrow. "No." I'm firm in my response. "I should have been there. He asked me to. Liam asked me to come over and watch his brothers with him. I should have gone. Maybe that was supposed to be some sign."

"How could you have known this would happen?" Reason obviously isn't going to work with me. "It wouldn't have changed anything, Tessa. This doesn't change things. It just puts the pieces together."

I'm on my feet, looking for something to strike, a wall to punch, but the air around me feels just as solid and I shove my fist into it. "Then why would I want this?" I scream. "Why would I want to be a part of something that allows things like this to happen? Why would I want to be involved in something where three-year-old boys are killed and families are ruined?" My words hit him. "Joel, give me *one* good reason why I want to be a part of something like that!"

"Tess, I don't know why it happened. But the fact that we can see *how* it happened and see that there was some reason to it—that should make it easier, right?"

"Make it easier? Like it makes it okay that Sammy is dead?" I scream, my body shaking.

"Of course not, Tess. You know that's not what I meant." He's dejected and grave. "Before, if something like this happened, you'd feel completely hopeless. You'd have no explanation—"

"I still don't have an explanation," I correct him.

"Okay, maybe not an explanation, but you have signs," he says. "You have parts that fit together to show that this was going to happen. That it must be some part of a plan where we only get to see the bits and pieces." I refuse to believe the logic in his words. He'd convinced me before that being a Tracer was a good thing. I'm not certain I want him to do it again. It feels like a betrayal—a sort of slap in Liam's face—if I acknowledge that somehow his brother's death is justified. Maybe not justified, but at least intended.

With his arm around me, he walks me back to the couch. An act intended to comfort, I'm sure, but sitting in one place is paralyzing. I want to run. For miles out into the darkness. To run away from all of this. From this reality. To run until everything is behind me instead of staring at me square in the face.

"I need to know."

"Know what?" Joel's eyebrows arch into a questioning curve.

"I need to see my records. I need to know if I've been immunized," I say.

Joel exhales. "Tessa. It's obvious that you haven't. You're a Tracer. You need to accept that." His words are gentle, but have a minimal calming effect on me.

"There has to be a reason for why it's so hard for me to do that. All you are saying, as much as I don't

313

want to believe you, it makes sense. So why am I having such a hard time accepting it?"

A sigh slips between his parted lips. "I don't know, Tessa. Maybe it's just easier for some Tracers to accept than others. But I'm hopeful one day you will."

I'm not at that point where I feel any ounce of hope in this situation.

We talk for a while longer, Joel attempts to console me, and then we just sit in silence which feels much more appropriate.

It's been quiet for so long that I startle when the handle to the front door jiggles and the clanging of keys hits the entryway table.

"Hey kids," Dr. McBrayer chimes from the door. "Late night?"

"Yeah, sorry Dad. We've just gotten some pretty bad news. Tessa's gonna stay here for a little while tonight, okay?" Joel defends my late-night presence.

"Of course. Everything okay?" It's one of the few interactions I've ever had with his dad and the compassionate, protective nature they share is uncanny.

"It will be. Thanks Dad."

Dr. McBrayer loosens his tie from his collar. "I'm headed to bed. I've got another long day tomorrow; the Med Sector is really cracking down on logging hours. Shut off the lights when you're done?"

Joel nods and his dad's feet echo down the hall.

"I should go." It's near ten and I need to leave this space; the words 'Sammy is dead' still hang in the air here.

"You don't have to, Tess. Seriously, it's fine with my dad and it's fine with me."

But I'm turning to go already. "No, it's okay, really. I want to try to get some sleep." I know I won't be able to sleep, but I have to get out. "I'll be fine. I'll see you in biology."

"See you in biology."

It's the stupidest thing to say as we part, but I don't know how to do it any other way. I sit in my car, the moonlight outlining the house, a silhouette against the dark sky. The keys are in the ignition, but I don't turn them. I don't know where to go. I want to go to the ranch, but no one is there. I want to go to the hospital, but I can't face Liam.

Minutes pass and I click the car door open, tiptoe back up the path to the McBrayer house, and place my hand on the cold handle. The front door falls open. Two feet inside the entry my fingers find what they came back for and snatch them up, careful not to rattle as I lift them into my palm. Just as quietly as I entered, I slip back out into the night and into my car.

Fog rolls in, blanketing the valley with a dense layer of haze. A haze like I'm used to and it brings me comfort. It's memorable and familiar and I've almost missed walking around with it everyday. My car pushes into it and it wraps me in its welcome, misty fingers.

I've only been there once before, back when they held the grand opening, so I'm surprised I remember the route. My headlights are off, they have been for the past mile, and I guide my way into the lot and park at the edge in the shadow of the trees. There's a light

315

above the entrance, one that flickers and begs to be changed, but it's not enough to illuminate the door entirely so I retrieve the flashlight from under my seat.

The stolen key finds the lock and I twist it, praying I won't be met by an alarm on the other side. I'm greeted with a chilling silence. My bag is heavy on my arm and I shove it up to my shoulder. There isn't any map—any specific path I know to take—so I stumble and fumble my way through the halls, past the examination rooms, and into a cold, gray space at the center of the building.

Four tall filing cases stand against the wall on the left, looming and towering, their steel exterior a barrier between me and what's contained inside. The vision is surreal. To think that copies of actual medical records from each adolescent in our town are housed within them seems crazy and almost ancient, especially in a day where the Tech Sector has so much power. I imagine the Hub commanding the Med Sector to dispose of them and a huge, burning bonfire flashes before my mind. All history erased. No paper trail. That has to be the reason for the physical, rather than electronic, copies. That or Med doesn't want to rely on Tech for more than they have to.

My eyes continue across the room and find a large, stainless refrigerator filling up the remaining space along the wall of cabinets.

Joel will never forgive you, Tessa. He was very clear that stealing our medical records is illegal. But I'm pretty sure breaking and entering is equally as punishable, if not more so. Despite all that's happened tonight I laugh a little. Liam was joking about my tardiness, my presumed cheating—he'd probably get quite a kick out of what I'm doing right now. That is, if he believes me. I hardly believe myself. It's like watching someone else plan the course of action and make the moves. For so long now I've been wavering back and forth between two realities. No more. I need to decide this for myself. This I have to know.

The filing cabinets are cold—colder than the temperature of the surrounding room—and I shudder when my palm meets the metal. *You have to do this, Tessa. For Liam.* My subconscious pressures me. He's had no choice in any of this. I have. I *do*. If I choose him, I have to choose this. There can't be any other way.

My fingers are still tingling from the freeze against them and I recoil, pulling back away from the cabinets and papers they house inside. The pages that contain my past; the decisions my parents made for me without my consent. Funny that Joel said my dad must have wanted me to have the opportunity to choose for myself. Well, I guess it's time to start making my own decisions. Maybe my dad might even be proud of me for this blatant rebellion against the Hub. What real power can the Med Sector have over me if I discover the truth about myself hiding in those documents? I'd know all there is to know.

But does knowing even really make a difference?

My fingers fall onto a handle, but not the one containing the files. I yank it open. It's even colder now, more chilling as the air trapped inside rushes out and onto my face, raising goosebumps on my arms, and tingling my neck. My eyes search for the right label and I find it surprisingly quickly. It takes a moment to register but I'm sure it's what I'm looking for.

It's almost like it has my name on it. I'm not certain if I'm envisioning it or if it's actually inscribed. I can't make it out clearly through the veil over my eyes, but I know it's meant for me. I pull it out and take it with me to the empty chair at the edge of the room. My book bag falls to the floor with a thud and I instinctively hush it, worried that someone will hear and appear to try to talk me out of this. Or throw me in jail. I'm not sure which would be worse since I've already begun to feel like I'm in some sort of self-created prison all my own. It's time to break out.

I grit the flashlight between my teeth, biting down on the plastic to keep it in place. I lift my hand up in examination. I don't know how to do this but it can't be all that difficult. I've seen it done on television before. It's just not in my nature to do something so secretive, to make up my mind without consulting anyone. I usually have Joel do that for me. To have the final say be all my own is a foreign experience.

I blink hard twice, shake off the fear that threatens, and plunge it deep into my arm, the icy liquid burning as it shoots through my veins, twisting and snaking into my body. My teeth clench harder, a scream forms around the flashlight, and the object falls from my mouth, plummeting to the ground. Batteries spill out with a clatter and the room goes black.

The inside of my elbow's throbbing, a pain ripping through me that's freezing then burning, the sensations so similar in intensity that I can't tell one apart from the other. My head goes faint; my vision darkens at the edges, a vignette of black around the already near-black room.

I had anticipated the initial discomfort, but not the steady stream of searing agony. And it's difficult to discern if the pain is all physical or not.

Tracer.

I say it in my mind, hoping my brain won't register its meaning.

But it does.

Visions and déjà vu feelings sweep through me. I'm not a blank slate wiped clean. All is not lost from my memory. I don't know what I had expected, but I'd wanted to be completely rid of it. Isn't that what vaccinations are supposed to do? Immunize you against the disease? Rid your body of its toxins?

The needle's still deep in my skin when the room illuminates, the small bit of light from my phone tucked in my bag spilling into the dark corners and crevices. It must be Joel calling. He's discovered his dad's missing keys. I'm found out. Funny how nervous I was when I thought I'd disappointed Uncle Mark in some unknowing way. I don't have that same sensation with Joel. I know I'm a disappointment to him already. That I don't accept being a Tracer fully, that I'm not as committed as he is. This final act will only solidify what he already knows about me. I'm not a good Tracer. I'm not even a good citizen. I might not even be a good person anymore. And I'm no good for him. I'm holding him back. He deserves so much more. What I've just done here infinitely reiterates that fact.

He's the good one. I'm the one who's bad. The one who's lost. And though Liam might not be lost, he's unaware, and maybe that's the same thing.

The light shuts off and it's just me alone in the room again, no caller hanging on the other line. I jerk the needle from my arm and edge my finger over the empty vial. *Come on. Do what you're supposed to do.*

But I'm no different. I don't feel any differently. I don't think any differently. I ponder retrieving my medical record like I had originally planned before spontaneously reaching for the needle. I'm still tempted to see if I was immunized to begin with, but it's all a moot point. I made my decision and acted upon it. That should be enough. I finally made a choice.

Dejected, I stash the needle in the biohazard container mounted on the wall. Biohazard. The word strikes me. Like the hazard is the needle. Shouldn't the hazard be the disease the needle protects against? Confused and disoriented, I recount my steps back through the winding halls to the building's entrance, locking the door shut behind me.

The fog surrounds every inch of the lot, my car barely visible from where I stand. I reassemble the flashlight and flip it on to navigate my way back to the sedan. I don't care who finds me now. I've done what I came to do. Let me be found out. That was the whole point, after all, wasn't it? To find something?

Sinking into my seat, I toss my bag onto the floorboard and remember the call. Joel's probably worried. Or furious. Whatever he is, I at least owe him some explanation for the thievery.

One missed message.

234-1112.

Liam.

The one who's life I have some responsibility in ruining. The one I had just tried to give up Tracing for in an attempt to make things right, and the reason for the stinging puncture in my forearm. *Liam.*

I'm half-trembling, half-steady as I lift the phone to my ear, his voice quaking and cracking in the recording.

"Tessa—I really need to talk to you. I know you know what happened…"

There is a pause and remorse sweeps over me.

I think of Sammy.

"…Joel called me…"

My heart jolts and anger rises. What did he do that for? That wasn't his place.

"…He told me about you, Tessa. That you might have some explanation for why this happened…"

The tears that I wouldn't allow earlier begin to flow freely.

"...Tessa, if you have something—some way of looking at the world that makes sense of all of this—then I want it, too. I need it, too."

He's begging into the silence. I feel shame for not answering and not giving him the opportunity to at least have an actual person to plead with.

"I can't go back to the way things were before this. Sammy's gone..."

The curls, the matchbox cars, the first morning at breakfast when he asked me to play. This golden-haired boy, a younger version of Liam, consumes my thoughts and distracts me from my once firm resolve to throw it all away, like I owe him something.

"And I don't want to live in a dark world where his death was for nothing. I need a reason for all of this, Tessa..."

His voice pauses and I fill in the silence with sobs.

"I need you to be my sunshine, Tessa. Please don't take that away."

The recording stops abruptly.
So does my heart.

TWENTY-TWO

My bed feels unwelcome, like I don't deserve its comfort after what I've just done. The keys were placed back on the table, never hinting at their brief escapade. I'd gotten away with it. It was almost too easy. No one gets away with anything with the Hub in charge. But I did. And it doesn't feel as freeing as I'd imagined.

I'm actually surprised there's anything left of me, really. I'd expected it all to be washed away. I'd hoped the immunization would blot everything from my memory, or at least empty me of it all, leaving just a shell of what I used to be before I even knew what the word Tracer meant.

But that's not what remains. There is still a glimmer of something tangible left of me. Some real parts rattling around in the hollow sheath, tinkering against the walls, a quiet reminder that I'm not all lost. That something meaningful still exists in me.

I'm still a Tracer.

When everything else is stripped bare that one truth endures. No amount of poisonous fluid pumped through my veins can push that out of me completely or erase it from my memory. I'd wanted a clean slate, but even a chalkboard with its letters swept away still has a faint outline, and the words still exist in the shadows. You have to look closely—examine the curves and the shapes which were at a time so clearly written—but the dusty figures remain, serving as symbols that something meaningful may have existed. I hadn't been wiped clean like I'd wanted. And it's an overwhelming relief. A relief that I haven't completely ruined myself with my own stupidly rash decision.

My thoughts go to Joel and wonder if he'll be able to recognize me past the deceit or if he won't be able see around my chalky exterior. I'm smudged and smeared, but deep down I'm still visible if you look hard enough. Will he even want to make the effort to try to see me anymore? He had wanted me to make a choice so badly and I chose wrong. I chose to deny it all; to give it all up. Will he be able to forgive me for pushing it all—pushing him—away? Is something like this—denying such a gift, breaking into his father's office, attempting to erase all meaning from my life—*is this even forgivable?*

I'd always thought maybe I was broken before when my parents died. But that wasn't a broken life, that was an interrupted one. I might have been fractured, but I wasn't fully shattered. But *this*? This has to be brokenness. To forsake everything without thought, without thoroughly pondering the consequences, not realizing whose life would change apart from your own—that can only come from a completely broken person. And when things break you either discard them or put the pieces back together. And I'm not a Discard. As tempting as it may be to sweep myself away, I know two people that will never let me do that. My only option is to rebuild.

This time I know that I can't remain silent. Maybe that was my dad's ultimate problem; he was too quiet in his resolve to change the system. After all, the term silent disobedient came from the Hub itself. It's the description they'd approved. If anyone was to disagree or disobey, they had to do so in silence, behind closed doors. But I don't want to stay in the shadows anymore because I'm a Tracer. It's what I do. It's who I am. I can't pretend to be anything different.

With knowledge comes action and my eyes have been opened, even if it did take a while to pry them apart. I have to change my reality. My *one* reality—no more shifting back and forth between two versions of myself. I don't want to be either of those, and definitely not some mediocre combination of the two. I think I've proved that doesn't work. And like Joel had said, I need to shout it from the rooftops and take ownership of this gift. Maybe it's time that I reclaim my future, what's rightfully mine.

Maybe Joel's right. After all, he's been right about everything else so far.

Megan Squires lives with her husband and two children just outside of Sacramento, California. A graduate from the University of California, Davis, Megan is now a full-time mother, wife, and dreamer—though her characters don't often give her much opportunity to sleep.

To follow The Outlier Chronicles, or to connect online, visit:

www.theoutlierchronicles.com
www.facebook.com/MeganSquiresAuthor

Tessa's Story Continues in
RECRUITED
available Spring 2013

Made in the USA
Charleston, SC
01 November 2012